THE GRUMPY BILLIONAIRE

A STANDALONE ROMANTIC COMEDY

THE BILLIONAIRES OF MANHATTAN
BOOK EIGHT

ANNIKA MARTIN

CHAPTER 1

STELLA

My new roommate, Kelsey, comes to my bedroom door while I'm unpacking my socks-and-ceramic-owls box.

"If you're in a place to take a break, some of us are going for a picnic in the park. Just food truck stuff. You can meet everyone!"

Kelsey's loud and fun and she wears the biggest earrings of anybody I've ever met.

"I would love to, but I need to finish," I tell her. This is mostly a lie.

"There might be hula hoop dancers," she tries.

"Tempting," I say.

"No, I get it. You just moved and you have a big day tomorrow." She picks up a small ceramic owl with big retro eyes. "You sure love owls."

"That's Chester, one of my first."

"Love." She puts him back on the shelf. "Next time!" With that, she's off.

I sink to the floor amidst the chaos of my new bedroom and silently freak out.

Yesterday while the movers were hauling in the last of my boxes, Kelsey confessed to me how relieved she is to have found a subletter with a decent job who she actually likes. She said it three times—"Somebody gainfully employed who I actually like! And is fun and sane!"

Like she hit the jackpot with me. She was so impressed that I moved here for my dream job...which fell through not fifteen minutes ago.

They called me—on a Sunday—to inform me of this.

I don't know how I'm going to tell her.

Landing my dream job was this big bright spot in my life after my fiancé crushed my heart. It was terrifying to move to New York all by myself, to sublet a room in an apartment with a perfect stranger, but I closed my eyes and took the leap.

"There's been a change in direction with the position." –That's all the HR person at Zevin Media would say.

Translation: I can't tell you.

I've been in the business world long enough to know that it's bizarre to pay for somebody to move hundreds of miles only to fire them—on a Sunday—the day before they start.

How could they do this to me? How am I supposed to pay my rent now?

Supposedly they were impressed by my award-winning work. The team and I had amazing chemistry over endless Zoom interviews. Everybody was excited.

Something big changed.

What?

I sit there feverishly thinking through my social media history. Too many owls? Too much Taylor Swift? Do they hate Team Jacob? But shitty social media is a rookie mistake I'd never make.

I do some self-pep-talking.

You're okay.

You have a few weeks to figure out rent.

You've been through hard things before.

It's probably not even about you!

But I'm pretty sure it *is* about me—why else would they call me on a Sunday? That's how badly they don't want me to set foot in there?

Did they think I'd wreck the place or something?

I sit Kelsey down that night on the red velvety couch that takes up half the living room and tell her the bad news.

She twirls her giant earring, long fingernails glinting in the light. If she thinks I'm a delusional liar, considering how much I gushed about my amazing new dream job, she doesn't say.

"No, I get it," she says. "Shit happens." But I can tell she's worried. She calls her friend Mia, who gets me lined up with a part-time gig delivering sandwiches dressed as a cat, of all things.

No way will it be enough to make rent, but it's something.

I tell her not to worry. The great thing about New York is that there is no shortage of little advertising agencies who need somebody with my expertise in branding and all things video.

I network like a demon in the days that follow. I sit at a busy Starbucks going gonzo on LinkedIn. I reach out to contacts of contacts.

Things get even more bizarre after that when a few jobs materialize and seem like sure things only to vanish, and nobody will tell me why. Like it's this state secret!

Around week two, I start going for jobs I'm ridiculously overqualified for, and the same stuff happens.

What's going on?

Do I share a Social Security number with a serial killer? Is my name attached to a "Let's bring back cannibalism!" manifesto on the dark web?

Mom is unhelpful on the phone that Friday. "You can always move back and take your old room. Actually, Crafter City has a help-wanted sign up."

"Seriously? That's where you think I'm headed? Back to my old room?"

"Honey. Did you not just tell me you can't land a job where you are?"

"It's under control, Mom."

I hear the telltale sigh that says Mom is not convinced.

No matter what I do out in the world, I can never live down the irresponsible baby-of-the-family brand that I earned as a girl, where I'm completely inept and clueless and everybody has to tell me what to do.

My greatest branding fail of all. And I'm in the branding business!

"What about Hugo?" she says. "Hugo could get you a job where he works. It's the perfect idea!"

They keep trying to get Hugo involved. Hugo, my older brother Charlie's best friend.

"Oh my god, no, Mom! Remember how I asked you not to tell Hugo to write that confidential letter of recommendation for me? Because I had my own people to write them? Remember how I forbade you?"

"Uh, yes."

"That applies doubly here. Do not tell Hugo! Or Charlie!"

"Why not?"

I groan. I can only imagine the way Charlie would describe my predicament to Hugo.

Stella's big New York job fell through, if there even was one. You know how Stella is.

4

"Hugo would love to help you," Mom says.

"No, Hugo would hate to help me. I'd rather sell a kidney than involve Hugo. Plus every drop of my plasma. And an eyeball!"

"Oh, Stella."

"Have you forgotten our entire childhood? Hugo is not in the Stella Woodward fan club. Hugo is in the opposite of the Stella Woodward fan club. Hugo is a card-carrying member of the Stella-haters lodge. He has the furry hat and the golden staff and a secret book of Stella-hating rituals that he reads in the dead of night."

"You're being silly now."

"It's under control," I repeat.

We get off the phone.

To say I'm the black sheep in my family is an understatement. Imagine a loud, extroverted cheerleader getting air-dropped into a family of serious math nerds—that's my life in a nutshell.

My parents didn't know what to do with a kid who hated to study, got average grades, and loved reality TV and Britney Spears and filming dance routines with her friends in the basement. My brother found me unbearable.

I'd act like I didn't care, and I'd always bounce back, because I'm a person who bounces back from things. And I'd be happy again until my parents yelled at me to tone it down, because they liked our home to be silent as a tomb so they could do math things.

I really did try, but then I'd forget myself—especially when Hugo was over.

And Hugo was over a lot.

The second Hugo walked in the door, *Star Trek* bookbag slung over his shoulder, this exuberance would just come over me. Hugo was beautiful and completely antisocial, with walls impenetrable as Alcatraz, a prince on his throne, tall, dark and harshly handsome, regarding me with utter annoyance.

And god how I worshipped him.

Hugo Jones was more brilliant than Charlie and my parents put together and everybody knew it. An off-the-charts genius.

And his annoyance toward me? Also off the charts. Hugo found me so annoying he could barely even look at me.

As I grew older, my infatuation evolved from dorky childish excitement to imagining Hugo in sexy scenarios he'd definitely find problematic, if not downright disturbing on an acrobatic level.

He was a harsh beehive of seriousness that I couldn't stop poking at, desperate for any reaction.

The last time I saw Hugo was ten years ago. I was twenty-two and we were both back in Percy Groves, Illinois, for Thanksgiving, and he was coming over to say hi and pick Charlie up for something.

God, how I primped that day.

I imagined Hugo's eyes lighting up when he saw me… "Wow! Stella…"

Cue the loss for words due to my cute outfit and my mature demeanor. And then he'd hear about the cool job I'd landed as a video editor at a creative marketing firm in Madison, Wisconsin. My job in media was unimpressive to my family, but I felt sure Hugo would appreciate that I was making something of myself.

All that hope and hairspray for a two-minute hello where he could barely look at me.

Just like old times.

Sadly, all of the passionate longing for Hugo was still there on my side, raging like a bonfire. My obsession over Hugo twisted me up with joy and pain, as only unrequited feelings can.

I vowed to get over him—and get over him I did.

Now that I'm in my thirties, my infatuation with Hugo has been pulverized and therapized and negative-reinforced out of me.

Gone.

Dead as a doornail.

Still! I don't want our first interaction in ten years being him having to rescue me like I'm the dipshit who crash-landed in New York with a purely delusional job, which is what it looks like.

In summation, do I want somebody to reach out to Hugo?

That would be an Empire-State-Building-sized no, thank you!

CHAPTER 2

STELLA

"Hey, great news!" Mom says the minute I answer the phone. "Your father got ahold of Hugo and explained your predicament, and he has a job for you!"

I blink, hoping this is a nightmare. "But I don't need a job from Hugo. I very specifically told you that, remember?"

"It turns out that they have an emergency need on the admin team at Hugo's hedge fund—Quantum whatever—and he already cleared it with HR. It's yours. Starting tomorrow."

"I can't believe you involved Hugo."

"He was happy to help. We can't let you be homeless."

"Homeless? This is what Dad presented to him? I was about to be homeless! Oh my god, I was handling it! I didn't need you guys to strong-arm Hugo into getting me a job."

"It's not strong-arming, it's networking," Mom says.

"No, it's interfering, because I specifically asked you not to."

"Stella, this is a good thing! They need somebody. You'd be helping Hugo out."

My blood races. I might be low-key panicking. High-key panicking.

My short life has contained two mortifying incidents between Hugo and me that my family doesn't know about. I don't need a third act. *Best friend's annoying little sister III: All grown up and still a problem.*

"There's no shame in it," Mom says.

"You know who says, 'there's no shame in it'? People who know that there's shame in it."

"I don't know what to say," Mom says. "Should we tell Hugo you're not interested? After all the trouble he went through to arrange this job? Even though you don't have something better?"

"Actually, I do have something better," I tell her. "It's a startup for a new app."

"Really?"

"Yes, it strangles people right through the phone when they do things you begged them not to. I'm gonna call it Python Solutions. What do you think?"

Mom is not amused.

In the end, I take the job. I do need it, and I'm not irresponsible, contrary to what my parents and brother think. I also want to take the path of least peskiness. Since Hugo already reached out and got me the job, I don't want to make him go through the trouble of undoing it all.

She gives me contact info for the details. I'm supposed to call ASAP.

"Oh, and you're not to bother Hugo. When it comes to Hugo, you're just another employee."

"Hugo wants to pretend we're strangers?"

"Charlie says Hugo's working on a very difficult and important project and cannot be distracted. Anyway, it's a huge company, and your job has nothing to do with Hugo's. And since

Hugo has clearly pulled strings for you, it makes sense he wouldn't want a fuss."

"Don't worry. But I would like to thank him," I say. "I mean, that is what adult people do. Maybe like a card or a bottle of nice scotch or something?"

"Hugo wouldn't want that. You know how Hugo is about gifts and displays of affection."

"It's not like I was planning on hunting him down and tackle-hugging him." I say this breezily, but I hate that they act like I don't know how Hugo is.

I know how Hugo is. I spent the entirety of my youth feverishly studying the ways of Hugo.

"So you promise?" Mom says.

"I don't need to promise. You know why? Because I'm an actual grown-up who knows how to act like a professional."

"Of course you know how to act professional!" This line is not delivered convincingly, let's just say.

I know what's on her mind—on all their minds: If you're so professional, why did your supposed dream job pay to relocate you to New York City and suddenly decide to claw back the offer?

What did you do?

Or worse, how could you have moved to a new city for a job that wasn't even nailed down?

Thank her and get off the phone, thank her and get off the phone, thank her and get off the phone, I chant to myself.

"Thank you," I say. "Thank you for...reaching out on my behalf."

"Of course, honey. Now what are you gonna do the minute you hang up from me? Are you gonna call Hugo's contact in HR to set you up?"

I assure her that I will and click the call end button, grateful, at least, that I'm not facing a mirror, because I have no doubt that my face has transformed into a rictus of pure agonized mortification.

CHAPTER 3

Stella

Back in my old life in Madison, Wisconsin, I'd worked my way up from video editor to creative director at a super-hot marketing agency, and I was awesome at it.

I'd think up creative digital content that would grab eyeballs for our corporate clients—just enough to be edgy without upsetting the C-suite, as we liked to say. Idea in place, I'd wrangle my underlings into working with me on it.

It was mostly video stuff. Some animation—scroll-stopping reels showing things like the wonders of MapleKrunchers or the thrill of driving the new Ascot Turbo.

Clients would sign on with that agency specifically to work with me. Things were good!

I'd wear jeans and tees and Vans, sometimes even pajama pants—in the world of ad creatives, the better your ideas are, the more you should dress like you don't care.

Nobody trusts a creative in a business suit, after all.

For the big meetings, I'd bust out the oversized blazer, Lycra shorts, and blue cowboy boots and go in there like colorful girl Johnny Cash.

Clients loved to see colorful girl Johnny Cash. Colorful girl Johnny Cash inspired confidence.

What do I not have? Clothes appropriate for an administrative assistant. And what else do I not have? The skills of an administrative assistant.

As Charlie always pointed out, I'm hopeless with numbers and organization, which is a big part of administrative work.

So when I call the number and discover they really do want me tomorrow, I spring into action.

First stop: Target's business casual section. Next stop: YouTube tutorials on software that administrative assistants use. I spend most of the night learning a thing called Outlook and a little bit on PowerPoint.

My new work home, the Quantum Capital Partners admin pool, turns out to be a sea of cubicles in a big open area on the fifth floor of a Wall Street skyscraper. There's a massive window on one side where you can look down and see gloomy, gray Wall Street. A glass wall on the other side showcases important-looking people rushing back and forth. Every once in a while, somebody comes to the desk at the front of the pool. My new supervisor, Viola, tells me that it's the courier desk even though hardly anything is couriered anymore.

Viola has short blonde hair, dangly beaded earrings, and lots of suspicions about my qualifications. She's been showing me procedures that involve functions in the obscure, outer-space reaches of the Microsoft Word toolbar, things I never had to use as a creative director.

Not thirty minutes into my training, Viola fixes me with a

hard gaze. "You're telling me you know Word? That's what you're telling me here?" This in the most accusatory of tones.

I did tell them I knew Word, or at least my résumé did, but the Microsoft Word that marketing people use is a simple fella. He wears a straw hat and rides around in hay carts and helps write documents.

Who knew MS Word had a whole secret life at the MS Word References rave bar?

"Just open up the clipboard panel," Viola says like it's the simplest thing in the world.

Which it might be if I knew what a clipboard panel was. Sweat begins to trickle down my spine.

She turns to talk to somebody, and I quickly pull out my phone and Google "MS Word clipboard panel." A diagram appears on my phone screen. I furiously commit it to memory before tucking it away, because I'm nothing if not resourceful.

When Viola's back, I call up the clipboard panel and await my next task.

She seems surprised that I know that clipboard panel after all. She gives me another command. This one I figure out by sheer intuition, pulse racing all the while.

I feel like I'm doing an extreme sport, pretending to know way more MS Word than I do.

She tells me to do mail merge things I don't understand. Just then, somebody comes up and distracts her with a question.

This is my chance; I go full defcon five—I reach around and loosen the connection to the mouse and keyboard to make it look like the computer froze, a trick an underling once used on me.

I start jiggling and clicking the mouse. I'm desperate. I cannot let Hugo down!

"What now?" Viola takes over the mouse. "Oh god, seriously?"

"I'll get it back up," I say.

She sighs.

"I'm a wiz at fixing things like this," I add confidently. "I'm a figure-it-out girl."

"A figure-it-out girl, huh." Viola's skeptical.

"Yup," I say brightly.

This is Branding 101. If you repeat things about yourself enough times, people will come to believe those things. Being a figure-it-out girl is a great piece of branding for me on this job because it suggests that I'm competent and resourceful, even if I don't know something right away.

She stabs a few keys. "Damn."

"I'll get it fired back up and ping you," I say.

She checks her phone. "It'll have to be after lunch." With that she's off.

Score!

I'll duck out somewhere and cram mail merge tutorials. I can nail this job.

A voice from somewhere nearby: "You're telling me you know Word? That's what you're telling me?"

I sit up. Is a cubicle neighbor talking to me? Making fun of me?

The voice continues, coming from the cubicle to my right. "Mail merge. Get on it!"

"Excuse me?"

The voice is behind me now. "Hey."

I spin around and see that the voice belongs to a grinning red-haired woman. "Don't let Viola rattle you. She expects everybody to come out of the womb knowing mail merge." She holds out a hand. "Jane."

"Stella."

"Once you unfreeze that thing, pop over and I'll quick show you. It's not that hard."

I reach around and restore the connection. "Unfroze it."

Jane snorts when she sees what I did. "You *are* a figure-it-out girl. A-plus."

CHAPTER 4

STELLA

I survive through to the afternoon and demonstrate to Viola that I actually do know mail merge, though she still seems unhappy with me.

Jane promises me that it's just how Viola is.

I meet my cubicle mate on the other side, Hesh. Hesh has round glasses and wicked things to say about Viola's constant use of the term "proactive." We take a break together and walk to the snacks area on the first floor, and I'm surprised to find a vending machine that's actually stocked with gummy worms.

"Yay!" I purchase a pack and rip them open. "Things are looking up!"

Hesh groans. "We were boycotting them in hopes they'd stop stocking them."

"They could be pretty old," Jane warns.

"Gummy worms don't get old." I grin and pop another in my mouth.

I'm back at my cubicle finishing my second pack of gummy worms while proofreading a PowerPoint presentation when suddenly everything goes dead still, like a forest when a large predator arrives, or a vampire or something.

Somebody whispers something that sounds like Houdini.

I look up. Our eyes meet. Shock arrows through me.

There he is, up at the courier station, larger than life.

Hugo Jones.

Is he looking at me? Staring right at me? He has a half-smile… or is that my imagination? Is this some kind of test where he's seeing if I screw up the whole directive where I'm not supposed to know him?

Of course it is!

I look back down. He said I'm not supposed to know him and now he's testing me.

"Who's he here to terrorize now?" somebody in the next cubicle over whispers.

Hesh wanders to the panel that separates Jane's space from mine. "Looks like he's picking up a delivery," he says.

"Is Brenda out sick?" Jane asks. "Still. He knows we'll deliver it to Brenda's desk or directly to him if it's urgent."

Up at the desk, a nervous-looking woman hands Hugo a FedEx envelope, and Hugo regards said envelope with the harshness I remember so well. He's very much the same, but filled out —strong jaw, hard cheekbones, and a solid build in place of awkward angles. He has a nice haircut rather than the choppy home job I remember.

It looks nice.

The courier desk woman is literally wringing her hands as he burns a hole through the envelope with a hawk-like laser focus.

I force myself to take a breath. It's not that his appearance is surprising after this long, Hugo-less decade. Stock market websites run his picture all the time. They love his severe beauty and his controversial market models.

And it should be no surprise that he's traded in his nerd T-shirts for a button-down. Even from here, you can see the way it stretches tight across his shoulders, as if to say, here be muscles.

Hugo. In the flesh. So serious and grown up.

I bite my lip, trying my best to hide my smile. Butterflies are whirling in my belly, but I give them a stern glare. I am supposedly over Hugo and all Hugo types.

The past years have included not only an awesome, self-esteem-building career path—if you ignore these past weeks—but also what amounts to aversion therapy to any and all Hugo types. A team of scientists in a top-secret lab orbiting the earth couldn't design a better course of Hugo aversion therapy protocols than the dating history I have lived since I last set eyes on Hugo.

This very painful therapy involved my jumping into relationships—two casual and one serious—with icy, brilliant high achievers with harsh personal standards—in other words, men like Hugo.

It's not as if I sought out only Hugo-like men. I had certainly tried dating nice men who liked me the way I am. But sadly, they didn't do it for me. Why couldn't my first blush of love have been for a golden retriever type, loving and uncritically appreciative?

My serious Hugo-style swains would always find my whimsical attitude enchanting at first. "You're a breath of fresh air, Stella." "You're comic relief, Stella."

Eventually, the whimsy would get old, and the disapproval would build. More and more I would find myself at arm's length in all categories that didn't involve food and sex. The razor-sharp talons of criticism would emerge, followed by total disdain.

Trust me—disdain feels like a jagged, rusty knife in the gut when it's coming from somebody you adore.

I'm so done with Hugos. So done with not measuring up. I learned my lesson.

The butterflies settle down and act busy doing whatever butterflies do when they're not circling and fluttering like little jackasses. But what can you expect? A butterfly has a brain the size of a pinhead, if that.

The woman at the courier desk has stopped wringing her hands; now she's gripping the edge of the desk as if Hugo might decide to use his vast mental powers to cause an earthquake.

So, clearly it's weird that he's come down from his ivory tower to visit the courier desk.

He doesn't look happy.

Why would he be? I'm a blast from the past to Hugo—and not the good kind; I'm an unfortunate fashion choice, a horrible earworm burrowing into his brilliant and beautiful life in the Big Apple. Though Hugo wouldn't call it the Big Apple. He'd call it whatever brilliant brainiacs who live in New York call New York.

"Since when does Hugh-dini pick up his own deliveries?" Hesh asks.

"Houdini?" I say.

"*Hugh*-dini," Jane says. "That guy who's standing up there? That's Hugo Jones. He's the brains of this operation."

"You call him...Hugh-dini?"

"Sometimes just *Dini*," Jane whispers solemnly.

I nod, biting the insides of my cheeks to keep from smiling or, God forbid, laughing. This would be a bad time to laugh!

I wish I could tell them I knew him growing up, but I promised I wouldn't, and I would never want to get him in trouble after he did this nice thing for me.

It would be so wrong to laugh, but...Hugh-dini? "So...he doesn't know you call him that?"

Hesh spins around and widens his eyes. "You can never say anything. The entire floor would probably be fired!"

"Lips zipped!" I would never tell. For one thing, I'm not an asshole. And also, Hugo's opinion of himself is already inflated enough.

Up front, Hugo holds the envelope by the edges like it's hot, confident fingers and big knuckles on full display. I know those hands almost as well as my own.

And of course, there go the butterflies, back in the old Hugo routine: flutter around until he somehow reveals how much he hates you, and then slowly drop to the pit of low self-esteem. Rinse and repeat often.

Newsflash, butterflies: Adult Stella is in charge now. Adult Stella is a successful, confident woman with a brain the size of a grapefruit, or maybe two grapefruits if you smushed them partly together, or maybe let's go with a largish somewhat misshapen mango to more accurately represent the oblong shape of a brain. Whatever, it's a big-ish brain. Definitely bigger than a pinhead.

What's more, as adult Stella, I possess a butterfly-sized swatter, and I'm not afraid to use it.

Up at the courier desk, Hugo's laser focus is still fixed on the envelope, though is it really? Hugo sees things you don't think he sees, what with his raptorlike vision able to detect the tiniest movement from ridiculous distances.

And that scowl! I remember it well, being that it was turned on me from the moment Hugo and I met at math camp that fateful summer.

Yes, I was once at math camp—not due to any math abilities, mind you. The camp desperately wanted my brother, Charlie, so they bent the rules and the prices for me. It was a convenient form of childcare for my parents, and an entrée into new realms of self-esteem sadness for me, being that I sucked at math.

Up front, Hugo mumbles something and then storms off with the offending envelope, long legs eating up the space on the other side of the glass.

Murmurs go up all over the room.
I'm looking down at my desk.
Swat swat.

CHAPTER 5

STELLA

Hesh leans in. "He sometimes sends his assistant, Brenda, to snap people up for special projects. Do what you can to not get caught up in that net."

"Special projects?"

"Mostly stuff that needs to be researched," Jane says. "He has a team on the tenth floor for things like geopolitical or financial analysis, but now and then he comes up with questions for us to look into like we're the voice of the common dipshit. Usually we have to fill out questionnaires or else go on social media and see where we think opinions are trending."

"And you have to drop everything," Hesh adds. "It's a lack of respect, but what Hugh-dini wants, Hugh-dini gets."

"If you're ever in the same room as him, keep your head down," Jane suggests with a concerned expression. "Unless he asks you a direct question, don't talk to him. Don't even look at him or you'll be sorry. Even if you're filling in at the courier desk."

"Don't even look at him or I'll be sorry?" I ask incredulously. It's just kind of funny.

"It's true!" A woman with purple hair pops her head up on the other side, jack-in-the-box-style. "Do not, repeat, do not make eye contact with Hugh-dini."

"Okay. No eye contact with Hugh-dini."

"It's sad," Jane says. "All that hotness, completely wasted on the most antisocial person ever."

Hesh adjusts his glasses. "If there's an ASAP delivery that needs to get to Hugh-dini, try your hardest to leave it with Brenda. In situations where Brenda isn't there, you're going to need to bring it directly in to Hugh-dini. Minimize your interaction at all costs."

Once people who work in an office get into full-on gossip mode, especially when there's a newbie to get up to speed, there's no stopping them, and the Hugo warnings roll on. People are a little ragey about an incident involving a sweet older woman named Vera. She used to be at the courier desk, but she was summarily moved to a far-away office at Hugo's request.

"Moved to Siberia for no apparent reason," the woman with purple hair hisses. She comes around to stand next to Hesh. "Not just to a different floor, but a remote site. She was like a mother to a lot of us. He took this mysterious dislike to her and had her banished."

"Banished for no reason at all!" Hesh adds. "Hugh-dini's a power-mad prince."

I nod, but I happen to know that Hugo never does things without reason. Though the reason could be something like untied shoes, a lopsided hairdo, or a tendency to use the word *fewer* when the word *less* would've been grammatically correct.

God, if Hugo had that level of power growing up, he would've sent me to Siberia so fast. As it was, he seemed intent on banishing me with his mind, icy cold whenever we passed in the hall, averting his eyes when I'd be dressed up to go out with my girlfriends or showing too much exuberance. Like he was using every ounce of his energy to will me away.

"And Wulfric Pierce, the owner of Quantum, will back him up on anything," Hesh warns. "Wulfric will chop off your head for nothing, and Hugh-dini's his golden boy."

"The two of them are easily billionaires by now," Jane says.

"Hugo?"

"Oh, yeah," Hesh says. "Wulfric's a zillionaire, but Hugo would be a billionaire in bonuses alone."

Viola appears at that point, and we all scramble to get back to work, but I'm stunned. I knew he was rich, but a billionaire? Does Charlie know about this? Do my parents know?

I force myself to focus on the PowerPoint, which practically has every word capitalized, and it annoys me so much, I spend most of the time imagining a slogan for a T-shirt that would say, *"An initial cap does not make the word seem more important. Just stop."*

The rest of the time I'm stressing out about Hugo. Is he mad I didn't thank him? Is that why he made that stunning cameo at the courier desk? To see the face of the ingrate who didn't thank him?

Charlie wouldn't even forward a thank-you text over to Hugo when I asked him. "Not making any fuss is how you thank Hugo. Thank him by leaving him alone."

I assumed the directive was coming from Hugo, being the utterly antisocial and highly annoyed-with-me creature that he is, but what if that's just Charlie's thing? Am I the asshole?

I could figure out where he lives and send him a card, but he might think I'm stalking him—if his people even bother to show him random cards. As a billionaire, he probably has people, right? Is that a thing? I have no idea how billionaires live.

I don't have his phone number to text him myself, not that he'd look at a text from an unknown number anyway.

My face gets hot as I feel that old rush of shame and awkwardness where I never know what to do or say, which usually makes me get loud and energetic, and then everybody says to tone it down, and I can't.

In the end, I decide that's a problem for future Stella, and I focus on being an amazing worker. It's not complete bullshit that I'm a figure-it-out girl.

I offer up ideas for reordering the PowerPoints, and I figure out how to convert some of the narrative paragraphs into visual charts. I may have been rejected for every marketing job in the city, but I know how to get a message across.

CHAPTER 6

HUGO

The minutes I spend walking from one part of the office complex to another to get a sparkling water, what I think of as hall time, is typically time where I get good insights. A focus for my mind while my subconscious mulls over the really important questions in the background.

It's precious, valuable time to me. I've made some of my most important breakthroughs walking from one place to another.

And right now, I need a breakthrough.

Desperately.

Half the financial industry is holding their breath, waiting for me to reveal my secret data model, which Wulfric and I refer to as QuantumQuilt. The other half is praying I'll stumble—or, worse, show up with the kind of mediocre iteration that signals the end of my career.

The QuantumQuilt will be a mediocre iteration over my dead body. The solution is out there, just beyond my reach.

What, then, do I not want to spend my precious hall time minutes on?

Wondering why Stella would pretend not to recognize me. Or is it possible she actually didn't recognize me? I had allotted a bit of time for a quick hello, but it's not as if I don't have other uses for that time. Better uses for that time.

I breeze past Brenda, blood racing.

Maybe she doesn't want people to know she got the job through family connections.

And what was so hilarious? Of course, with Stella, something hilarious doesn't need to be happening for her to think things are hilarious. Given the right mood, Stella can find a bloody pair of scissors hilarious.

And why does any of this matter? Trying to work out why Stella does anything is as impossible as it is pointless.

Brenda spots the envelope in my hand and pops up from her desk, alarmed. "Mr. Jones, is there a problem? I could have gone to the courier desk for you. You didn't have to go all the way to admin—"

"There was no problem. I was there."

"B-but..."

"I was there. I grabbed it. It would've been idiotically inefficient not to."

Brenda nods. If there is anything we both hate, it's idiotic inefficiencies. Beyond that, she knows not to question me.

Nobody questions me. It's one of the greatest perks of success. The money and the prestige are fine, but the exemption from social interactions and expectations? Priceless.

I spent a startling amount of my youth practicing smiles in the mirror and copying the way normal kids interacted with each other.

The solution, as it turns out, wasn't to level up my social

game. It was to become rich and powerful enough to not have to care how I act or what anybody thinks.

I storm into my office, which I keep as spartan as my social life, and throw the thing on my desk. I continue on to the window and flatten my hand to the cool glass, adjusting myself to this strange new reality: Stella. Here at Quantum Partners.

The street below bustles with trucks and taxi cabs under steel-and-glass skyscrapers and historic buildings festooned with flags.

This uncomfortable sensation of heat blooms in my chest. Lunch at the Korean deli usually doesn't bother me, but Jesus Christ! Is this heartburn or what?

I sit down and yank open my drawer, rummaging around in the back, grateful my Tums Chewy Bites are still in there. I cram a purple one in my mouth, set the timer that marks the beginning of my focus session, and head over to stare at my whiteboard.

I make a few notes. I erase a few notes. I ponder.

Anybody can create a data model that predicts the markets when people behave sensibly; the problem is that people can be obnoxiously irrational, constantly operating against their own self-interest. In short, throwing monkey wrenches left and right. Because that is what people do.

How do you make a data model that will hold up to monkey wrenches—or, better yet, predict the monkey wrenches?

That's my job.

And suddenly, here she is, Stella Woodward, the world's greatest monkey wrench. A walking, talking monkey wrench fucking up my concentration on the project of predicting and accounting for monkey wrenches.

It would be hilarious if it weren't so maddening.

I go back at it, jaw clenched. This is not a distraction I can afford.

Stella Woodward, my best friend's kid sister. Jelly on her face, mischief in her eyes. And later on as a teenager blowing the upstairs fuse with her hair-grooming rituals, completely disrupting our gaming. Because of course she had to have her hair in a shiny, wavy waterfall-like style designed to reflect light in a totally distracting way at all times.

And yes, when we got older, I could see that she was what my high school peers might have considered hot, if they had any intelligence at all—debatable. Yes, obviously she was attractive what with her sparkling eyes and curves, just a whirlwind of laughter and rebellion and cheeky energy.

But any attraction I might have had to her was overruled by general decency. Only an asshole goes after their best friend's little sister—I didn't need Charlie to warn me off of her all those years ago to know that.

Stella was practically family for all the time I spent there, and Joyce and Warren Woodward were like second parents. The debt I owe them is incalculable. "It's like Stella has two older brothers looking out for her," Warren once said to me. I always admired Warren, a stand-up man with the bearing of a four-star general and an old-school sense of humor.

Off-limits. A man has to have codes, after all.

I go back to work. I stare at the board, determined not to think about her being in the same building.

There's that ridiculous saying that if you try not to think of an elephant, suddenly all you can think about is an elephant. It's the pathetic sentiment of a person with an undisciplined mind.

When I tell myself to stop thinking about something, I stop thinking about it.

End of story.

CHAPTER 7

HUGO

I hit the timer when I realize I haven't been working on the new data model for some time.

I'm trying to expand my focus minutes by 1 percent every day, and I track it on one of my whiteboards. My QuantumQuilt data model is hugely ambitious—it'll take enormous effort, but it'll skyrocket our market leadership—unless somebody else figures it out before me. Then we'll lose market share, and all my work will be wasted.

I gaze out the window. What, exactly, was so funny?

I shouldn't be mad; it's all my fault she's here. What did I expect?

And that expression.

Some people might call it smirking, but that would be wrong. It's this mode her face gets into when she's suppressing completely fucking inappropriate mirth—her lips smush together into a plump little line and her cheeks harden, as if with the immense effort to contain an outburst. She thinks she's fooling people. She thinks she looks serious. Like nobody can tell she's a micron away from laughing.

She takes nothing seriously. She never has. She is impulsive, undisciplined, disruptive, rebellious, inappropriate, impudent, and, in a word, trouble.

I trudge over to my focus chart and scrawl a dark X in the block for this time period to signify a failure of focus, then I grab another Tums. This heartburn is twisting me up.

Yes, some men might find her attractive. Some men would probably enjoy her devil-may-care attitude and the way her eyes dance when she's dreaming up something outlandish. I could see some men focusing unwholesomely on her button nose with its light dusting of freckles, on her strong, solid legs, on the gentle curves of her lips. It's possible certain sorts of men would be entertained by her obsession with retro owls or her love of the artist Salvador Dali. Yes, I'm sure a lot of men find her attractive.

But she's not my type. She's the total opposite of my type. In fact, if you described the kind of woman I very specifically avoid, you would find a description of Stella Woodward, double underlined, pencil tip broken.

Yes, she does have her charms, but she is so impossible.

And anyway, I have a code. If you can't stick to your own codes, what do you have? Weakness. A lack of integrity. Dissipation.

I hit the timer and go in for another focus session. A major iron-clad focus session.

My attention does not wander. It doesn't go on flights of fancy. It doesn't gaze at the clouds or gather wool or stop to smell the roses or trot elephants around the room. I do not let it get distracted by gummy worms or the memory of how a shiny waterfall of brown hair feels in my fist.

I do not let it get distracted by Stella Fucking Woodward's badly contained mirth due to whatever she thinks is so hilarious.

My mind is the fucking Roman legion. It crawls through mud when I tell it to. It sleeps when I tell it to—on jagged rocks if need be.

I work uninterrupted and hit my morning goals.

CHAPTER 8

Stella

The walk home takes a good forty minutes, but it's a lovely late September evening. The sidewalks are mobbed, yes, but I'm starting to get the hang of how to move as part of the human river that is Manhattan and I'm working on my attitude.

It was a tough first day, yes. It's hard on the ole self-esteem to be working at a job I'm not qualified for while being back in the orbit of Hugo and his displeasure at my existence and the weirdness of having to pretend I don't know him—all made a hundred times worse by the hideous fact that he gave me the job.

And apparently I still have remnants of that crush. Which, how is that even possible? How many times does my soul need to be crushed by Hugo types?

"So done with Hugos," I say to myself. Not that I ever had a chance with the original Hugo.

I remind myself to look on the bright side. I have two awesome co-workers. I have a great apartment and a new roommate who I'm becoming friends with. I'm living in the best city in the world.

I can figure this out.

I finally reach my cute new neighborhood and pause at the Cookie Madness window to see what the cookie of the day is. They make a special cookie for each day, commemorating a holiday. Apparently every day has some weird holiday. It's September 30, extra virgin olive oil day, so there are cookies with olives on them.

The purple-haired clerk behind the counter waves. We bonded over owls the other day. She points to a tray of samples, but I shake my head and continue on. Some people might buy themselves a nice cookie as consolation for the kind of demoralizing day I've had, but I have a better plan.

I smile at Flo, who's arranging flowers in her cart, and cross the street to check out the bookstore window. I'm stalking the third book in a certain trilogy, which would be an amazing cheer-up gift to get myself, but it's not out for a week, and my goal is straight ahead: the Gourmet Goose, my favorite new store.

I walk in and say hi to Greta, the spiky-haired owner behind the counter. She's a forty-something foodie who's currently arguing with somebody about honey.

The store's floor-to-ceiling shelves are stuffed with pasta and crackers from faraway lands, colorful little jams, and strange pickled things and chocolates of every kind, but the refrigerator case is where the action is. There among the spreads and dips and cold salads are cheeseballs.

And I'm not talking about the crunchy puffed-snack kind.

I'm talking about the kind of old-fashioned cheeseball that a person would put out for party guests—a large, delicious orb of soft cheese mixed up with yummy things and covered with crunchy things and surrounded by crackers.

Though I skip the crackers. I skip the party guests, too.

I'm eating that thing all by myself, just me and a spoon. Solo cheeseballs are my ultimate cheer-up food.

I discovered this place when I got pre-fired from my dream job. It seemed irresponsible to buy such an expensive gourmet treat when I had no source of income, but I promised myself a future cheeseball, and today's the day.

Greta has the best selection of cheeseballs I've ever seen—from her "Blue Velvet and Honeyed Walnut" cheeseball to her pesto cheeseball with toasted breadcrumbs. She told me she creates the recipes herself and runs an offsite kitchen where they're made.

I immediately home in on today's special: a cranberry pecan cheeseball with white cheddar. I'm dying, imagining the goodness of it.

The great honey debate seems to have ended—badly from the sound of it—and Greta wanders over to me.

I point. "I'd love one of the specials. That large one in the back, please."

Greta's excited. "This batch turned out primo. What are you going to serve it with? Veggies or crackers?"

"Oh, I'm not serving it. I'm just going to eat it."

She stiffens. "Excuse me?"

"It's just for me. To eat."

She doesn't seem to comprehend, so I continue. "Like in a bowl with a spoon?"

"You can't eat a cheeseball like that!"

"It's a great way to eat it," I say. "You get the pure flavor."

"Cheeseballs are designed to be shared and enjoyed with loved ones."

"One person can enjoy a cheeseball—and if they really love cheeseballs, they can enjoy it more than an entire group."

"You can't eat a cheeseball alone," Greta says angrily. "Cheese-balls are for sharing, not for gluttony."

"It's not gluttony when you love them." I point at the case. "I would like to purchase that big one. Any one of them." Because I'm guessing she won't be giving me the best one at this point.

She crosses her arms. "I'm sorry, I can't sell a cheeseball to you."

"What do you mean?"

"You'll have to go elsewhere. Get your cheeseball from some-body else."

"But I wanted that one."

"You're not getting one."

I straighten. "You won't sell it? Isn't that...illegal or something?"

She points to a sign that says she reserves the right to refuse service to anybody.

"But..."

"You're not getting one."

"I had such a hard day, and cheeseballs make me happy, and—"

"Cheeseballs aren't for mopers." Once again, she points at the sign.

"Okay, how about if I share it? I'll share it with my roommate."

"I don't believe you."

"So now I'm a liar?"

"I'm gonna have to ask you to leave."

My jaw drops. Is this happening?

Some people come in and I think they sense the weirdness. She smiles and asks whether she can help them, and then hits me with the side-eye.

I get out of there before she can ask me to leave in front of them.

I stop at the window, gazing dolefully at a display of jellies and jams surrounded by dried flowers as people stream by, jostling me now and then. I wanted that cheeseball so badly. How can she not sell it to me?

An older man stops to examine the display of balsamic vinegars in the next window. I smile at him, and he smiles back. He seems friendly.

I finally get up the courage to ask him, "Are you going in there?"

"I don't know," he says warily. "Why?"

"I was wondering if you'd, uh…see, the woman in there won't sell me a cheeseball, and I really needed one."

"She won't sell you a cheeseball?"

"So weird…" Breezily I wave my hand. "She doesn't approve of…how I'd eat it."

He looks at me strangely.

"No! It's not anything weird or uncouth—"

Greta appears at the doorway. "She doesn't get a cheeseball!"

The man looks alarmed. He mumbles something and heads off.

"It's not anything weird!" I call after him.

"It's wrong!" Greta calls after him. "The way she eats it is immoral."

"It's not!"

The man picks up his pace.

I spin around to face her. "I will get my cheeseball elsewhere, and I will enjoy it more than anybody ever enjoyed a cheeseball in the history of time."

"Seriously doubt that."

"In the history of time!" I repeat as I spin around and march down the sidewalk, trying not to cry.

CHAPTER 9

STELLA

"I can't believe she cheeseball shamed you!" Kelsey's putting on her shoes. "Greta is a freak. Somebody should've warned you about her. Tell me the kind you wanted."

"You don't have to do this," I say.

"Fuck that. My girl wants a cheeseball, my girl gets a cheeseball. An elevator ride and a walk down the block. I think I can manage it."

I hand her some cash. "The one I want is today's special cheeseball with dried cranberries and pecans. And thank you!"

She's out like a tornado of bling.

I stand there in the middle of her living room—now our living room—feeling so grateful.

I've spent so much of my life with emotionally unavailable brainiacs who saw any kind of upset as excess drama, I'd forgotten what it was like for somebody to get in there with me. To be an ally.

I head to my room to change out of my uncomfortable work clothes.

I'd given her the headlines—I didn't have the right skills and felt like an asshole; weird vibes from the family friend who got me the job which also made me feel like an asshole; and the last straw: the cheeseball shaming.

I tidy up the kitchen while I wait for her.

Ten minutes later she bursts into the kitchen and sets two Gourmet Goose boxes on the counter.

"I only needed one," I say.

"The other one's for Willow and Lizzie. They're dropping by later. I hope you don't mind if I serve it with crackers."

"Just because I eat them alone doesn't mean I'll get ragey if you serve one the normal way. I know it's weird."

"It is weird, but it's kind of cute."

I plop the thing into a bowl and grab a spoon.

She follows me to the living room, which is full of colorful furniture and art. Front and center is a poster for *Anything Goes*, the Broadway show she's in. My roommate, in an actual Broadway show!

She sits on the beanbag chair and texts somebody while I dig in.

"Oh my god," I gasp.

"It's okay?"

"This is the best cheeseball I've ever eaten," I say. "It's so…delicious."

"Just…a bowl o'cheeseball."

"Cheeseballs are amazing. You have this incredible cheese and you mix it with little things, like treasures, and the crunchy outside to balance the cheese. Cheeseballs are created for maximum pleasure. Beautiful to look at and eat."

"You just saw a cheeseball one day and said, 'those crackers have to go'?"

"It's more of a historical thing with me. My parents had a math department party once, and I was really sad, and they'd put out all of these mini cheeseballs, and I stole one and brought it to my room and ate it with a spoon, and I don't know, I felt like a queen. And later I graduated to full-sized ones. I mean, they are completely useless, put on earth for maximum pleasure."

"You think about cheeseballs a lot," she observes, squinting at her phone.

"I do. And did you know, there's never been a perfect dish for the cheeseball—especially if you eat it with a spoon like me. If you put it in a bowl, all of the fun side stuff gets stuck to the sides. And if you eat it off a plate, it moves around unless you smash it down, and then, what's the point? And on a plate with crackers? Don't get me started. Someday I'm gonna find a way to eat it where it keeps its fun, festive shape."

"A plate with a spike?"

"A spike would be a start, but it would need to go way beyond that."

"Life goals!" Kelsey says, scrolling and scrolling.

I snort and take another bite.

Kelsey's friend Lizzie stops by with her sister-in-law, Willow, and of course Kelsey immediately tells them all about how I was cheeseball shamed by Gourmet Goose Greta.

"Greta sucks!" Willow says. "She and I had a huge argument about baked brie. I mean, is it a waste of triple-cream brie to bake it in puff crust? Fine. Maybe. But is it worse than murder? No, Greta, it is not."

"But did she still sell you the brie?"

"She did."

"What a freak!" Lizzie spreads some of the communal cheeseball onto a cracker. Lizzie owns Cookie Madness, the cookie store I pass every day. Kelsey says she's building a whole empire of them. "If a person wants to shove a cookie up their ass, we'll still sell it to them."

I nod politely.

"So your new job sucks?" Willow asks, crowding onto the massive velvet couch.

"It's not that it sucks, it's just not the job I moved here for."

"A company paid for her to relocate here, and they let her go the day before she was supposed to start," Kelsey informs them.

"And you don't know why?" Willow says.

"No! We had three Zoom interviews and one in-person where they literally flew me out here and put me up in a hotel. They loved my reel—my work samples. I had great chemistry with the creative team, and suddenly they're going in another direction?"

Lizzie frowns. "That was their excuse?"

"Yeah—*going in another direction with the position.* I actually had competing offers—I turned down other jobs for this one, and they nix me?" I tell them about my weirdly fruitless search, all the supposedly sure things that evaporated like morning dew in the Gobi Desert.

"Weird," Lizzie says.

Kelsey points at Lizzie with her cracker. "Lizzie would know. She hires and fires people all the time."

Lizzie narrows her eyes. "It's suspicious that they changed their mind after they *paid* for your relocation, because they would've vetted you by then. So what happened?"

Kelsey grins. "Lizzie has an idea. I can tell."

"I just want to check something," Lizzie says. "It's probably nothing." She asks me for my contact info.

"My new job isn't that bad," I say. "It's in the administrative pool at Quantum Partners. The people are great, but I'm completely underqualified, as in, I'll be spending tonight watching Microsoft Office tutorials."

"Quantum Partners," Willow says. "They're the best."

"Yeah. My older brother's best friend works there. He got me the job."

Kelsey turns to Willow. "Not just any brother's best friend. It's Hugo Jones."

Willow's eyes grow wide. "*The* Hugo Jones? The quant?"

"You've heard of him?"

"He's legendary," Willow says.

"Willow runs her own tech company," Kelsey explains. "She's all about the math and tech world."

"What's he like?" Willow asks.

I gaze out the window, unsure how to answer or even where to start. I'd need a month to fully describe Hugo. "He's incredibly intense. Brilliant. Super loner."

Willow grabs a cookie. "I've heard he hates people."

"More like he hates talking to people, aside from a chosen few, like my brother."

"Really," Willow says.

I study my fingernails, remembering the intense set of his jaw that showed he was irked. The flash of his gaze when he was intrigued—I'd do anything for that intrigued flash. There were times I thought it was aimed at me, but it was my imagination. "People say he's oblivious to anything that's not math, but that's wrong. He's aware of everything—excruciatingly aware, a fact that is obvious if you watch him closely enough, which I did. I had the hugest crush on him."

Kelsey sighs. "Brother's best friend. The ultimate forbidden love."

"Did he know?" Willow asks.

"No way. It was Hugo's life's goal to ignore and avoid me. Though there were these rare moments when we'd connect. Like sometimes we joked that we were switched at birth because Hugo's parents are lively and colorful, always having parties. There were times you could hear singing and laughing, even standing on the sidewalk outside their house. Hugo would seem embarrassed, but singing in the middle of the day? Sign me up! Not that I didn't love my family, but it was the quiet math nerd experience with me as the black sheep. He'd be like, 'It's not all fun and games at the Jones house.' And I'd be like, 'Hugo, even fun and games aren't fun and games to you.'"

Lizzie has her phone out. "Googling."

"He's the ultimate perfectionist," I continue. "He has these severe standards that people need to rise to. He'd hate when people seemed lazy or wouldn't follow through. Even my brother, Charlie, would get frustrated, like, 'Oh, Hugo won't do this or that. It's against his code.'"

"His code? Yeesh," Kelsey says.

"Little things would drive him batty. Like God forbid that my shoes were untied. He'd tell me to tie them, and I'd say, 'You tie them.' And he'd really want to, but that was way too interactive for him, so he'd just stew about it. I'd sometimes untie one in front of him, just to tease him."

"This you did to Hugo Jones," Willow says. "THE Hugo Jones."

"No wonder he avoided me like the plague, right? He and my brother were always into some project, and he ate dinner over all the time. I'd tease him like, 'Roboto, please expedite the salt ten inches at a ninety-degree angle' instead of asking him to pass the salt. And then he'd be like, 'That's not even a thing.' So disgusted with my antics. He's no robot, though—that's the truth."

"Because you were crushing on him," Lizzie says.

"Yes. Totally unrequited. I was the cat who went for the ultimate cat hater, or in this case, the ultimate Stella-hater. I wanted to curl up on his lap and have him pet me. And I would nuzzle him."

"Maybe a nice tongue bath," Kelsey says.

"You want to know the weirdest thing about him? Antisocial as he is, he has this shocking talent for giving the perfect gift. It's like a magic trick. He once gave my mom a 3D-printed model of the Mandelbrot set, which is apparently a famous fractal, whatever that means. It's sculpture made of resin that's covered with intricate patterns and it was her favorite gift of all time, over and above most of the stuff her own kids gave her. Charlie got a few perfect gifts from Hugo, too, his favorite being an actual tricorder used in one of the Star Trek movies."

"Did he ever give you a perfect gift?"

"No," I say sadly. "It's okay. I'm so over him."

"He is hot." Lizzie passes her phone to Kelsey. "Did you see him today?"

"From afar, but I'm not supposed to bother him or act like I know him. It was totally weird. I know we haven't seen each other in ten years, and I'm this annoying person who used to be in his life, but it feels wrong. I'd at least like to thank him. A thank-you is what an adult does, right?"

Lizzie grabs another cracker. "Can you send him a thank-you card?"

"How? Even if I knew where he lives, he'd think I was stalking him."

"Interoffice mail?" Willow tries.

"I don't want people at work to think I'm sending him things. That would be weird, right? What if his assistant opened it? And I doubt he reads his own email, so email's out."

Kelsey turns to Lizzie. "Have Antonio do a singing telegram?"

Lizzie snorts. "Yeah, if she hated him."

"No, thanks," I say. "I want to thank him, not terrorize him."

"Do the admins ever do deliveries to him?" Willow asks. "Maybe you could do a delivery and personally slip him the card."

"That has potential," I say. "Hugo likes it way better when

people thank him with a card rather than thanking him with words. And I could keep up the pretense of not knowing him. I could discreetly hand it to him."

Later that evening, I pop out and buy a beautiful card with a cute bear face on it. On the inside it says, "I can bear-ly thank you enough," and it's printed the old-fashioned way on really thick paper. It's sort of dorky.

Back in my room, before I settle in for a night of tutorials, I work out what to write inside. I do several drafts on paper before I hit on the just-right thing.

I can't wait for him to read it, to see the look on his face.

CHAPTER 10

STELLA

Hesh pops his head over the wall that separates our cubicles. His small glasses reflect the rectangular light fixtures on the ceiling. "Diamond Thai day. Get your order in by eleven."

"Diamond Thai day?"

He comes around, takes over my keyboard, and calls up a spreadsheet. "Put your name here and your order there by eleven. Any special instructions or spice level notes go here." He clicks a link, and a menu opens up. "Best Thai in the city, no cap."

"Okay, I'm in." My night of software learning has me exhausted—a big, delicious lunch will help!

I choose a large pineapple pad Thai with four stars and make my payment.

Five minutes later, Tinley from the courier desk is standing over me, nervously wringing her hands. "Did anybody explain to you about pineapple?"

"What about pineapple?"

Jane comes around from her side. She has her red hair down

today, and her curls are giant, like soup-can curls. "This building is pineapple-free. You can't have anything with pineapple anywhere ever. It's, like, a really important rule."

"The entire building?"

"You want to do regular pad Thai with peanuts?" Tinley asks. "I need to get the order in."

"Perfect."

Tinley heads off.

"This entire building is pineapple-free?"

Jane lowers her voice. "Hugh-dini is deathly allergic."

"He is?"

"Deathly."

I frown. Hugo's deathly allergic to pineapple? I feel like I would've known about such a severe allergy. And Mom makes a killer fruit salad that's full of pineapple. Surely we ate it when Hugo was over, being that he was always over.

"Deathly allergic to pineapple? Are you sure?"

"Deathly. You shouldn't even have pineapple candy, because if Wulfric came around and smelled it? Off with your head. Instant termination."

"Noted." I frown, feeling baffled. Could it be a new allergy? But even then, there would have been some kind of near-death incident to kick it off. I would have known about it. Charlie would've said something.

Though Hugo is so weirdly private.

Jane lowers her voice. "The Quantum team was at this industry banquet one time? All the top Wall Street movers and shakers were there, and Wulfric discovered a pineapple tart on the dessert cart after he'd confirmed that there would be no pineapple served. He had the whole thing shut down."

"He was literally flipping tables," Hesh adds from the other side.

"I don't think he *literally* flipped tables," Jane says. "But there was yelling. Wulfric threatened some people."

"I heard he flipped the dessert table," Hesh says. "Hugh-dini is Wulfric's secret weapon. He's the sacred billion-dollar oracle of math whatsits. He'll do anything to protect him."

"And when they travel?" Jane adds. "Wulfric will pay entire hotels to take pineapple off their kitchen menu and scrub down their fruit storage areas."

"Wow," I say.

"You know whose problem it really is? Lola—Wulfric's assistant," Hesh says. "I'm sure she's terrified that she'll ever overlook a pineapple. She's probably the one that has to call ahead to restaurants or whatever about the whole situation. On top of everything else she has to endure from Wulfric."

"You couldn't pay me enough to do Lola's job," Jane says.

"Hell no," Hesh says. "Most of his assistants are gone in a week."

"Wait, though..." Jane narrows her eyes at Hesh. "Has Lola been here an entire year already?"

"Is that possible?" Hesh gazes up at the ceiling, seeming to calculate this in his head. "Jesus Christ, she started in June of last year and it's October. Over a year."

"That's...stunning," Jane says.

"Okay, then," I say. "No pineapple. Noted. And I'll take the position of 'Wulfric the ragey megalomaniac's personal assistant' off my job aspiration vision board."

Viola comes by and we act like we're working. Meanwhile, the card is burning a hole in my bag. I wander up to the courier desk now and then, but there never seems to be a delivery for me to take to Hugo's area.

Until the following day. I'm up making copies at the machine when somebody throws a white cardboard mailer on the courier desk with a clipboard. "ASAP needs a signature from Mr. Jones."

I gather up my copies and wander by. "I gotta go that way. Want me to bring it?"

Tinley widens her eyes. "You would?"

"Absolutely. And it needs Mr. Jones's signature?"

"Right here on the clipboard, but Brenda'll sign if she's there. You don't have to bug Mr. Jones with it."

CHAPTER 11

STELLA

Hugo's office is up on the ninth floor. You have to take a special executive elevator to get there, and then walk down a long hall and pass through the office of his very serious admin, Brenda. Her brown hair is in a high, sleek bun. Her suit is sleek, too, as are her glasses. Everything about Brenda is sleek, like a scary racecar.

I walk up and smile. My card for Hugo is stuffed inside the clipboard sheets. "I have an envelope that needs Mr. Jones's signature. Should I bring it on through?"

"Set it here and I'll stamp the sheet."

"It has to have Mr. Jones's signature," I say.

"The stamp is fine," Brenda says.

"This one's special. It needs a personal signature specifically from Hugo Jones."

"No," Brenda says. "It doesn't."

"It really, really does," I say. I fully realize here that it would have attracted far less attention if I had written "anthrax" across the front, but there's no stopping now.

"Well, he's not here."

"Will he be back soon?"

"Possibly."

I take that as a yes. "I can wait."

Brenda adjusts her glasses to better showcase the scowl she's aiming at me. "I've never heard of any delivery where the stamp isn't acceptable."

I shrug.

"He's gonna want me to stamp it. When he comes through, he'll say, 'Stamp it.'"

"Well then…"

"Your funeral." Brenda turns her scowl back to her work.

"How long have you been Mr. Jones's admin?" I ask.

"I'm not an admin. I'm a junior analyst and executive assistant."

"Like a protégé?"

"If you want," she says. "Yes."

"For how long?"

"Almost three years."

There's a squarish gray rock on the corner of her desk—it has a strange and lovely luster, and I have to pick it up. "Heavy."

"Galena." She snatches it from me. "Nearly eight times as heavy as water."

"Really."

She holds it up to the light. "See how it's slightly translucent? Very unique. A gift from Mr. Jones. I don't know where he found it, but…" She sets it back on his desk, turning it just so. "This specimen is very rare."

And suddenly I know what it is—it's not just a rock, it's the perfect gift. "Galena," I say.

"Yup. My favorite mineral."

"You have a favorite mineral, huh. Do you have a favorite number?"

She grunts, annoyed.

I grin. I know she has one, and I know she'll answer. I didn't grow up with nerds for nothing.

"Tau is my favorite number, if you must know." She looks up. "Chia is my favorite vegetable. Gallium is my favorite element, and my favorite color is blue."

"Chia's not a vegetable, it's a seed," I tease, even though it probably *is* a veggie. Somebody like Brenda would get that right.

Brenda glares. "Chia's a vegetable."

I can see why Hugo likes working with this woman. "Why blue?"

"Because of its position on the spectrum."

"Uh-huh. I like the color pink."

"I'm sure you do," she says.

"What's wrong with pink?"

"It's your criteria that I take issue with."

"What's that supposed to mean? You don't know my criteria for liking pink."

"Fine. Why do you like pink? Tell me your criteria."

"Pink makes me happy." I know this answer will annoy her, but I can't help it. Something about how stern she is transports me back in time to my teen self, saying annoying things to my brother. But it's true—pink makes me happy!

Brenda is disgusted. "Not to be rude, but can you wait in the chair outside the door?"

I snort. "Not to be rude?"

Brenda points to the door I came in through.

I go out and heave myself down onto one of the chairs at the far end of the hall. It's a ways down, but I can still see who goes in and out of Brenda's office.

There was a time when I would've sold my soul for Hugo to

give me the perfect gift. The fantasy wasn't getting the gift itself, but that Hugo would have taken the time to figure out what I would most want in life, which would require him understanding me, caring about me, pondering my deepest desires.

My favorite iteration of this fantasy had Hugo coming into my bedroom at night via a secret door he'd created himself. I would be startled, of course. And he'd sit next to me in bed, and the gift would be beautifully wrapped. He'd tell me that he didn't want the others to see because of how special the gift was, and how much it would reveal about his feelings.

I always let the gift be a mystery in my fantasy—it felt more magical not to have any idea what it could be; I only knew it would be perfect, the result of his vast love and attention all zeroed in on me.

A more public version of the fantasy was him walking up to my middle school lunch table to give me a gift in front of my girl-friends—who all agreed he was hot and utterly unattainable due to his antisocial ways and the fact that he was in high school. He would beg me to stop ignoring him, and he didn't care who heard. And I'd open the gift, and everyone would be in awe.

In other versions, he'd come to me when I was sitting on the outdoor couch—an orange plaid thing Mom and Dad had dragged out the front door of our ramshackle split-level in Percy Groves. It wasn't proper porch furniture, but they were nerdy high school teachers who lived the life of the mind, not to mention the life of deep debt.

This couch was a favorite phone-scrolling spot of mine, and that's what I was up to in this scenario. Hugo would lean over me, hands on the couch back, caging me with all that stormy intensity, staring into my soul with those killer gray eyes, and he'd kiss me fiercely, like his life depended on it, confessing his love in breathless whispers between kisses. And the gift would be so amazing.

I liked this fantasy because it had the highest probability of coming true. I spent a lot of time on that couch, and Hugo really could've come out at any moment with the perfect gift and a heartfelt declaration.

Ding.

I sit up. There he is, storming out of the elevator at the far end of the hallway. He makes a beeline into Brenda's office, seemingly lost in thought.

I spring up and head back in. He's standing in front of Brenda's desk.

"Excuse me, uh...Mr. Jones?" I say.

He whirls around to face me.

Gray eyes burn into mine.

My mouth goes dry. The floor seems to dip beneath me.

"It's a delivery specifically for you, Mr. Jones," I say.

Brenda pipes up, sounding Hugo-level annoyed. "She's got something that needs a signature, and she insists the stamper won't do."

"It's special circumstances," I mumble, unprepared for the mind-bending reality of being near Hugo after all these years.

"Fine." His deep, gravelly baritone sends pleasure waves through me. "Follow me. I've got research anyway."

I follow him down a long, slim hallway, through a small waiting room, and on into a brilliant office lined with windows on one side and computer screens on the other, and three whiteboards covered with angry scribbles.

He spins to face me. "What are you up to, Stella? What is this game?"

I forgot about this feeling—the sheer joy of being near Hugo, the wild brightness in my chest, just like old times. He'd be so stern, and I'd smile from the pure joy of him, and he'd get even more annoyed.

I'm squeezing my lips together, trying to quash that smile. I don't want him to be mad, but he's frowning so perfectly, and his mussed hair and oh-so-serious glasses…

"What am I up to?"

"Yes. What?" he demands again, so stern and gravelly.

I forgot how sexy he is when he's stern! I swallow nervously. "I wanted to thank you for getting me this job. I got you this card." I pull it from its clipboard hiding place and hold it out to him.

And wait.

The way he's staring at it, you'd think it was a dead mouse.

"It's for you."

"You didn't have to bring me something."

"No, I did. You came through with this job when I was in a pinch, and I want you to know how much I appreciate it. I don't know if Mom told you, but I had this one other job lined up—it was a great position, and it was one hundred percent locked down. Double and triple locked—"

"Don't worry about it." He takes the card. "It's fine. Thank you. And, welcome and all that. Is there anything else?"

My gaze falls to his fingers on the envelope. I'm remembering the feel of those fingers touching my neck and grabbing my hair during a certain long-ago kiss—the mistaken-identity kiss, as I call it.

The mistaken-identity kiss was the result of Hugo napping in the wrong place at the wrong time during a teen drinking game my friends and I were playing in our basement back in Illinois. The game involved blindfolds and boys hiding in dark rooms around the house, not knowing who would come to kiss them.

Our parents were away at the time, needless to say.

I went into the dark music room, having drawn a scrap of paper that sent me there to kiss whatever boy was there, not knowing it was Hugo. Hugo was supposed to be holed up in Charlie's room.

But there he was—taking a nap, as I later figured out.

And I sat myself right down on the daybed and leaned over and kissed him.

He jolted up. He grabbed me and kissed me back. He was so warm and strong, all pine shampoo and a smattering of whiskers.

I instantly realized it was him.

Hugo.

Hugo and I were kissing! It was like every dream I'd ever had, coming true. Better, even, because Hugo's kiss was full of raw need. It was like he had an earthquake inside him, gripping me, holding me, needing me. He whispered something that I thought was my name, but surely it wasn't, being that I'd accosted him while he was sleeping with a kiss in a dark room.

And he was kissing me—passionately, like he was out of control with lust, gripping my hair, all knuckles and breath and heat.

It was the hottest thing I'd ever experienced—until the moment he seemed to come to his senses, fully awake.

"Stella?!" He was irritated or angry, or I didn't know what.

"Oops," I said. "Uh...wrong person." I got out of there in a flash, reeling. Mortified.

We never spoke of it again, and Hugo would barely look at me after. I'm sure he put it out of his mind, but me?

Hell no.

I thought about it constantly. That kiss burned so hard and deep into my heart that it changed me in some fundamental way. It changed my soul. That kiss stayed inside me, acting on me like a powerful forbidden drug, and I was addicted, chasing after that high ever after, and never coming close.

So the mistaken-identity kiss is the wrong thing to be thinking about here, but I can't stop remembering. Though to be honest, remembering is the wrong word for what I'm doing. I'm luxuriating in the echo of the kiss, letting the feel of him resonate through my body.

It was the hottest moment of my life—by a mile, and I've had some hot moments.

When I raise my eyes to his, I think he might be remembering, too.

Though his memory is probably the opposite of mine. Instead of amazing hotness, he's likely recalling the amazing awfulness of being accosted in such a way during his nap by his best friend's stupid kid sister. Or else he forgot about it.

I shake myself out of it, averting my eyes from the way his shirt stretches tight across his chest. "Your guard dog almost wouldn't let me in," I say. "What's up with her?"

"I don't know that there's anything *up* with Brenda," Hugo says.

"She treasures the galena that you gave to her."

"Is there a point to all this?"

I grin. It's just so, so, so nice to see him again, and I know he wants me to leave, and I know he spent years avoiding me. And of course there's my Hugo moratorium where I stay away from Hugo and all Hugo types, but somehow, I can't bring myself to leave.

Self-discipline never was my strong suit.

I trace the crisp corner of his glass desk. "How'd you know a hunk of galena would be her favorite present in the world?"

"It's a little something I like to call *observation skills.*"

That's such a Hugo response. "It's more than that. You act like you don't get people, but with these gifts? It's like you see right into a person's heart."

He shrugs. "Primitive humans thought thunderclaps meant that the gods were angry at them. That turned out to be wrong, too."

I snort. Of course he acts like it's nothing. Hugo the sexy, untouchably icy detective.

And the sad truth is, he could've given me a bent paperclip and I would've treasured it like the Diamond of Sheba.

"Brenda is also under the impression that chia is a vegetable and tau is a number, I'll have you know," I say.

"She would be right on those counts."

My heart pounds. Hugo being Hugo is my catnip.

"That would be news to my mom. Remember how she'd collect all those Chia Pets and have them growing?"

"Oh, I remember," he says darkly.

"Hugo," I whisper, barely able to contain my happiness. "Do you hate Chia Pets?"

He gives me the stern eagle eye. "A hunk of clay designed to grow sprouts that badly resemble hair? Cultivating a plant where it shouldn't be and in the place of hair, but it deliberately doesn't work as hair and is wasted as a plant?"

I'm biting my lip so hard. Is it possible he's become sterner and sexier? Yes.

It's bad that I want to kiss him.

And kind of distressing that I still feel this infatuation.

I remind myself that I have sworn off all Hugo-style men and that would include the original Hugo, but I can't help it. I plaster on a serious expression. "So that's a no on the Chia Pets?"

He growls.

My heart flutters.

I have to get out of here.

"There was always one on the dining room hutch," he says. "Visible from each and every spot in the room, no matter where you sat. Your mother—a mathematician. Yet these Chia Pets she'd be growing everywhere—"

"Oh my god," I say. "It was you! You're the one who'd move them around and put things in front of them!"

Hugo's eyes flash with humor. It's so subtle, most people might not see it, but I do. I may have gotten shit grades in high school math, but I earned straight A's on the subject of Hugo Jones's nearly imperceptible expressions.

I point. "You!"

His eyes narrow. "Sprouts. Growing on a cheap sculpture."

"You know I was blamed for that, right? Thanks a lot, Hugo!"

His lip quirks. "I wasn't hiding them, more like shifting them so they weren't visible from my seat at the dinner table."

"Her pride and joy," I tease.

"I'm sorry, a sculpture. The sprouts—"

I'm laughing. "All this time!"

He straightens here like he suddenly remembered we're not supposed to have fun. "Look, I have to get back to work."

"What are all those X's?" I point to the whiteboard nearest to the window.

"Nothing," he says.

I stroll over. "What are you tracking?"

CHAPTER 12

HUGO

The thing with Stella is that sometimes answering her questions leads to more questions. Other times, answering her questions gets her to let go of whatever she's decided to grab on to. You never know which way will be best in a given circumstance, but I go with the latter.

"If you must know, I'm tracking focus sessions," I say.

Stella examines the board, trying to make sense of it.

The light brown streaks on the lower part of her hair weren't there in the photo Christmas card her parents sent last year, but her hair is otherwise the same, a shiny waterfall of waves. Her periwinkle skirt matches her periwinkle jacket—she's more dressed up than I've ever seen her—for the job, I imagine. The color complements the warm tones in her skin and hair. Everything about her is deeply pleasing to the eye, a phenomenon that would probably be best explained by a color wheel.

"Lotta *X*'s for today," she finally says.

Yes, there are more *X*'s than usual, and the reason for the *X*'s is standing right there. "Those are unsuccessful focus sessions," I say.

"What? You get a punishing and angrily scrawled black *X* when you don't do the session right?"

"What's measured is managed." I go up and stand beside her. "My goal is to improve the length and quality of my focus sessions by one percent every day, which is 39.78 percent per year."

"Are you being funny, Hugo?"

"No."

She turns to me. "You know what's so weird? I have a whiteboard at home, but it's for getting one percent worse every day. My goal is to be negative a hundred."

"Funny," I say, unamused.

She turns back to the board. "Don't you think life is too big and unpredictable to be quantified by numbers?"

"Nope," I say. "I can put numbers to anything."

Stella gives me a look I remember well: an exasperated sideways glance that communicates utter disagreement.

"Anything." I go back to my desk and sit down. When I glance back up, her face is beet red. God knows what she's imagining. Some people really cannot control their thoughts.

"Soooooo…" She points at the card. "Don't forget."

"I won't."

She puts her hands on her hips, a motion that widens the V of her button-down shirt, drawing the eye in the direction of her chest.

"I'll open it later." I turn to my screen, ignoring the V.

Most women leave those top two buttons unbuttoned, but on Stella, it's highly distracting. A less disciplined man might imagine pressing his hand to that V of skin, to feel the warmth there, and maybe even imagine sliding it downward, to the edge of where her breast begins to swell, the edge of whatever lacy undergarment…

I jerk my mouse to wake up my screen, expecting that my abrupt focus on my computer will give her the message to leave.

Of course Stella in a business suit is a kind of dissonance after so many years of seeing her in jeans and T-shirts. Except when it was time for her to go out with her dubious girlfriends, at which point she'd wear a sequined tube top or strappy little dress or whatever else she could find that was inappropriately revealing.

I look up. No sign of getting back to her job anytime soon. I'm used to people monitoring me for signs of displeasure and instantly reacting, but Stella isn't like other people.

I give her a look that would send most people packing.

She smiles. What is she waiting for? An engraved invitation to leave?

"We're done here," I finally say.

"Is that how the prince dismisses people?"

"Other people know better than to bother me."

"Come on! Aren't you gonna open it?"

"What? The card? I'll open it later."

"Why not now?"

"Because opening cards with the person standing right there staring at me is in the category of things I no longer do."

She looks amused.

I shouldn't be surprised. The set of individuals who find me amusing contains exactly one member: Stella.

Why did I get involved in her life? Why?

"Hugo." She lowers her voice and turns up the conspiratorial energy to ten. "You have an entire category of things you no longer do?"

"And now you know one item that's in it." I say this more harshly than I meant to, but this has to end.

"I'm sorry, you used to always say that you prefer greeting cards to interactions. Remember?"

"I prefer that if the card is sent in the mail, not if it's hand-delivered by a person who stands there staring at me. If that's the case, go ahead and talk at me, because unlike some square of cardboard, you have the ability to adjust your communication to real-time reality, the real-time reality being that I neither want nor need whatever heartfelt effusion is on deck right now."

"Whatever heartfelt effusion is on deck?" Stella's eyes sparkle. "Oh, Hugo."

"Is that it?"

"What if I want you to see what I wrote?"

"So the card is actually for you? The card is an obligation, and I'm supposed to react to it like a circus monkey so that you can watch me see what you wrote? If that's the condition of the card, I'll pass. Gifts with obligations do not interest me."

She sucks in a breath looking highly entertained in spite of the fact that she's using the energy of five nuclear reactors to suppress that smile of hers.

I grit my teeth and concentrate on my pad. I can't afford to be distracted, but it's no use. Her presence is magnetic, and the way she takes over a space...it's just all very Stella.

Not that the magnetism is about her, specifically. Homo sapiens are hardwired to monitor the unpredictable individuals within their community.

"What?" I bark.

"Oh my god, Hugo! Fine! Read it when you're home in your little hermit cave or whatever. Is that what you want?"

"It's exactly what I want."

"Under the cover of night, Hugo sits in his hovel. He opens his card. He steams it open, so as not to rip it."

"It's not a hovel, I'm not a hermit, and I won't be steaming it open."

"But you won't rip it."

I tap the screen, pulling up the currency exchange rates.

"Do you wish I wouldn't thank you at all?"

"Yup."

"Well, I guess you can toss it or whatever."

When I look back up, I can see that she's unhappy.

Something tugs at my chest. I yank open the drawer and grab a Tums. "I'm not tossing it; I'll look at it later."

"Okay."

It comes to me that I've gone too far. In trying to minimize the disruption that is Stella Woodward, I'm being an asshole. I ask her how she's fitting in.

"Are you asking me that because you just realized how mean you're being? Is this you throwing me a bone?"

"Are you gonna let me?"

Stella sighs happily and sinks into the chair in front of my desk. "It's good. I like the people for sure. I had to scramble on the skills acquisition front, but I'm up to speed. I won't make you look bad, don't worry."

"Not a concern."

She plucks a pen from the pen holder and clicks it repeatedly as she describes her new work friends, Hesh and Jane. It's so Stella to go right to the people she likes.

I'm relieved the position is turning out to be tolerable at least. She needs to find something else, though. I'm surprised she hasn't. She's hardly the incompetent her family makes her out to be.

She crosses her legs and continues on. The skirt pulls tight, accentuating the line of her thighs, not that I'd dwell on it, being that she's still Charlie's little sister.

Instead I concentrate on unwrapping the Tums. I had Brenda re-up my supply this morning.

Stella sets down the pen and picks up a Post-it pad now, flipping through it as she describes her boss, Viola.

I'll open the card tonight—it wasn't a lie.

Most people leave me alone, and the few people I allow in my orbit know not to come at me with cards or gifts or emotional outpourings. They know that if they did that, they would no longer be welcome in my orbit.

It's awesome.

If somebody had told teenaged me that when I grew up, I could reject 99 percent of all social obligations and interactions and get to spend my time on math, it would've sounded like heaven.

Though teenaged me would also want to be assured there was still fucking in the future...and would therefore be thrilled to learn that future me would know several ambitious, career-minded women in Manhattan who were down for no-strings hookups.

Stella exchanges the Post-its for a USB adaptor which she immediately begins to twirl.

The other upside of no-strings hookups? They are the opposite of distracting, the opposite of tormenting.

"You probably think I'm a screwup for not being able to land a job in my field."

"Not at all."

"I need you to know, I had a killer job with Zevin Media Group, this hot boutique agency in Soho. They were bringing me on as Associate Creative Director. It was a done deal." She waits for this to sink in. It's important to her that I believe the job was real.

Of course I knew it was real. All too real.

In the light streaming in from the window, you can see how her face has lost the baby-fat roundness she still had in her teens. There's a majesty to her cheekbones, and she moves with poise.

"It was a done deal. They paid my relocation and everything—

not cheap, right? And then the day before I was supposed to start, they're like, 'We're going in another direction.'"

"That's what they said?"

"Yeah. Another direction."

"You probably wouldn't have liked it there," I say.

"I would've loved it! I hit it off with that team like fire." She describes the elaborate interview process where they apparently started brainstorming a campaign.

How have I let this interaction with her go on for so long? What am I doing?

Now she's describing her efforts to land similar jobs, and how people would be excited to hire her, and then the jobs would mysteriously vanish.

"And you can't go back to the other places that offered you jobs?" I ask.

"Too late." She sighs. "So now I'm applying for practically entry-level positions where I could not be more overqualified, just to stay in the industry, you know? And the same thing keeps happening! Which makes no sense. A couple of months ago I had my pick of great jobs, and now it's like, 'Sorry, we won't touch you with a ten-foot pole even for assistant film editor.'"

I frown. It *is* strange.

She twirls the adaptor. "The more I think about it, the more I think there's something strange going on, because why would Zevin Media pay for my relocation and then change their minds? My roommate and her friends think it's suspicious, too."

"Huh," I say.

She stops twirling the thing and narrows her eyes. "Maybe it's something with my background check. But no. They would've run the check *before* making a job offer." She resumes the twirling, moving it this way and that. "It makes me think I should do some sort of postmortem."

"What do you mean?"

"Aggressively investigate why the job was pulled away at the last minute." She flips the thing back and forth in a distractingly random pattern, now. "Go all *Law & Order* on their asses."

I'm not a fan of that idea for a number of reasons. "I think you should leave it alone."

"What? You're a data scientist; aren't you all about getting to the bottom of things?"

"Not all things are worth getting to the bottom of."

Stella looks hurt. "Are you saying that because you think I won't like what I find?"

"Chasing sunk costs is a major waste of time, that's all."

"Oh my god, that *is* what you're saying. You think I'll get a negative outcome." She flips it faster and faster. "You think I'll be disappointed."

I go around the desk and pluck the adaptor from her hand. This works to halt the visual chaos, but we're too close now, and her sadness is palpable. Most people are mysteries to me, but I've always been able to feel Stella.

"I don't think you'll be disappointed, but sunk costs shouldn't affect future actions."

"It's not a sunk cost if there's something I need to know," she says.

"What is there to know other than Zevin Media is the kind of place to relocate a worker only to leave them high and dry?"

She sighs. It's a sigh I know well, one of the many Stella sounds that have played over and over in my mind.

But my favorite sigh of hers I only heard once. I was seventeen, home from college for the summer, napping in the small room where the Woodward kids would practice their instruments. If you drew the blinds, it was completely dark, save for the glint of Stella's rented saxophone.

The perfect place to sleep while Charlie carried on his sometimes annoying Skypes.

And suddenly somebody sunk onto the daybed next to me and started kissing me, all flowery shampoo and lips like berry alcohol.

Kissing me. It seemed like a dream—a girl who smelled like Stella. Felt like Stella.

Something inside me crashed open, and I was ferocious with lust. I fisted her soft ponytail. I consumed her lips like a starving man.

I still remember the surprised catch of her breath, and that glorious sound when she sighed into that kiss. I can still feel her small hands gripping my shoulders, fingertips digging into flesh as she kissed me back.

And I kept on.

There in the otherworldly zone between sleeping and waking, I became unhinged from any sense of decency. My code was nowhere in sight. I was a runaway freight train, steely with power and unstoppable force.

Out of control, and I didn't care.

I can't even use the excuse that I wasn't fully awake, because by that time, I was.

The intense pleasure of kissing her destroyed all reason, obliterated the codes that held my life together. Kissing her was suddenly more important than my word to my friend.

I was an addict, willing to trade anything for one more moment.

Until I came to my senses and pushed her away.

She mumbled something that sounded like "I didn't know..." followed by something unintelligible, and then she ran out of there and left me reeling.

She'd kissed me—snuck in and kissed me.

Gradually, it occurred to me that this kiss was likely part of a drunken teen dare game. A boy had burst in on me some time before, blindfold in hand, stammering something about looking for the music room before I ran him out of there.

It was him she was supposed to kiss—not me. She thought I was the boy with the blindfold.

And I lost control. I hated myself for losing control. Losing control seemed like the worst thing somebody could do.

"I need to get back to work," I say.

"Hint, hint. I get it!" She heads toward the door, but then spins around, because nothing is ever simple with Stella. "Hey, since when are you deathly allergic to pineapple?"

"How is that relevant?"

"Isn't death always relevant?"

"Do I need to have Brenda escort you out?"

"Deathly allergic, Hugo. I mean, hello, did you not spend years eating Mom's fruit salad? I can't imagine her not putting pineapple in that. How did we not know?"

"You think I made it up? Who would make up an allergy?"

"But I'm almost sure we ate pineapple when you were over."

"There's such a thing as a late-onset allergy, isn't there?" I say.

"Is that what it is?"

"So." I straighten, resolved to end this. "An obligation card, a ridiculous refusal to understand sunk costs, and an interrogation? Am I going to regret getting you this position?"

Her smile fades. Her sparkle goes. "Excuse me."

I regret my harshness, but it's always best to rip off that bandage. She needs to steer clear of me.

"I just wanted you to know how much I appreciate your help," she adds.

"You are welcome."

"Right. Um...okay."

I hate that it's come to this, but she gets the message now. Leave me alone.

This is how it has to be.

I watch her leave with a queasy twist in my gut.

CHAPTER 13

STELLA

"Hugo's bad boyfriend material, that's for sure."

Charlie said that to me once when we were on the outside porch couch watching Hugo drive off in his parents' beater car.

I staked out that couch a lot the summer I turned fourteen—not only was it cooler out there, but Charlie and Hugo would have to pass by for all of their comings and goings. I was a one-girl toll booth with a crush the size of a tank.

Charlie was pretty oblivious as a rule, and I was careful to feign disinterest whenever he'd talk about Hugo and his antisocial ways, which I, fool that I was back then, found hot.

Hugo was growly and difficult and unpolished, but I felt sure that he was hiding a heart full of love and tenderness, and that I was the only one in the world who could ever bring that love out. Not that I had evidence for it, aside from times he'd look at me with what I tried to convince myself was adoration but was likely disbelief or possibly gas.

So when Charlie dropped this little not-boyfriend-material

tidbit, I'd no doubt pretended to concentrate on Candy Crush or Tetris—while burning with curiosity. I was an inferno of curiosity, desperate for him to say more.

Why was Hugo bad boyfriend material?

When Charlie didn't elaborate, I'd allowed myself a grunt, desperate to elicit the tiniest drip more, but it was a no go.

I knew that any further sign of interest in Hugo would shut that faucet forever. I had no choice but to bide my time.

Still.

Bad boyfriend material? Why?

Was there something wicked about Hugo's sexual appetite? An outrageous sexual proclivity? A voracious drive? Dark desires?

Needless to say, Charlie's little warning only fired my interest.

A few weeks later, he did seem to elaborate—we were on the bench outside the high school—I'd walked up from middle school to catch a ride home with my dad, who was teaching at the local community college. Charlie was waiting, too.

"No Hugo-mobile?" I'd asked, plopping down next to him.

Hugo was mostly attending classes at the University of Chicago by then, driving the hour into the city, but he usually still managed to get back for robotics club with Charlie and then drive him home so they could do their games between bouts of eating like locusts.

"Hugo's off with Norma," Charlie said, wide face scrunched into a mask of concern, lips pursed under his button nose. He then added this tidbit: "I don't know why they like him; he gives them nothing."

My antennas perked up at that, if not outright springing from my head like surface-to-air missiles, because what did that *even mean?*

Gives them nothing.

"Nothing?" I'd asked nonchalantly.

"Trust me, you wouldn't want a guy like that," he'd said.

Of course Dad pulled up right then.

I turned that one over in my mind for days afterward like one of those impossible questions that Zen masters sit in caves and ponder.

What was the meaning of the word *gives* in that sentence?

What was the meaning of the word *nothing* in that sentence?

Did he give nothing emotionally? Or was it more of a literal thing, like no birthday gifts? No box of chocolates on Valentine's Day? Or was it nothing physically?

I ruled that option out. Hugo would give and give and give on a physical level. My infatuated teen imagination would accept nothing less.

From time to time I'd walk in on Hugo and my brother lifting weights in the basement—usually on my way to the downstairs freezer to get something that nobody actually needed.

Charlie and Hugo would be shirtless and sweaty, pointedly ignoring me, doing their reps, skin gleaming.

This vision of shirtless Hugo doing squats, a barbell hoisted on his shoulders, it's burned into my mind.

Isn't it a rule of the universe that brainiacs are supposed to be gangly and bespectacled with pimples and pocket protectors? How was it fair that Hugo got to be smart *and* good-looking?

It was not fair.

Hugo's good looks, intelligence, and standoffish attitude made him catnip to the girls of Percy Groves High School. He dated several of them, but those relationships never took.

Was it because of the *nothing* he gave them? Would they know what the *nothing* was if asked? By a kid from the lower grades, for example? I wished I could interview some of them. I considered trying to befriend them, but I was so much younger.

So I was left to wonder. And pine. And pine.

Hugo graduated from UChicago in record time. The finest

grad schools fought over him, Roman-coliseum style, all swords and spiked clubs, and MIT won out. After he burned through MIT's grad program, the finest business leaders fought over him, but he went with the controversial Wulfric Pierce, moving to New York City at the tender age of twenty-one.

I stayed back in the Midwest, following his brilliant career from afar, rife with desperate longing—longing that I tried to fill with a string of guys who were brilliant (though never so brilliant as Hugo), beautiful (though not even close to Hugo), and icy.

How many times did I have to burn my fingers on the icy-hot stove that was the Hugo sort of man, causing myself horrible pain, before I would swear off Hugo types forever?

Three.

Viola accosts me the next day as I'm hanging my coat on the pop-out hook on my cubicle wall, pink frosted lipstick accentuating her very large frown. "You're not to bother Mr. Jones unless he's made a specific research request," Viola informs me the next day. "There will never be a case where Brenda can't stamp for his signature. And if there were, Brenda would be the one to determine that. Not you."

"Got it," I say. "Won't happen again."

"There are two people here you want to absolutely minimize your interaction with, and Mr. Jones is one of them."

"Understood." I shuffle some papers around my desk, still feeling shitty from my asinine visit to Hugo, hoping that this is the end of my conversation with Viola, but Viola doesn't go away.

In fact, when I next look up, she's staring at me weirdly. It's here that I realize she's waiting for me to ask who the other one is.

I really hate when people do that. It makes me feel like a trained seal. *Arp! Whooooo's the other one, Viola?*

The side of me that doesn't want to be a trained seal is warring with the side of me that knows I should be nice to Viola, because she's my boss, and she obviously wants me to ask.

I suck it up and decide I'll make it good for her. I lean in, all conspiratorial. "Who's the other person?"

Viola straightens. "Let's just say it's somebody you'll never meet." This in a really ominous tone that suggests *she* has met this person, but I never shall.

Oh my god. I played her game, and she won't tell me? I feel like such a chump.

Again she stares, waiting for me to ask who this very important and frightening person is.

"Thanks for the warning," I say. "I'll keep my head down. I'll keep my nose to the grindstone."

"Good thinking," she says.

I wake up the computer. When I look back up, she's still staring at me.

"The other person would be Wulfric Pierce," she adds. "And I'm telling you right now, do not accost him. Like Hugo, any business you have with him can be handled through his assistant, Lola, or whoever follows once Lola's head rolls."

CHAPTER 14

Hugo

I spend ten minutes looking at the whiteboard before I realize that I'm looking at the whiteboard, but not seeing the whiteboard. I run my hand through my hair.

My concentration is officially destroyed, just when I need it.

I sit down at my desk and grab a yellow legal pad and a nice, sharp pencil; sometimes that helps my focus. Instead I make a string of triangles.

A secret presentation has been scheduled. My deadline is screaming up. Half the quants on Wall Street are hot on my heels.

And I'm making triangles, but really thinking about Stella.

I go back to the board. I remind myself I trained all my life for this.

Growing up in Percy Groves, I would've traded anything to laugh like an idiot at something on TV or flop onto a couch in a naturalistic way. I studied other boys exhaustively. I made flow charts. I copied physical movements.

I spent a lot of time, in short, approximating human behavior.

You might think that all that time was wasted, but if you look at the job I have now, it's all about approximating human behavior, though instead of smiling in the mirror or trying to re-create the conversational stylings of popular kids, I'm creating data models that predict and approximate the way market forces are impacted by people's irrational, emotional, and frequently idiotic tendencies.

I couldn't have asked for better training.

An alert from my phone jolts me to attention. It's one word from Brenda: *Wulfric.*

The door bangs open.

"Jones," Wulfric barks. That's the extent of niceties. He's at the board.

His assistant, Lola, gives me a quick smile, stylus poised at her iPad to take notes. She has short, dark hair and a quietly observant demeanor. I realize with some surprise that she's lasted fifteen and a half months. Made of strong stuff.

"You're still at the board," Wulfric grumbles.

"I've gone down a lot of paths."

"Down a lot of paths? If you do this thing by the process of deduction, we'll be here until 2060."

"Good thing that's not how I'm doing it," I say.

Wulfric's a big man—a brazen Wall Street cowboy with a bright blond crew cut, the build of a linebacker, and one of the fiercest intellects I've ever encountered.

He gives me a hard look and I throw one right back. You never show Wulfric weakness.

"I've put a lot of chips on this, and it's not close," he says. "You promised this could fly."

"It's moving."

"Any ETA?" he asks.

"If I had an ETA, it would be cracked."

He turns back to it. "A lot of chips."

As if I didn't know. I've already gotten an extension from him, and we're screaming up on the big presentation.

He asks me about one of the side elements, and I explain. Wulfric doesn't know math like I do, but his market knowledge is keen as a diamond-tooth saw.

Everybody warned me not to work for Wulfric, but I knew he'd give me the freedom to call my own shots, and that's what I care about. In the end, it was the right decision. The model I created made us a fortune, and more importantly, it broke new ground. Models going forward were largely based on mine.

Lola wears a neutral expression. I wonder, and not for the first time, how much she's seen. Wulfric checks the time on his phone, and the two of them blow out as quickly as they swept in.

The goal I've set for myself is ambitious. Some might say I've bitten off more than I could chew, that I should just settle for iterating on my old model.

No way.

Settling and iterating is what a lazy thinker does.

It only takes a second to make a breakthrough. One stroke of the marker.

I force myself to review the board from Wulfric's eyes; sometimes that's the way to get back in. But after ten minutes, I realize that I'm just pretending to review the board while Stella is simmering on the back burner.

What was I thinking? I roll out the red carpet for Stella Woodward, and here she is, invading my sanctuary and taking up precious space in my brain.

Stella Woodward, who lives to throw monkey wrenches and knock things down; Stella, who can always be counted on to laugh at the most inappropriate times, and whose favorite artist is Salvador Dali, and have you seen the works of Salvador Dali? I can think of no artist more inane than Salvador Dali with his ridiculous melting clocks and warped reality.

She is not without her charms, as established, but she is the opposite of women I go for.

There are not enough permutations of the word wrong to cover Stella Woodward.

CHAPTER 15

STELLA

I saw this movie once where a guy liked watching women crush bugs under their shoes. He would lie on the floor and watch it.

It was a strange and oddly chaste fetish that, if the script writers are to be believed, originated in the man's childhood thanks to an incident of him watching his mom crush a bug under her heel.

I guess I should be glad that watching men crush bugs isn't my thing, being that it would really limit my prospects on the ole dating scene and sound bad on a Tinder profile, but I suppose you could argue that my thing is worse because of how men like Hugo have crushed my heart.

I pursued several Hugo types in college, but the rejection was swift and fierce. Until Arjun, a nerdy but brilliant—and of course icy—perfectionistic chemist. He had a great laugh, and he shared my love of hiking and *Gilmore Girls*. Things were good with us.

But little by little, he began to find character flaws, and he was happy to spell them out. I was too silly, too rambunctious, too sloppy in my logic. "You're too much," he'd said when he finally dumped me, acting as if I fooled him or something, like I'm a carton of eggs that you think is perfect, but then you crack one open and there's a yucky chick blob inside.

So that was over.

Was it my fault for pursuing icy, perfectionistic brainiacs? Was it my fault for chasing after that initial Hugo high?

I eventually moved to Madison and landed that job with the creative marketing firm. It was an early naughts-inspired workplace full of modular seating, blond wood, and Ping-Pong tables. The creative staff would hang around late into the night brainstorming big ideas for clients.

I loved it. We could hammer at it until three in the morning and I'd be energized. Flying. Ten years I was there, rising up through the ranks, building my personal brand as a somebody who can think up campaigns that will move the ball for clients.

I had a little apartment near Capitol Square, a cute flowerbox out the window, and a steely determination to steer clear of brilliant, handsome, remote, perfectionistic men who'd find me flawed after a test-drive period.

I even went so far as to identify golden retriever types with the help of a couple of concerned friends. I dated two different men like that—kind, outgoing, fun men who were really into me. Those relationships went well enough that the guys wanted to be more serious, but I couldn't do the wagging tails and excited happiness.

I only wanted the icy brainiacs. It was like a disease.

I ended up with Jonathan, a dashingly hot statistics professor, an enchanting conversationalist and an enthusiastic wearer of Obsidian Valor cologne for men, which features peppery bergamot notes, as he liked to point out.

He was brilliant and perfectionistic, yes, but he seemed more easygoing than the other Hugo types, and certainly more easygoing than Hugo himself, so I thought it would be different.

Jonathan and I laughed a lot. We made ambitious recipes. We watched old movies. We had decent chemistry that seemed like it could evolve into love.

We spent two great years together. We even bought an SUV that we called the baby-dog mobile, because we planned to fill it with a baby and a dog.

Until he went to a Coldplay concert one night. The concert made him realize our relationship was him settling—that's what he told me when he got back. He wanted to be with me, but he simply couldn't. There were problems that couldn't be repaired. He couldn't settle anymore.

"Settling?" I'd asked, distraught. "What does that mean?"

"It's hard to articulate," he'd said.

My heart was pounding out of my chest on full déjà vu mode, because I knew what he meant even if he didn't.

"It won't work."

"You just can't with the character flaws?" I tried. "The reckless, overzealous thing? Too loud, too much, too cheerleader-y, light as gossamer, lacking in *gravitas?*" These were a medley of observations Hugo once made about me.

This look he gave me right then. I'd hit the nail on the head.

"Never mind!" I'd added, wishing desperately I hadn't supplied him with those words. "It doesn't matter."

It mattered to Jonathan, because one of the features of icy, brilliant men is a need for getting the perfect description for a thing, even if it devastates a person. "No, you're right. That's how I feel, but that's me, that's my loss. Other men won't feel that way, I promise," he'd said.

Why couldn't one of these men have fallen for a hot, leggy model-type and dumped me on the basis of looks? It had to be my horrible character flaws? I had to be the carton of eggs with the bloody, partly formed chick blob running roughshod over their perfectly ordered lives?

I walked away with money for my half of the baby-dog mobile and a total Pavlovian reaction to the smell of Obsidian Valor for men by Jack Hermann.

Even now, when I catch even the faintest whiff of the peppery bergamot notes of that cologne out on the street, my entire soul cringes.

I went to a therapist who showed me a thing called an emotion wheel and had me identify all the emotions I was feeling. I didn't like the emotion wheel. I didn't want to sit around naming my emotions, I wanted to get away from my emotions. I wanted to never feel like that again.

I was done with Hugo types. I put caramel streaks in my hair, fought like a banshee to land my dream job in New York City, pulled up stakes, and moved to New York.

Not only was it a geographical fix for the heartbreak of Jonathan, but it was the next logical step in my career. I might be failing in the love department, but I was killing it in the short-form video niche, where coloring outside of the lines and being overzealous and extra are highly prized.

And Zevin Media was the best. The team wanted me. Our Zoom interviews were brainstorming lovefests.

What did they discover about me? Did they go to a Coldplay concert, too? And why did it have to be Coldplay? Jonathan couldn't have had his epiphany at a cooler concert? Something more badass and rocking or exciting? I would've even accepted classical or jazz.

According to the cookie display in the front window of Cookie Madness, today is Kangaroo Awareness Day. I wave at the clerks and continue on, past the flower store.

Square of cardboard.

I spent forever picking out that square of cardboard, and even more time figuring out what to write on that square of cardboard.

But does Hugo care?

I get it, he wants to open it alone. He doesn't like surprises, but did he have to be so eager to get rid of me?

I stop at the bookstore to pick up a little pressie for Kelsey—the newest in a mystery series where an old woman and her cat solve mysteries at a retirement village.

I wait for the clerk to ring me up hating that Hugo still has the power to hurt me. How is that still possible? I thought I was past that!

I need a way to shock myself every time I think smitten thoughts about Hugo. I had a friend who snapped her wrist with a rubber band when she thought about chocolate. I need something stronger. An electric shock. Salt-coated spikes that dig into my arm.

According to the gossip rags, Hugo dates brainy supermodel types—women with big important Wall Street jobs and nary a hair out of place. Perfect women with perfect pedigrees. The opposite of me.

I walk into Gourmet Goose, all smiles, as though I don't remember what happened the last time. It's a two-cheeseball night—one for me and one for Kelsey and anybody who might stop by. I can say with full honesty that I'll be sharing this time.

I grab a pack of crackers and examine today's cheeseball offerings. "My friends are going to be so excited!"

"I'll sell you the crackers, but you know I can't sell you a cheeseball," Greta says, somehow seeming both bored and angry at the same time.

"But I'm having guests! It's practically a cheeseball party!"

Greta arches one eyebrow. "I think we both know what your idea of a cheeseball party is."

"Are you calling me a liar?"

She comes up to the counter and looks me square in the eyes. "Can you guarantee me that none of these cheeseballs will be eaten with a spoon?"

I hesitate, taken aback by her directness.

"Cheeseballs are for entertaining. End of story. Buy yourself flowers."

"I don't want flowers," I say, fighting back stupid, stupid tears.

I want a cheeseball.

I want to not have gotten pre-fired from my dream job.

I want off the wheel of emotions I've been on ever since catching sight of grown-up Hugo, but I'm trapped here, wheeling away like the saddest hamster ever.

CHAPTER 16

HUGO

I lean Stella's unopened card against the lone candleholder that marks the precise center of my dining room table and then I head to the kitchen and get to work on a savory roasted vegetable medley, diligently cutting each piece to uniform size to ensure even cooking. While the veggies roast, I grill a chicken breast, paying meticulous attention to time and temperature.

Fifteen minutes later I'm at the head of the table, mixing the vegetables to get a uniform distribution of colors and taste. My perfectly grilled chicken breast rests diagonally. The silverware is positioned symmetrically on the left side of the plate, forming an acute angle that complements the dish's visual balance.

And there in front of me sits the envelope.

I can't smell it from here, but I happen to know that the scent is bright flowers mixed with something earthy.

The mix is very Stella; she loved all kinds of different things. You'd see her shooting hoops with neighborhood kids, all messy hair and unruly bravado, and then a couple hours later she and her wild girlfriends would head out with their blow-dried hair and sparkly outfits—hidden under oversized shirts when parental eyes were around.

Charlie didn't approve of Stella's girlfriends—he seemed to think they were corrupting her. The way Charlie would talk about Stella sometimes, you'd think she was a doltish hunk of clay. I'd frequently point out how wrong he was, but it never seemed to affect him.

There was one day when he called her a "hopeless waste of space." I remember this wild, burning sensation in my chest, and my voice sounding strange to my own ears. "Don't talk about her like that," I said to him. "You're her brother, for fuck's sake! How can you not see how bright and capable and persuasive she is? If anything, her friends are copying her."

Charlie was usually a good judge of character—it baffled me, how wrong he was about her.

He did stop after that. I was glad that he'd apparently reconsidered his ignorant opinion. It really was unfair. She wasn't book-smart like Charlie and their parents, but she was optimistic and interested in everything, and she had an artistic flair that nobody seemed to appreciate. She loved taking pictures, and she was incredibly observant, constantly pointing out the way trees and houses out the window changed in the shifting light, or marveling at the different shades of green in the yard.

She was also wild and reckless at times—an adventurous spirit who hated being told what to do. She'd run into trouble now and then, but she always seemed to find her way out of it.

Almost always.

I finish dinner and clean up, then I fix a cup of decaf coffee, and set it on the upper right-hand corner of the placemat. A bowl of ginger candies is on the upper left-hand corner, and Stella's card is there in front of me.

I eat a candy and sip the coffee. Then I pick up the card, loosening the envelope by its flap, trying to get it up without ripping it. It annoys me when people rip presents open or rip envelopes open. It annoys me even more when they open them from the small side with a paper knife.

Letters in general annoy me. All paper can be electronic.

The card is thick, printed with an old-fashioned letterpress. There's a bear image front and center above the words "I can bear-ly thank you enough."

I read the inside.

I'm sooooooo grateful you got me this job, Hugo. It means everything that you're in my corner. Hundreds of gummy worms set nose to tail, circling the earth over and over, could not encompass the hugeness of my gratitude. I want you to know that I won't let you down.

Warmly,

S

This followed by several hand-drawn cat faces.

Something churns in my gut.

I set it aside and finish my coffee.

I think there's something weird going on, because why would they hire me and then change their minds? My new friends thought it was suspicious, too.

The German philosopher Immanuel Kant argued that it's never wrong to tell the truth, that telling it's a moral duty, regardless of the consequences. And I had a good reason to tell the truth in that letter of recommendation.

A very, very fucking good reason—and good intentions, too.

But the road to hell is paved with good intentions, as they say.

I go back to the card. It comes to me that the grinning cat face she drew is supposed to be an emoji. Leave it to Stella to *draw* an emoji, defeating the purpose of the thing on several levels.

A quick check of my phone tells me that it's the smiling cat emoji; it means extreme happiness.

I doubt she put real thought into the choice of emoji. It was probably just topmost on her emoji panel or something. Because it was clear she's not happy at that job, though it seems like she's making the best of it.

Pretending not to know me for whatever Stella reason. Waltzing into my office with the ASAP delivery so that she can hand-deliver the card. The pouf of her ponytail. The way she took my chair, legs crossed. Periwinkle and brown.

And now it's official: she's taking up entirely too much of my attention. What's done is done, and no amount of thinking and rationalizing will change that. Eventually, she'll get another job; in the meantime, I'll avoid passing by the admin pool as much as possible. And reiterate that I am not to be bothered.

I don't know why she hasn't found a different job. She seemed to think I needed to be convinced of her value in the career marketplace, but I know about her success. Her family seems to see her awards and promotions as participation trophies, but it's obvious that's not the case.

And with that, I really am done thinking about her. I said I was done, and I need to be done.

Stella's off-limits. That is the rule. She's Charlie's little sister. Warren and Joyce Woodward considered me to be a second son, which makes Stella like my sister.

What's more, thanks to the Jones household, I got a front row seat for what life looks like when people break their codes, their vows, their promises—to themselves and others.

"We're going to stop drinking this month, Hugo!" "No more big parties!" "Wednesdays will be grocery trip days—just say what you need, Hugo!" "Only one drink a night!" "This is the last time somebody sleeps in the bathtub, Hugo, but for now, just ignore him!" "We're turning over a new leaf!" "Okay, we really, really mean it this time—new leaf."

That will never be me.

CHAPTER 17

STELLA

I've just settled onto the living room couch with a bowl of popcorn and a juicy true-crime documentary when Kelsey bursts out of her bedroom door, phone in hand.

I perk up—I was hoping she'd come out. "If you're in the mood for buttery popcorn and a grisly murder in a quiet seaside town," I begin, but I trail off.

She looks upset.

"What's wrong?"

"I got a text from Lizzie. It's intel about your mysterious job thing."

"Lizzie got intel?" I hit pause. The grisly crime scene can wait.

"You want the good news or bad news first?" she asks.

"The bad news?"

She sits down. "I'm forwarding you a few texts. The screen-shots are what you're gonna need to see."

I grab my phone.

I spot my name right away—it's the header for an entry in

some kind of forum. The next line is my address and former place of employment. And the centerpiece of it all: a PDF of a confidential letter of recommendation.

The next screenshot is the text of the letter.

"I've known Stella Woodward for years. She's reckless, unruly, and refuses to follow orders. Completely incorrigible."

Each and every word is a punch in the gut.

The identifying information is blurred out, but I know who wrote that.

Reckless. Unruly. Refuses to follow orders. These are classic Hugo things to say about me.

Other screenshots show bosses spilling the beans on employees for things like poor work habits, social issues, hygiene issues.

"Where is this website?" I ask her.

"Lizzie says it's some kind of human resources chatroom, like for marketing and advertising businesses in the area," Kelsey says.

"Like a secret forum."

"Illegal and secret," she says. "But I don't really get what this letter is."

"I know what the letter is," I say, putting it all together. "Part of getting that job at Zevin Media was that I had to ask two or three people to send confidential letters of recommendation on my behalf—you know, those letters where they send them directly to whoever's thinking of hiring you?"

"Right," she says.

"Usually you ask old bosses or somebody important. And you have to be pretty sure they're gonna say something nice about you."

"Because you don't ever get to read it?"

"Exactly. It's confidential. The idea is that the person will tell the truth about you if they know you'll never see it."

"And you thought this person was gonna say something nice about you?"

"This person is Hugo Jones—that family friend who got me the job. And no way—I never asked him. I never would've! This is the handiwork of my mom and dad. I told them not to ask him when they suggested it. I thought they would respect my wishes, but my family is really into micromanaging my life. Like, really into it."

"They must've thought Hugo would say something nice."

"Yup." I pretend to study my phone, but I need a little time before I can speak in a non-weepy voice. "They thought wrong."

"And now Hugo's letter is on a forum where people post mean letters of recommendation and employee horror stories."

"Just like those forums about horrible landlords and cheating boyfriends. Except I'm the one getting posted about now. Guess that explains my problems getting hired."

Kelsey makes a sympathetically angry face.

"I can't believe Mom and Dad asked him after I said not to. Hugo's not even in the marketing industry, but my parents think that everyone stands in awe of him. Mom was like, 'It would be such a feather in your cap, Stella!'"

"That's one shitty-ass feather," Kelsey says.

"Right?" I flop back on the couch. "Also? So much for confidential."

"Why would Hugo Jones get you a job at his hedge fund if he thinks you're such a terrible employee?"

"Guilt? Pity? The opportunity to enjoy his evil handiwork, maybe? Keep me under his thumb in some perverse way? Though all of that would suggest he cares, whereas obviously he just wants me to leave him the hell alone. So...file it under *Who knows?*"

"What a jackass."

"All the jobs that I almost got—they probably came to check

this board before hiring me. This is why they all changed their minds."

"Being unruly and not taking direction are awesome traits," Kelsey says. "Women would still be begging their men to cosign on credit cards if not for some unruliness and refusal to follow orders."

My heart practically melts with gratitude. "Fuck yeah!" I spin around. Nobody keeps me down—not even Hugo Jones. "So what's the good news?"

Kelsey goes to the kitchen and comes back out with a bowl that contains a Roquefort and fig cheeseball. She hands me a spoon.

The kindness of that gesture makes me want to burst into tears.

"When did you get this?" I ask.

"Today. I wanted you to have another one. Greta can fuck herself."

"You are such a sweet friend."

She sits down and grabs the bowl of popcorn. "We'll figure this out. But first up: a horrible murder!"

I start the show back up and dig into the cheeseball, but my attention is only half there. Hugo went out of his way to ruin my job prospects. Does he hate me that much? I feel like such a fool for ever wanting him to think I'm pretty, or hoping he'd look at me and see an impressive woman.

But slowly, slowly, as the detective begins to put together the clues and close in on the mild-mannered insurance agent, my hurt turns to rage.

CHAPTER 18

STELLA

I storm into Brenda's office, breezing past her, not caring that she's guarding Hugo's inner sanctum like the world's most assholey lion.

She follows me down the little hallway. "You can't go in there!"

"Well, then you can fire me. Or he can fire me. Whoever wants to can fire me. Everyone can fire me!" I blow on through the waiting area and pound on the door, and then I pull it open.

Mr. Antisocial McStern rises up and comes out from behind his desk.

"I told her she wasn't to bother you," Brenda says.

"I'll handle it," Hugo says.

"This should be a write-up," Brenda says.

Intense gray eyes pierce mine. "I got it."

Brenda heads out with a huff.

Hugo shuts the door and turns to me. He's wearing yet

another one of his shoulder-defining shirts, finespun gray fabric outlining triceps and biceps and various other fetching muscles.

"The rules don't apply to you, is that it? You think you can walk in here whenever you please?"

"Yeah, well, you know me." I march right up to him, glaring into his stupidly chiseled face. "Unruly. Reckless. Refuses to follow orders."

A muscle fires in his jaw. He remembers what he wrote in that letter—he has a memory like a steel trap.

"So, Mom and Dad asked you to write a confidential letter of recommendation to Zevin Media on my behalf?"

"They did," he says.

"And you thought, 'That's a good idea, but I'm gonna put my own unique twist on it and make it super mean.'"

"Mean was not my intention," he says. "Quite the opposite."

"I see. So, that was your idea of a supportive letter? I gotta tell you, it didn't read that way, what with the recklessness and unruliness and all."

"Stella—I know it looks unsupportive."

"*Looks* unsupportive? It tanked my dream job. And then it tanked every other job I applied for afterwards. How could you write a letter like that? The process is confidential. Mom and Dad would've never known whether you wrote anything at all. Nobody would've known. So why would you do it?"

His powerful gaze feels like a searchlight on me. "I had to." This he gusts out with feeling.

"Why?"

He shakes his head. "I had my reasons."

"Like what?"

"I can't tell you. I'm sorry."

"So your reasons are a big secret? No. I think you owe me an explanation."

"I can't tell you," he says.

"So...secret reasons. That's why you wrote it. Secret reasons. Are you fucking serious right now?"

He nods, gray eyes serious as can be.

"Well, I wanted that job, and you wrecked it. Thanks to you, I'm now doing spreadsheets and proofing and travel arrangements—me, the least detail-oriented person on the planet. That job is crushing my soul because of how much I suck at it. But guess what? It's the only job I could get. I hope you're happy."

"I'm never happy," he growls.

"Poor Mr. Roboto! What's wrong? Did they leave the happiness out of your coding? Along with empathy and human decency? How could you? Seriously—*unruly? Reckless?* Do you really think those things, Hugo? You think I'm reckless and unruly and incorrigible and—"

Warm fingertips settle against my throat sending electricity radiating across my skin.

The words evaporate from my lips.

Hugo's gray eyes spear into mine, dark and serious as he traces a molten path down my throat, two strong fingers sliding down, down, down to the tender divot at the base of my neck.

Desire shivers through me. My knees wobble.

This is wrong—I hate Hugo with every fiber of my being.

But I can't look away. I can't move. Also, every fiber of my being wants to wrap around him like a horny and slightly depraved gymnast.

"What..." I whisper raggedly.

His fingers continue on their wicked way, down the center of my chest, and all the while he's watching my eyes in that gravely serious way that makes me feel like a shy, naked deer in the headlights of a predator.

This man, ruiner of my love life, destroyer of my career, blower-upper of my serenity, has my body humming with need for him.

I should stop this, but I don't. I'm in his thrall and I don't even care. He clamps the nape of my neck.

"Somebody's eager to show off his robot hand upgrade," I mumble nonsensically.

"God, Stella." He yanks me in for a kiss—a punishing kiss. He's raw and forceful and everything the opposite of smooth.

God, this man can kiss.

I tunnel my fingers into his hair, grabbing it like a handle for his head.

I'm kissing him back—feverishly, ferociously—like if I kiss him deeply enough, my hunger for him will be sated, but the more we kiss, the more I need.

I'm mauling him, because the pleasure is melting my mind and I am a lips-and-hands monster for him, hungry for him and his hard shell with the soft, secret insides.

His breath comes coarse and fast. Large Hugo hands close around my shoulders and he hauls my body up against his, deepening our kiss, aggressively invading my mouth with what feels like a stunningly muscular tongue. My tongue comes out to tangle, sliding across his.

It's mind-bendingly sexy—just these tongues of ours, tangling hotly.

Confident hands slide over my ass. He lifts me onto his desk. His lips come back over mine, and my mind is completely lost.

He fists my hair and turns my head in a new way, like he needs a new angle of kissing. "The scent of you. The way you feel. You are the most distracting woman alive...can't think..."

He kisses me with terrifying but delicious intensity.

My legs clamp incorrigibly around his waist. I'm a human-sized chip clip that's clipping my sex right to his steely erection, panting. Reeling.

As if of their own volition, my traitorous and very nonrobotic hands are at his stomach, grabbing on to his muscle-outlining shirt, little wads of fabric in my fingers, freeing the shirt from his belt.

The hard jut of his erection rubs between my legs.

My horney lizard brain likes that. Presses in. Frees more shirt from his waistband, and now my hands are on his abs, hard and warm. My greedy palms eat him up.

"Relent to me, Stella."

Is that even the right way to use the word *relent*? I don't know, and I don't care, because my hands are skimming over the taut contours of his stomach, the smattering of hair there, and the soft line of it trailing downwards. I feel the movement of his breath, the hard slash of his hip bones.

"Is relent a nerd way of saying submit?" I ask.

He kisses down my neck, hot, lusty kisses punctuated by the zing of teeth grazing over sensitive skin.

"I think that's what it is," I whisper. "I think it's a nerd way to say submit."

He growls, frustrated and turned on. Does he have a problem with that? Maybe he does, and he's disciplining me with some very intense kisses, and I am way into it.

His body feels strong and warm, and touching him is everything I dreamed about and longed for all those years. It's everything I imagined.

Maybe his secret reasons are some way of helping me—that's the thought my libido is having now. *And surely he doesn't think I'm unruly and reckless and all that!*

"Stella," he breathes, back at my lips. He pulls me in, fitting our bodies together.

"Mmm," I say.

It occurs to me here that he never did answer the question of whether he really thinks all those horrible things about me—instead he kissed me.

But a kiss is a form of communication that says "I like you!"

And Hugo doesn't lie.

Screeeeeeech. My brain kicks in here. Thoughts start spinning. Hugo doesn't lie! Which means he truly thinks those mean things that he said!

Did he kiss me to just distract me from the question?

"What am I doing?" I push him away. "You think you can mess up my career, insult me, and now I want to kiss you and whatever?"

For the record, he would be correct in thinking that I want to kiss him, and I very much want to whatever with him. But I'm officially out of my fugue state.

Hugo looks disorganized. Undone. Hugo undone is the hottest thing I've ever seen in my life. I want to go to him and put him back together with more kisses and hand ministrations.

Hugo undone almost breaks me, but I resist.

I scramble out of there, clutching my last remaining shred of dignity.

CHAPTER 19

HUGO

I ascend the polished stone steps to the historic and somewhat grandiose Gotham Club on East 64th Street and head down the lushly carpeted hallway, still reeling from my failure of self-control today.

It was a colossal failure of self-control. Unforgivable. Shocking, even.

Try as I might, I can't parse what happened. It was something about her scent, the tone of her voice, her high emotions, her anger, her chaotic attitude, her aliveness—all I know is that I was overcome with such a violent surge of lust, I barely knew myself. I watched myself go to her, helpless to stop.

And before I could think, I was pulling her to me, kissing her, unquenchable desire rushing through my veins. The deeper our kiss went, the more I needed. She tasted so bright and sweet and warm and good. And the sounds she made—pure Stella.

If I'd been a vampire, I would've sucked every last bit of blood from her—uncontrollably, mercilessly. Every last bit.

She was right to stop us. It's a pretty sad thing when Stella is the one to put the brakes on an out-of-control situation.

And she was right to be angry. This situation with the letter—what the hell happened? Did it get passed around? Apparently so, and that is absolutely outrageous. I would send somebody to look into it—not in a nice way—but that could just result in them passing it around even more. I have to think of something. It's not right, what happened. None of it.

I open an unmarked door and walk into a richly paneled room with a roaring fire at one end.

"Look who the wind's blown in!" It's Fergus, his Scottish brogue thick as ever. He comes and slaps me on the back. "Hugo Jones, thinking he'll be taking our money. But it's a new day, my friend."

"We'll see about that," I warn.

I've been coming here every Tuesday night for years to play high-stakes poker with this group of men, or I suppose you could call them friends at this point. I missed last week working overtime, but I need to blow off some steam.

I hang up my coat, get my chips, and take my place at the heavy oak table.

I have to ante up ten times what the other guys do; it's a handicap we established because of how much I win. They don't let people like me into Vegas.

Maybe Fergus will make out tonight. Maybe all five of them will. I'm off my game already and we haven't even started playing. I've always been excellent at compartmentalization, but my disgust with myself is clouding my mind.

Ronan takes the seat across from me. Even in this relaxed setting, the man has impeccable posture. Regal posture. Luther says Ronan's some kind of minor royalty, and he looks it, from his tight, dark curls to his Roman nose to the precise, confident way he moves.

Cooper hands me a scotch. "How's the top-secret data model going?"

"Shitty," Leon barks from a leather chair next to the roaring fireplace. "Can't you tell from his expression?"

"It's fine," I say. "Though I am still on the whiteboard."

"You should be in testing now," Leon says.

"Uh-oh," Fergus says.

"It's under control," I say. More under control than the Stella part of my life. I pull up the custom app that Leon developed for our group.

Did they leave the happiness out of your coding? Along with empathy and human decency?

Apparently so. Jesus Christ, kissing Stella like that. Touching her the way I did. What's wrong with me? I am a man of codes. Codes, once established, are not optional. Once you start breaking your own codes, everything starts to unravel.

Everything was unraveling.

She's off-limits, and I was out of control. A creature driven by craving.

I'd always wondered how my parents ended up the way they did, feeding their cravings for alcohol while their lives went to shit. This thing with Stella was a window into that—I wanted her so badly, nothing else mattered. That's the very definition of weakness in the face of addiction.

It's good that she's angry at me, good that she thinks the worst of me.

Cooper watches me closely. "Attila the Hun with an axe or Wulfric Pierce with his infamous blue iPad? Who I want less on my ass? I'll take Attila the Hun."

Fergus laughs. "I'd take Attila the Hun and give him a free shot at that."

I grab a seat. "With an axe? No way."

Ronan deals with concise, elegant movements.

The cards fly. I lose one hand after another. All I can think about is the kiss. Her scent. Eager little hands pulling at me shirt. The way she locked her legs around my waist, like she couldn't get enough.

I met Stella the summer I turned eleven, an age I was pleased with, being that eleven is a prime number and a palindrome.

My parents had just moved us to Percy Groves. We'd set up house in a hotel—we stayed in a lot of hotels before the money ran out, and my parents sent me to lots of camps.

Camps had their downsides—namely other kids—but I enjoyed the structured activities and regular meals.

And this one was math camp.

I met Charlie the first day. He'd been the star of the camp two years running. He'd already skipped a grade and was deep into geometry. He tried to compete with me at first, but I ended it quickly, and we became friends after that.

He was my first real friend, but he came with a major liability: Stella.

Math camp was the last place Stella should've been sent, but her parents must have gotten some sort of deal, being teachers. Stella was an outsized presence there; she'd laugh and whisper during quiet work times. She'd call out ridiculous answers to the equations posed by our long-suffering camp counselors. When she wasn't doing that, she'd be busy corrupting the younger kids with her worldly, nine-year-old ways, or moping around bored, all untied shoes, haphazard ponytails, and blindingly bright outfits.

Needless to say, Charlie and I spent a good deal of energy avoiding her. This only spurred her to bother us more and create more chaos.

I had a daily routine at math camp that involved a walk to the welcome center vending machines during a twenty-minute break between sessions. Most kids went for the dining hall vending machines, but the welcome center ones had almonds, and almonds are amazing brain food.

I had inserted $1.00 into the vending machine when I discovered I was a quarter short. I hit the button to get change, but change wouldn't come out. The machine stood there waiting for my last quarter.

I didn't know what to do.

If I walked back to our cabin to get another quarter, some other kid would come up and see the $1.00 in LED lights on the front of the machine and realize they could get any snack they wanted for a quarter. I thought about writing a note but that would only encourage somebody.

I stabbed the return button.

"It's probably out of quarters," said a voice from behind me.

I turned around and there she was, snapping her gum, bracelets stacked halfway up her arm. Charlie's little sister.

"It doesn't give bills in change. Only quarters. But it runs out sometimes."

"Do you have a quarter I can borrow until later?" I asked.

"Nope," she said.

"Would you do me a huge favor, then?" I asked. "Will you guard the machine here and not let anybody use it until I come back with a quarter? I can be back in under four minutes."

She'd sauntered up and leaned on the machine, clinking quarters around in her hand. "You go ahead and run back there, Hugo."

"You'll guard it until I return?"

"I won't let any other kids get a cheap snack if that's what you mean."

This all seemed too good to be true. I'd only just met Stella, and we'd never even had a conversation, but I'd observed her enough to be wary. "I'm asking if you'll guard it for me."

"Sure, I'll guard it. And you see that hill up there? The second you're out of sight over that hill, I'm gonna get a pack of sour gummy worms for a quarter."

It took me a little while to process this. "You can't do that."

She widened her brown eyes, as if in shock.

"It's my money in the machine," I explained.

"Get it out, then."

"Obviously that's not possible."

Glittery toenail polish sparkled through the sandals that she wasn't supposed to be wearing—camp rules called for sneakers. "I don't mind waiting."

"But as soon as I turn my back, you're gonna buy gummy worms for a quarter."

"You catch on fast, genius boy."

I couldn't believe it. I was the king of math camp. The god of math camp. Nobody messed with me.

Except Stella.

"Fine. I'll pay you a quarter to guard it," I said.

She tilted her head, eyes sparkling. "I may not know algebra, but I know I'm about to save a buck on a nice fat pack of gummy worms, and I think I like that better."

This girl. I couldn't believe it.

"I'll wait, too."

She seemed delighted that I'd said this. "Five minutes until the bell, according to my phone."

I gritted my teeth, wishing some other kid would come along with a quarter for me to borrow. Any kid would be glad to help me, especially if it meant putting Stella, the math camp pariah, down a few pegs.

"The bell applies to you, too," I tried.

"Does it, though?" More gum snapping.

Stella was always late, always getting yelled out, even getting after-dinner screen time taken away.

It's here I saw my angle. "You might lose screen time."

She shifted her pose and let out a dramatic sigh. "I suppose I'll just have to wipe my tears with my gummy worm wrapper."

I could not make sense of this wild, irrational, and untamed girl, willing to take a hit—for gummy worms.

The three-minute warning sounded, and there she stayed.

Fuming, I headed back and took my seat in the front row with Charlie.

Stella sauntered in a few minutes later, making a point of eating a purple gummy worm right there in front of me.

Undisciplined. Scrappy. Reckless.

Infuriating.

I lose another hand.

Luther settles in next to me. "You okay?"

"All good."

"Except for the part where you're playing like shit." Leon rakes in the chips. "Are we gonna have to reduce your ante, Hugo?"

"Definitely not," I say.

"He's trying to lull us into a false sense of security," Ronan suggests.

"Hugo doesn't bluff," Cooper says. "He doesn't play mind games."

Cooper's right. I play numbers and the odds, pure and simple. No bluffing, no mind games. Poker's easy to win if you pay attention.

A new deal goes around. I examine my cards. I track the play.

I need to see her again—not for a replay of what happened, but to discuss what happened. To affirm that it won't happen again. To institute some form of ground rules between us.

I pop another Tums and organize my chips.

"Dude, it's not candy," Cooper jokes.

I grunt and toss away the wrapper.

The six of us have known each other for years, but we don't

do feelings or get into each other's personal business, so the comment was a bit odd.

It's also understood that what's said at the card table stays at the card table.

I'd always liked that rule. Simple. No room for interpretation. Nothing said leaves the room.

I've come to hate that rule, but I keep my promises. I uphold my rules. Except, apparently, when it comes to Stella.

CHAPTER 20

STELLA

Jane and I are collating packets up at the copier. She's doing the sorting and I'm doing the stapling and the bitter regretting.

I staple a sheaf and put it aside.

Unruly. Reckless. Refuses to follow orders. Exasperating. Incorrigible.

Not being entirely clear on the meaning of the word, I looked it up and found this: *an incorrigible person's behavior is bad—resistant to change or correction.*

It's awful enough to say that about a person, but coming from perfect Hugo? He may as well have called me an axe murderer; that's how much he hates a lack of order and discipline and all that.

And then I kiss him? Or kiss him back. Or whatever I did.

Staple smash smash smash.

"Stella." Jane's staring at me.

"Yeah?"

"The corporate style is one staple, placed in the corner at a forty-five-degree angle. The placement should be equidistant, like so." Jane staples a packet in the corner, saying something about four corners of a square. A visually balanced placement.

"Got it," I say.

I gather up the next ream, squaring it off and stapling like Jane showed me, specifically not thinking about how Hugo screwed up my career.

I staple another sheaf.

He ruins my reputation, says those jackass things, and when I confront him, does he apologize? No! He thinks he's entitled to a nice big smooch.

Staple smash.

To be fair, I did go for it.

Hell, I did more than go for it—I was a nympho maniac from hell. A monkey on aphrodisiacs. Like I was living on fake Hugos all this time and suddenly I get access to the real thing, and I want to mainline him directly into my veins.

Or, let's be honest, I wanted to mainline him directly into my vagina. Do not pass go, do not collect two hundred dollars, just get into the vagina.

Being with him was that hot. Horribly. Diabolically hot.

Uh!

Staple smash.

"No, no, no," Jane says. "You really need to get that forty-five-degree angle. Wulfric likes things just so." She turns her chair on a dime and tosses half of my stapled packets into the recycling.

"He's that particular? Will he give us concrete shoes and throw us in the Hudson if we don't staple perfectly?"

"Just to be clear, we're not stapling perfectly for Wulfric, we're stapling perfectly for Lola. Giving Wulfric less shit to be menacing about makes Lola's life easier."

"So what's the story there? Is he literally dangerous in some way, or is that some kind of rich guy vanity PR?"

"You don't become notorious with nothing behind it," she says. "You can't believe the line poor Lola has to walk. Good stapling is our way of helping our girl out."

"Got it. Okay. Definitely down with that." I go back to stapling —more carefully this time.

God, this place!

Jane passes over another stack of collated handouts for me to staple.

Precise staple smash.

I have to get out of here—that's all there is to it.

And I'm working on it. I have résumés out, because apparently I live in hope that not everybody knows about the trash-talking HR forum. I'm also working on a website showcasing my coolest projects—projects I singlehandedly dreamed up and led. A corporate marketing team might not know about the forum.

Staple smash staple smash.

I'll cold call—I'm not scared of that. I'll figure it out. I'm scrappy and resilient.

I'll get something, and Hugo will be out of my life.

Yes, his lips were deliciously glommable, and touching him after all these years—the guy I'd been obsessed with since I was a kid—it was beyond everything.

My palms skimming over his hot, muscular back, my fingertips tracing the stiff line of fabric at the top of his waistband, inches from the promised land that my wicked imagination had done mega-lascivious things with over the years.

Perfect staple smash.

I spent years replaying the mistaken-identity kiss.

I kissed other men after that, but no kiss ever measured up to that. Nothing even came close.

As the years wore on, I wondered whether I was remembering the kiss as being more exciting, more epic, than it really was. How could one kiss contain so much earth-shaking feeling? Was it because I was so young?

It turns out I wasn't remembering it wrong—not judging by yesterday's kiss.

Relent to me, Stella.

Who says that? In my mind, relent is a word you use for weather, as in, "we'll go hiking once the storm relents." Or a rule or policy— "when will they relent on the two-gummy-worm rule?"

But *relent to me?*

How do you relent to a person? Knowing Hugo, it's an arcane but accurate usage that is perfect in every way.

Unruly. Reckless. Incorrigible.

This is my bar? Ruin my career and insult me, but hey, if you kiss me well enough, I'll forget that I've sworn you off?

I know better—so much better. Can the red flag of Hugo's freak-level perfectionism get any redder?

If I kiss him again, if I so much as think hot thoughts about him again, I deserve whatever happens. I deserve to have my heart fed through a meat grinder because I know better.

I'm like a girl in a horror movie whose friends never come back from investigating the strange sounds in the basement. She knows not to go down there. And if she *does* head down there after them, she deserves whatever happens to her—the scary doll stabs her. A creep surgically sews her to some other people to create a human centipede or whatever else, just like I deserve to have my heart broken if I go for original, full-strength Hugo.

I'll be staying upstairs in the creepy-doll-and-meat-grinder-free living room, thank you very much.

A hush descends over the admin floor.

I know it's him without even looking up. It's like my thoughts conjured him.

He's up at the courier desk, mere steps away from my post at the copier, him and his dusky brow furrows and mighty, hawk-like harshness.

And let's not forget the stern frown that always seemed to cow everybody into submission, though it never worked to subdue preteen me. Quite the opposite—that stern frown would energize me. It would spur me on. It would make me turn myself up to eleven.

And it's having that effect on me now, because I'm feeling very eleven, and I really, really want to taunt him.

I force my gaze down, but my heart won't stop pounding. He's just so supremely serious.

When I next look up, our eyes meet. And before I can stop myself, I plump out my nostrils and lower one eyelid. This face was a Woodward dinner table staple, a very subtle face, very wrong face that I like to refer to as "nostril dragon."

Hugo's gaze sharpens, like he's suppressing disbelief and extreme exasperation.

He turns to Tinley, who is yet again wringing her hands, and speaks in growly tones.

"Stop making eye contact!" Jane scolds. "Trust me."

"Right. No more eye contact." I'm back to stapling, quivering with delight.

And because I have no self-control, I look back up and make the face again.

He glowers.

I do that thing where you scratch your face with your middle finger, and then coolly smash in a staple.

When I look back up, because that is the sad state of my self-control, he does this eye-signal thing where his eyes dart in the direction of the hall.

He wants a word with me—out in the hall.

My heart pounds with outrage. Think again, Roboto!

Again with the eye signal. Does he think I'll kiss him again? Am I his sexy girl Friday now?

Staple smash.

So done.

I'd rather quit than be his concubine. I should quit.

Though actually I'd rather be fired. In fact, I'd love to be fired from this job. I'd probably get some kind of bonus pay, but even if I didn't, I like it as a statement.

"Stella."

Tinley's staring at me. Was she saying something to me? "Can you come over here?"

"Fuuuuuuck," Jane whispers. "Told you."

I give Hugo a nice icy look and do another staple.

"You better go over there," Jane mumbles.

"Stella," Tinley says again.

It's not Tinley I'm pissed at, so I amble over, pointedly ignoring Hugo, who's standing right there.

"Could you be free for a research project this afternoon?" she asks. "Mr. Jones has a research request."

Hugo takes a pen from his breast pocket and initials a clipboard, so innocent.

I direct a burning stare at him. "No can do."

I can feel Tinley's astonished gaze. We're supposed to drop everything when Hugo needs research.

Tinley says, "We'll find somebody to take over any urgent tasks that you have. Research like this would take priority."

"It's simply impossible—"

"I'll expect you at two." Hugo nods, as if to show that this is the final word on the matter.

"But my project is very important," I say. "It's regarding the chia account. There's been mysterious movement."

Hugo's frown of grim annoyance is everything good in the world.

Tinley furrows her brow. "Is that related to Mattel?"

"This is not optional. You'll report to Brenda at two and she'll direct you." With that, Hugo heads toward the door.

My blood races. So he's just ordering me around now? Just because he can?

"Excuse me...Mr. Roboto?" I call just as he's pulling it open.

He stops dead in his tracks. Slowly he turns.

Everybody's staring, but I don't care.

I pick up the pen he left on the desk and hold it out innocently. "You forgot this."

Hugo's eyes blaze into mine, and my chest explodes with this strange, heart-pounding feeling that might be pure bliss. "You'll address me as Mr. Jones," he says.

I'm biting my lips to keep the smile at bay. Thrumming with joy, I hold it out farther. "Your pen, *Mr. Jones.*"

He comes in close. "Don't be late." He snatches the pen from my fingers and leaves.

Tinley turns to me. "W-what..." She's studying my face, confused. She has a bottleneck of questions, all crowding into her mind at top speed.

Jane rolls up and grabs my arm. "Did you call him Mr. Roboto?"

"Something came over me."

"You're gonna get fired," she whispers.

I turn to her—I'm sure she's bummed. We get along so well, and they really do need my help here. "Sorry—"

"No," she hisses. "You are livin' my dream."

"You're living my dream, too," Tinley squeak-whispers.

Hesh is there. "God, his face when you said that?"

"Chef's kiss," Tinley says.

Jane lowers her voice and looks around. "I feel like Viola's gonna storm in here at any moment and cut you loose."

"Tell them you have a medical condition," Hesh says.

I snort.

"Maybe she won't get fired," Tinley says hopefully.

Another admin comes by. "That's one way to get out of a research project," he says as he plops down a stack of folders.

"She didn't even get out of it," Hesh says.

Jane shakes her head. "Is it possible she won't get fired?"

Hesh shrugs. "It *does* sound like he still expects her."

"'Don't be late,' he said," Tinley reminds us.

"How much do I have to pay you to bring him a pineapple?" Jane jokes. "As an apology gift?"

"Oh my god, not even funny. He's deathly allergic!" Tinley says.

"But it's a little funny," Hesh puts in.

Everybody agrees it's a little bit funny.

Jane's worried. "It's gonna be a bitch of a project, and we're not gonna see you for the next five years."

"It'll be fine," I say, but I hate that I *have* to go, now, like a kid sent to the principal's office. He costs me my dream job and we have ill-advised sexytimes and now he gets to order me around?

It's not right.

I eat lunch at my desk, feeling angry.

But mostly I'm hurt.

Am I that shitty of a person that he felt compelled to warn future employers? It hurts. And the kiss, then. What was that? Some twisted power trip?

I should get tattoos all over my hands to remind me of the assholery and heartbreak of men like Hugo. Maybe the word "No!" or "It will not end well" in scrolly cursive. Or an *H* in a circle with a red slash through it. Or maybe some teardrops. But then I remember that teardrops are a sign you've killed somebody, and I'm having enough trouble on the job-getting front as it is.

Plop! A pack of gummy worms lands on my desk, nearly startling me out of my chair. Who threw gummy worms? I look around and see Jane, smiling at me from her cubicle.

"A little something something," she says.

I smile. "Thank you!" I sit back down and tear open the pack. It is so sweet that she remembered!

Five minutes later, another pack lands on my desk, startling me yet again. "Livin' the dream!" Hesh says.

Moments later, another pack lands on my desk. An admin comes by and tosses in another pack. "One word. Awestruck." Another hits me in the head. It's from Tinley.

People are showering me with gummy worm packs like I'm this folk hero.

"You guys!" I protest, but it feels good.

CHAPTER 21

HUGO

I can see that she thinks I want her to come to my office for a replay of what happened yesterday. Even so, that's no reason to address me so disrespectfully. She's miles out of line, which is pretty much home turf for Stella Woodward.

Anyway, we'll talk, and she'll see that I'm not looking for another kiss.

The kiss was a lapse in judgement. A failure of control. Not like me at all.

She'll see that.

It wasn't like her, either. We've always kept a chaste difference. In the years I hung out at the Woodward household, Stella and I touched exactly two times.

The first time was that mistaken music room kiss. The second time I touched her was about a year after that when I rescued her in Williston.

It was autumn, and I was shuttling out to UChicago by then, but it was a Saturday night, so I was at home in my room—doing some coding, as I recall. Probably working overtime to shut out the chaos beyond a flimsy door in our prefab house. The trust fund money that my parents lived on had run out by then, and things had devolved, let's just say.

And that's when I got the Twitter DM.

We found your sister drunk as a skunk with a dead phone on a bench outside the McDonald's on Fairview Road in Williston. We can only stay here for about ten more minutes. You need to come get her.

What kind of ridiculous scam is this? That was my first thought.

I was just about to block and report when…could it be?

Tell me her name.

Stella Woodward.

On my way.

I grabbed my keys and texted Charlie—*you there?*

I got nothing back. Not surprising—their parents were at some conference in Indiana, and I happened to know that Charlie and his girlfriend had plans that involved a box of condoms.

I headed out with a rush of anger at Charlie for not keeping tabs on his little sister. Not that a person could—she was fifteen by then and fairly wild.

And indeed drunk as a skunk in the next town, grinning at me from a bench next to a couple in their fifties. She looked surprised when I walked up. "Hugo! What are you doing here?"

"You had these people DM me."

I thanked them, and from our brief exchange, I gathered that Stella begged them to use their phone, but she couldn't remember any phone numbers, so she'd gone for a Twitter DM. How or why it got to me, who knows. Did she point out the wrong name?

They headed off into the night.

"I thought Charlie was coming."

"He's with Jeanette." I hoisted her up and tried to help her walk. Eventually, I resorted to carrying her. "What the fuck are you doing out here all alone?"

"Hugo," she replied, gazing at me like I was Prince Charming.

"You're wasted," I growled, getting her to the car as fast as possible.

From what I could glean, she'd been out with some boy who got her drunk and had been pressuring her into something she didn't want to do. It wasn't like her to be so drunk. Whatever she had, it was something strong. Not quite roofie strong, but grain alcohol strong?

Probably.

"Don't tell my parents. I'll be grounded forever." And then, in a loud, boozy stage whisper that I knew all too well, she said, "They won't understand, what with the switching at birth."

That was a running joke between us—that we were switched at birth, because her family is so studious, and she seemed to think my parents were fun and extroverted. I suppose they looked like that from the outside.

"I won't tell your folks if you tell me his name," I said.

"S'under control," she'd said defiantly.

Some people are boastful drunks or weepy drunks or funny drunks; Stella turned out to be the kind of drunk who tried to act hypercompetent. Like everything was under control.

"Just some miscommunication," she'd added.

For all her flightiness and disorganization, she always had a deep sense of loyalty—even, apparently, to the jackass who'd gotten her drunk and left her to fend for herself when things didn't go his way.

I got that name eventually.

And I carried her into the house, settled her onto the threadbare living room couch, and then pounded on Charlie's door. He and Jeanette wandered out, half-dressed, and they sprang into action when they saw how drunk Stella was.

And I drove off.

She and I never talked about it. I sometimes wondered whether she forgot about it.

I didn't.

My memory of that night is one of her soft skin, her extreme vulnerability, and murder in my heart.

CHAPTER 22

STELLA

I heave myself up from my desk and the pile of gummy worm wrappers, the remains of a very unwise round of stress-eating, and head out.

It's ten to two. People wince at me as I pass. Some look solemn. It's like I'm going to an execution.

"I'll give you fifty bucks if you call him Mr. Roboto again," Tinley says as I pass.

I grin.

"Don't encourage her," Jane says. "We want her back."

"I'll be back." This I say with more confidence than I feel.

I take my time ambling to Hugo's office; I even stop at the vending machines to get an orange soda, which is the most moustache-giving soda in the machine. The closer I get to his office, the angrier I feel.

"He's waiting." Brenda nods darkly at the private hallway that leads to Hugo's lair of fearsomeness.

"Thanks."

I breeze down the little hall and saunter through the doorway in what I hope is a defiant attitude. "What now?"

He looks sterner than usual. "Shut the door."

"That won't be necessary, Mr. Roboto."

He rises from his chair and walks over. Flames lick over my skin as he passes.

He closes the door with his foot. It's a sharp, sudden sound. "Wow, are you programmed for karate?"

His voice is low and rumbly. "The financial health of thousands if not millions of people rests in my hands, and you think it's funny to call me Mr. Roboto?"

"Is that a rhetorical question?"

"You will not call me Roboto again. Understand?"

I cock my head like I might be processing that. "Define *understand.*"

"We need to talk."

"About what? How you ruined my job prospects in my chosen field? Your emo detection program is running at full strength, Roboto."

"You'll make that the last time you call me that."

"Or what?"

He sucks in a ragged breath.

It shouldn't be hot, but it really, really is.

Really, really hot.

I tilt my head. "You gonna give me a horrible research project?"

His voice, when it comes, is hoarse. "No."

I take a sip of soda in a way that'll leave a moustache, knowing it'll bedevil him. He was always quick to point out when I had a grape soda moustache.

The top of my lip feels cool with unlicked soda, the face version of untied shoes.

His gaze is glued to my mouth. A muscle in his jaw fires.

I smile. "Will that be all?"

His pulse visibly bangs in his throat. "No."

"What? You've got more to say? More insults?"

His gaze seems to sharpen, harden. His look of raw need hits deep inside me, and it's more than the soda.

This one strange thought flashes through my mind: *His Alcatraz walls are breaking.*

I tell myself it's an illusion. A girlhood fantasy. Hugo's walls don't break, and he's never undone. He's rigid and exacting with an operating system coded for logic and decorum.

But god, the way he's looking at me—it's a very serious look that's scary and exciting all at once.

So done with Hugos, I remind myself. Teardrops on the hand. Creepy doll in the basement.

Incorrigible.

Unruly! Unruly! Unruly!

I shake myself out of it. "What I don't get is, why don't you fire me if you think so poorly of me?"

His Adam's apple bounces in his throat. Like he's swallowing down his agitation. "I'm not gonna fire you."

"Why not?" I go near him, feeling shaky. It's anger and a lot of other things that I'll file under heat.

And this need to kiss him again.

I hate him.

I want him. This all should stop, but a wicked part of me doesn't want it to stop. My pussy throbs with need. My pussy doesn't want it to stop.

"Fire me," I whisper-hiss.

He's fixated on my soda moustache.

Time stills. We're panting in unison.

"Fire me, Hugo."

The words come out sexy.

I could've said anything—*Style me. Clip me. Winterize me. Osterize me*—and it would've been sexy.

His nostrils flare. Something in him changes, like a rip in the fabric of his control.

Suddenly his fist is clamped onto my ponytail, and his lips are a hair's breadth from mine.

"Fire me—I want you to," I say.

His breath is a feather on my lips. His gray eyes pierce my soul. I think he's going to kiss me, but he's got something better —wicked fingers that settle between my legs. He presses his fingers to my sex, right through my skirt, pressing between my legs.

"Ungh," I say.

He's doing dark magiks upon my pussy while his hawk glare mesmerizes me. I nearly implode from the pleasure of it.

"Is that how you fire me?"

"That's not what I'm doing right now," he rumbles.

"Fire me harder, Roboto."

He changes his pussy-stroking style and a new burst of pleasure shoots through me.

Thump. I'm against the wall, shoulder blades pressed to the cool, hard plaster. The soda can is on the floor.

I'm sliding my hands over his shoulders, his chest, around to his back. I'm pulling him to me, urging him onward to further pussy rubbing.

He sucks the top of my lip, sucking off the soda. "Need you wet for me."

"Isn't your oil can around here somewhere?"

He yanks up my skirt, pressing it up until it's way above my hips. He slides a finger into my panties. "Don't need it, do we?"

No. I'm mega-wet for him. He strokes me directly now, going for a skin-to-skin pleasure explosion.

"Ten degrees to the front, Mr. Roboto."

He growls and adjusts his motion.

Going from the blunt pleasure of the vageen cup through a skirt to a raw finger at the wildly perfect angle, there are no words. I'm panting, mind blown by the harshly delicious moves of Hugo Jones.

"An eighty-eight-degree angle of approach, please."

"That doesn't even mean anything." But he changes his angle and it's exactly right, because Hugo's a quant who figures everything out.

He kisses my neck, my cheek. I'm clutching at him, kissing whatever face skin comes near my lips. My pulse might be thready.

Teeth clamp down on my earlobe, sharp and good.

I suck in a breath.

The teeth. The vageen angle of approach.

Rough words grumble into my ear. Something about firing. I'll always fire you.

I tunnel my fingers into his hair. He's doing a new angle. "Just like that, Roboto," I manage before my brain explodes.

He keeps up the sexy rumbling nonsense, like a sexy voice beckoning me from the far reaches of orgasmic darkness.

I'm just coming down when he picks me up and bangs me onto his desk.

Yesssss.

We're kissing again.

He's pulling at my panties. "Relent to me, Stella."

His chest is heaving and the way his fingers feel on my thighs? It's so incredibly hot. It's hot how bad he wants me, and I want him even more.

"What does that mean?" I pant.

"This," he says, pressing into me.

I want more—more of an explanation than that. But then I reach out and press my fingers over his steely erection and I'm done with words, because I have to see him, and by "him," I mean his cock.

I have to see how Hugo-ish it is, and then I will lick it and suck it.

I want him to be undone even more, and for him to dig his harsh and beastly fingers into my scalp and shove my face onto him while I suck him.

I kiss his neck. He smells like sage. "Yes, yes, yes," I say to his neck.

He groans.

I push off some papers. Things clatter to the floor.

"So fucking reckless," he growls.

"What?"

"Reckless," he breathes, coming back for a kiss.

"Don't forget *unruly* and *incorrigible*. Don't forget refuses to follow orders."

He sways before me, eyes fierce, hair mussed, probably regretting he reminded me. And now I can't un-hear it.

"Why, Hugo? What reason would you ever have to write that? In a letter to a boss?"

"I can't."

"But do you really think all that?" I want him to say that he really doesn't think it. I need him to say it.

He blinks, looking caught out.

My blood races. "It's an easy yes or no. Do you or do you *not* think it?"

"It's not…I know how it sounds—"

"Oh my god." I jump down from the desk. "Oh. My. God." I'm putting myself back together. "This?" I make a circle with my finger to include him and me and the desk. "Not in this life."

"Stella—"

"And for your information, I *am* incorrigible when it comes to you. I will not be corrected, and I will not be changed from my radical path of only being interested in being with nice guys who think I'm awesome."

I put myself together and get out of there.

CHAPTER 23

STELLA

Can I have worse taste in men? What is the matter with me?

This I contemplate as I head home. I get off the subway and walk to our neighborhood, past the flower shop and the cookie shop. I even pass by Gourmet Goose, because the last thing I need is more cheeseball shaming.

My taste in men is appalling.

It's not just the Hugo clones I went for all through my twenties; even back in high school I dated jerks. Guy who wanted to have a go at a cheerleader or put a notch in their whatever.

One of them even left me in a neighboring town after a night of weirdly strong drinks after I informed him that I wouldn't be having sex with him—something that I had told him up front.

Timmy Trask—Trasker to his friends on the football team. He dumped me in a gloomy park next to a shuttered strip mall with a dead phone battery, and it wasn't exactly a safe area at that time of night. I had to beg some passersby to use their phone, but I couldn't remember Charlie's number or even his Twitter handle.

The best I could do was to have them message Hugo to have Charlie pick me up.

Or at least that's what I was going for.

But who came? Hugo himself.

I don't remember a lot from that night, though I didn't puke in his car, which, considering my condition, was a major win. I mostly remember my utter mortification the next morning, and pretty much the whole rest of the year.

Hugo and I never spoke of it, and my parents never found out, lucky for me.

Timmy Trask. Definitely my worst boyfriend, and I wasn't alone in my low opinion of him, because a few days later somebody in a Chewbacca costume beat the crap out of him.

Nobody knew anybody who dressed as Chewbacca, so it was this big mystery, though my friends and I figured Timmy was being an asshole to the wrong person on their way to a Halloween party.

I evilly enjoyed his puffy face and big black eye at school the next day, but mostly I was relieved that he avoided me after that. He never so much as looked at me again, and he never spread around rumors about me—double stunner, because he said he would.

I definitely spread around the truth about him to each and every one of my girlfriends, plus the girls in gym class, band, and cheerleading.

I head in under the green canopy.

Sully, our gray-haired bulldog of a doorman, is right there, pulling open the door with a giant smile. "How're you doing, Stella?" he asks.

"I'm okay, Sully," I say. "How about you?"

"Dandy as candy!" he says like he always does.

$\sim$

Mom texts me a picture of a massive zucchini she managed to grow. I give her shit because there's nothing next to it to show its scale. I make her put a shoe next to it and send the picture again.

She calls, and we talk about her plans for making three loaves of zucchini bread.

"By the way," I say, "do you remember how I asked you and Dad not to have Hugo write that letter of recommendation? Do you remember that? Because imagine my surprise when I find out that you went ahead and asked him anyway."

"Did Hugo tell you about this?"

"It doesn't matter," I say. "You know I didn't want you to ask him, and you went ahead and did it, and I'm pretty upset about it."

"What? Well, we had so many conversations..." Mom says, putting up the old confusion smokescreen.

"I need to know I can trust you when you say something. And you need to trust me. I said I didn't need it, and I didn't need it."

"But maybe you did. Clearly it was competitive enough that you didn't get the job in the end, even with Hugo's help."

"Actually, Hugo's letter wasn't helpful at all. Like not at all."

"You're not blaming what happened on Hugo, I hope," she says.

I pick up Chester the owl and turn him over in my fingers. I definitely blame Hugo, but that's between Hugo and me. Also, I can't think of anything that would cement my position as family fuckup more solidly than all of the unkind things that golden boy Hugo said about me. "I'm saying I wish you would've listened to me."

"I apologize," she says. "Though a letter from somebody of Hugo's caliber is a real feather in your cap, and he'll always want to help you, contrary to what you seem to think. Of course Charlie didn't want Hugo to write a letter for his job, either—he was very fixated on getting that teaching position on his own merits. Well, you know, Charlie can be sensitive about Hugo taking up so much of the spotlight and all of that."

This is something I never heard her say before. Hugo definitely grabbed way more of the spotlight in school, though even in our family, Mom and Dad worked with him a lot to help make the most of his talents, and later on, to win scholarships.

Is it possible they worked with Hugo more than they worked with Charlie? Thinking back, it does seem so. I always thought they were just trying to balance out Hugo's loser parents. Did Charlie have feelings about it?

Right then I remember the big news: "Mom, do you know anything about Hugo being allergic to pineapple?"

"No, Hugo loves pineapple," she says. "He used to love my fruit salad."

"That's what I thought, but people here are telling me that he's deathly allergic to it. Everyone at the office says he'll keel over if he so much as looks at a pineapple."

"Allergic? Why wouldn't he have told us?" Mom says. "Some people do develop allergies later in life, but I'd think he'd tell us."

"Right? He's worked here for over a decade, and to hear the people talk, he's had the allergy the whole time."

"Poor Hugo. He should've told us! Why wouldn't he have? Though he always does go out of his way to be the perfect guest. Helping to clean up without even being asked. Always looking for ways to lend a hand."

"He does have a perfectionistic streak," I say.

"More like he doesn't want to wear out his welcome. You know, I don't think he ever really got a decent meal from Jeremy and Mara."

I nod. The shittiness of Hugo's party-hardy parents is a favorite topic of Mom's to this day.

"The way they'd carry on, it was a very chaotic environment," Mom continues. "I never felt it was my place to tell the Joneses how to raise a boy, but I always made sure Hugo knew he had a place at our dinner table."

"I think you made a huge difference for him," I say. It's what I always say in this conversation, and it's one hundred percent true.

"Still, I think I'd know about a pineapple allergy. Deathly!"

"I know!"

"No, wait…I could swear I've served him pineapple in recent years," Mom says. "My god, I'd hate to have sickened him. Did he not want to be an imposition? Hugo never likes to be an imposition on us. WARREN!" Her yell nearly breaks my eardrum.

Mom has a screaming-bejesus-cross-house conversation with Dad, a back-and-forth about whether Hugo is allergic to pineapple. Dad remembers that they had Hugo over for BBQ last year on the Fourth, and Mom says there was pineapple there and Dad says there might not have been pineapple.

"Hugo was there this summer? He was barbecuing with you without Charlie there?"

"Sure, we always make a point to invite him over when he's in town. We love hearing about his work and getting updates on his life. We couldn't be prouder!"

Later that night, my phone pings with several texts from Mom.

The first is one word: *Eureka!*

The next is a picture. It's Dad standing at the grill with a spatula standing next to Hugo seeming to eat pineapple.

I download the image and expand it, grateful that my mom doesn't know how to take pictures with a reasonable data size.

There he is, Hugo, holding a giant triangle of pineapple as big as a pizza slice—with one telltale bite taken out of it. I love his expression—he's been caught midchew, and there's humor in his gaze, as if to say, I'm going to look dorky in this photo with a cheek full of pineapple.

I pull the picture back up a couple times more over the following night. I can't help but smile. Hugo can be so harsh and remote, but now and then, his nerdy, socially awkward heart blazes through.

I try not to think about kissing him or how amazing his hand felt on my lady parts. I try not to wonder what would've happened. I try not to wish I hadn't stopped it.

Hugo is off my menu—for good reason—but I will not stop loving him in this picture and loving that he invented an allergy —and knocking myself out wondering why he would ever do such a thing.

CHAPTER 24

HUGO

I'm staring at my whiteboard, but what I'm seeing is Stella, up against the wall, eyes bright with pleasure.

Ten degrees, Roboto.

I've been replaying yesterday's events nonstop in my mind. The way her eyes changed. The feeling of her coming apart in my hands. The bold, recklessness of her requests.

And I couldn't not touch her.

So wrong. So deeply wrong.

Riding home, she's all I saw. Beating off in the shower. Beating off after my workout. Falling asleep, waking up, it was all Stella, all the time.

This bright, strange feeling flows through my chest whenever I think about the way she responded—was that Stella being wild and reckless, or is she attracted to me? She really was into it...for a while.

And now I've wandered so far from my project, I feel like I might never find my way back.

I force my attention onto the whiteboard, and suddenly I stop. Everything stops.

There's a stumbling block I wasn't seeing.

How did I not see it before?

It's the remnants of a prior concept I was attempting to weave into a string of variables, but if I take it out, I can use an alternative path to accomplish the same thing and eliminate the obstacle it's been creating.

How did I not see this?

I'm scribbling furiously. This is good. Very good.

It's okay. I made progress. It feels good to have made progress.

I circle back around to my desk thinking again about Stella. We never got to talk about rules, but we should. It's still a good idea. I could let her know that our little interlude was an anomaly.

I grab my phone, about to text Brenda to have admin send her up, but then I pause when I realize I'm deceiving myself.

I just want to see her.

I put down my phone and go about my day like a rational human being and not an obsessed Neanderthal in the habit of lying to himself.

The best thing is to keep away from each other—no meetings. No walking by. No nothing.

I pushed her from my mind once before.

I can do it again.

Walking into work the next morning, it comes to me that I really do need to at least talk to her about my wrong behavior.

And I think Stella would appreciate ground rules. She needs to know that I'm in no way interested in continuing a physical relationship, and more communication is always better than less. The presence of rules is always better than the absence of rules.

Even Stella would agree to that.

Or not. Stella likes to go in unexpected directions, which is doubtless why she's so good at her job with those attention-grabbing reels.

Back around the Woodward dinner table, she'd frequently come up with original perspectives, and then act surprised when other people didn't notice what she noticed. To Stella, the things she sees are just obvious. In fact, it would be very Stella to be surprised by the fact that her work won awards—she always did underestimate herself, though not as much as her family did.

At any rate, we can put guard rails around our behavior.

I text Brenda to have admin send her up to finish the project.

A few minutes later Brenda forwards me a text that Tinley had forwarded to her. It's from Stella.

> Stella: Mr. Jones is confused—he doesn't need me to come.

I get her number and text her directly.

> Me: We're not done. We need to discuss this.

> Stella: We are done.

It comes to me here that she thinks I'm calling her up for sex. Of course she would think it. But she'll see that's not my intention—once she gets here.

> Me: You may be mistaken in what you think I mean by "finished." While the past activities associated with the project are very much over and done, not to be repeated, a quick debrief is required with some ground rules established.

> Stella: No thanks.

> Me: This is not a request.

> Stella: Here's some food for thought for the next time you're tempted to throw your boss weight around.

The next message is just a photo.

Of me.

Eating pineapple.

Wild energy swoops through me. It's not anger. It's not anything that I know.

Judging from my shirt and the hackberry tree in the background, it was taken when I was barbecuing with Jenny and Warren Woodward this past July Fourth weekend when I was in town arranging various things for my parents.

My thumbs move furiously over the keypad.

> Me: you know AI could have done this.

> Stella: It would take your tech guys exactly two minutes to figure out the picture is real. But just in case...

Three dots appear and disappear.

An odd lightness fills my chest. You'd think I'd feel dread, but this light helium feeling is quite the opposite.

A new image comes through. It's the original—Warren Woodward and me at the grill. Scrawled across the top of the image, with the pen tool set to pink and ridiculously thick, is "Jennifer Woodward—309-555-0938" and "Warren Woodward—309-555-4559." And two additional words: "chef's kiss."

It's the vending machine all over again.

She wouldn't. Would she?

Wulfric would lose his mind if he found out I wasn't really allergic to pineapple, but I feel this curious lack of concern about it all. I just need to see her.

I stalk down the hall. People get out of my way, as usual. When I reach the admin pool with its fishbowl windows, everybody looks down.

Except Stella. She kisses the tips of her fingers and splays them outward. *Chef's kiss.*

My pulse races.

It's here I come to my senses. What am I doing? What?

I make my way through the building and down the stairwell, down to the street, and out to the corner where the bracing October wind whips off the Hudson. I let it lick my skin.

Calling her to my office to discuss not seeing each other? What bullshit. I'm lying to myself, plain and simple.

I model the effect of ridiculous human behaviors on the markets. I don't participate in them.

Kissing her, touching her, nearly fucking her, Jesus! Stella is off-limits. That is a code; a code is a promise to the world as well as a promise to myself.

The fact that I broke my code doesn't mean I should abandon it altogether. If anything, it's more reason to redouble my commitment.

Once a man starts breaking his codes, everything unravels.

CHAPTER 25

HUGO

Two days later, she's standing at the elevator bank, clutching a stack of files in her arms, her big everything purse slung over her shoulder. She's in a brown skirt suit, and her hair is up in a high ponytail, dusting of freckles over her button nose very visible in the harsh office light that she'd definitely hate.

She's with a knot of people who are all waiting to get onto one of the elevators—elevator number one, which appears to be about to arrive.

I nod and continue toward elevator five, away from everyone. I'll take the later, less populated elevator any day of the week.

In the days since she sent the pineapple text, I haven't called her to my office. I haven't contacted her. I'm content to let her think she's won. I'm making progress. Not the level of progress I need, exactly, but I'm in better shape despite everything.

I glance over and she looks away, but not before I catch the classic Stella resisting-temptation face—a glint of mischief in her eyes, lips drawn slightly to the side, as though she's fighting to contain an inappropriate smile and whatever very wrong urge is cranking through her like a circus organ.

She's the most distracting woman alive—she really is. But that's on me. I put her here. I screwed up her career.

Elevator one comes. People get on, but Stella's still standing there when the doors close. It's just her and me now, and the rush of pleasure that flows through me is nothing short of perverse.

I pull out my phone and force myself to look at the news feed.

She comes up and stands next to me. "I hear that your precious mentor, Wulfric, has spent untold millions keeping you safe from those deadly pineapples, clearing hotel kitchens and entire ballrooms over the appearance of one pineapple."

"Millions might be stretching it."

"But of course it's worth it." She puts on a fake concerned face. "A deathly allergy is a truly terrible thing!"

"And this is your business why?"

"Come on, Hugo! Why would you tell people that? *Deathly* allergic. It's been driving me crazy."

"Then stop thinking about it," I say.

"I can't—it's way too weird and funny."

I focus on the floor indicator. "Try a bit of self-control."

"Like the self-control needed to resist the temptations of certain deadly tropical fruits?"

I don't indulge the comment with a response.

When I look over next, she has this amused expression that tells me there's more.

"What now?"

"Tinley from the courier desk put this corkboard up in the admin break room and a lot of us have been printing out images of ourselves outside of work. It's all about building camaraderie. It's been nice to see people's kids and pets, or see them rooting for their favorite teams...or enjoying themselves at barbecues."

"You wouldn't."

"What do you have against camaraderie, Hugo? People would love to see your fun side."

I give her a hard look. A warning look.

Her dazzling smile connects to something deep inside me.

People have begun to gather nearby, waiting for the next elevator.

She lowers her voice so that the slowly gathering group can't hear. "Eventually somebody would look even closer. 'And wait—what is it that Hugo's doing? Whatever could he be eating?' And Wulfric—my goodness, wouldn't Wulfric be surprised!"

"You wouldn't dare."

"You know me—I can be a bit unruly. Also, incorrigible! Really, you just never know what somebody like me will do next. I mean, I hardly ever even know myself."

I turn to her. I'm not a man who bluffs in poker, but I know a bluffer when I see one. "You won't put up that picture. You may lack self-control, but you're not vindictive."

"Are you so sure about that? You haven't seen me in all these years. Anything could've happened."

"I'll take my chances."

"Mmm-hmm," she says mysteriously.

"I'm going to take the next car that arrives," I say. "I'd ask you not to be on it."

"Would you, now?"

"Yes, I would."

She lowers her voice. "Do you know what they say about pineapple, Hugo?"

I go back to my phone. "Don't know and don't care."

"You really don't know?"

"Sorry, I have actual important things to think about."

"Oh, I think you'd be interested. It's rather astonishing."

Of course she thinks I'm going to be curious about it.

Curiosity is something we have in common. But unlike her, I have self-control.

She looks down at her phone. She's practically sparkling with pleasure. Even those freckles look more vibrant.

I'm supposed to be searching for the answers to some of the most complex questions ever posed, and she just won't stop with the monkey wrenches.

In the interests of clearing my mind, I do a quick, discreet Google on it.

It is said that eating large amounts of pineapple not only makes your genitalia and related fluids taste better, but also sweeter.

My face heats.

Stella smiles. "Really too bad that you're allergic. Pineapple is delicious. Personally? I eat it all the time."

I grit my teeth, fighting back a ferocious rush of desire.

"All. The. Time."

I ball my fists. Images of tasting her crowd my mind.

Ding.

She strolls into the elevator and turns to me, gaze spearing mine.

Suddenly my feet are moving. I follow her and spin around, blocking the entrance with my arm, fingers clamped violently on the side of the opening. "Take the next one."

The people behind us scatter like startled birds. I stab the *close doors* button. I turn to her. "You will stop this."

She tries to look innocent, tilting her head and furrowing her brow. "Stop what? Stop eating pineapple?"

A rumble comes out of me unbidden as the doors close.

"Think of the food pyramid, Hugo. The food pyramid!" She gazes at me straight on, just a hint of a smile on her lips. The air is thick between us. I think she's going to come to me, but instead she backs up.

My pulse races.

"Pineapple's a nutritional powerhouse." She hits the wall.

Some chase instinct unleashes in me, and I slam my hand onto the elevator brake button. I go to her with a need that's dark and brutal. I grip her shoulders, pull her to me, and kiss her.

Files fall to the floor as she wraps her arms around my neck, kissing me back.

"Wait! Are there cameras?"

"Not in this one. Wulfric reasons." I push her against the wall and knee her legs apart. I kiss her like a lost man. A starving man. I press into her so that she can feel how hard she makes me.

"Yes, Hugo," she whispers, moving against me. "Yes." Her hands roam over my chest and then down over my ass. She cups my ass and arches into me.

I bend my knees to give her more of my length, trapped as it is inside layers of fabric. "Take it," I say, ferociously pulling up her skirt to give her better access. I reach down, needing to touch her, but of course there are panties.

Irrationally maddened by all of these layers of clothes between Stella and me, I palm them down, but they won't go. I drop to my knees and pull, but they get all twisted.

She grabs on to my hair, arching toward my face. I kiss her mound. She's bare down there, and the growl that tears from my throat is something I've never heard come from myself. I don't know myself and I don't care. I fist the fabric—two furious fists ripping the scrap of cotton into two parts.

She twists her fists in my hair. "Hugo."

I lick her slit. She gusts out a shuddery breath. I lick her with more ferocity, licking and sucking, mercilessly invading her pussy with my tongue. Her breath is coming in short bursts.

I find her bud with my tongue. I can't be gentle. I slide my tongue against it rough, then I slide against it softly. I pull her lips apart with my hands and shove my tongue into her hole. She whimpers. Her knees buckle. I hold her up, keep her with me.

"Two degrees harder, Roboto," she says.

I give her what I think she needs, and she gasps, small hands practically tearing out my hair.

I press a finger into her hole.

One hand clamps onto my shoulder, holding on, breath coming fast. I work her hole with my finger while I lick her perfect pussy.

"Say relent again," she mumbles.

"What?"

"Say it like you said it before." She grips both shoulders, back wedged against the wall, barely standing on her own.

I devour her like a wolf—teeth, tongue, fingers, snarls.

"Say it."

"Relent to me," I hear myself growl. "Relent."

"Uh, fuck!" she says, coming apart under my tongue. "Fuuuu-uck!" Her pussy convulses, small fingers dig into my shoulders. I'm eating it up, eating her up, cock straining under my pants.

"Relent," I say.

She's leaning on the elevator wall, one hand on the flat silver rail, one on my shoulder, bare pussy gleaming in the subdued elevator light.

I press my hand onto her pussy. "Cannot get enough of this," I rumble, sliding around her juices. "Need to be inside you. Need."

"Do it," she hisses. "Right now! Wait!" she roots around in her everything purse while I unbutton her top.

She produces a condom and hands it to me.

"No." I unbutton my pants. "You put it on me." My voice is a hard baritone. I'm reduced to savage need, yanking down my zipper, my boxer briefs.

She kisses my cock, sending shivers over me.

She puts it on me while I claim every inch of her breasts, hands down her shirt. I used to have some technique with a woman's breasts, but now it's just about roughly owning them, fingers and palms working in a way that might be more bearlike than human.

"Do everything. Anything and everything." She gazes up at me darkly. God knows what she sees that made her say that. Her words are like a red flag to a bull.

"Do me however you want—however you want."

"Turn around," I say. "Grip the rail."

She turns and grips the rail. I should stop this, but I can't.

I slap her ass and she hisses out some word I can't make out, or maybe my language faculties are simply offline. I'm spreading her dripping wet lips, spreading around the juices. She wiggles around and I slap her ass again, harder.

"Yeah, Roboto!"

"Up. Open for me." She tips up her ass and I position my tip against her sex and sink in.

"Ohhhh," she whimpers.

She feels like heaven, wet silky warmth. I press in, fucking her like a rutting, grunting bull and I can't stop. I don't want to ever stop. I don't know if I can stop.

"More!" She's doing herself, rubbing her pussy.

I grab her hair, lost in the heaven of her. "Relent."

"Omigod omigod omigod," she says.

The sound of her pleasure surges through me like lust and domination and hunger and a fever in my blood, and the only cure is thrusting into her, fucking her, owning her.

I feel as if a dam has burst, and as if I'm riding a tidal wave that's made of years of pent-up lust and longing.

She's coming again. I can feel it with my cock, her pussy walls clenching and releasing. I hear it in her breath. She's coming, spinning.

My fingertips dig into her ass cheeks.

I press deep into her one last time, an orgasm ripping out of me, ripping through my body. I come, making lord knows what sounds.

I'm panting after. I pull out of her, feeling like I've been turned inside out. I brace myself, one hand on the wall.

What just happened?

She turns and presses a hand to my cheek, eyes full of wonder. "Wow."

"Wow."

Her brow furrows. She looks...perplexed. "I didn't expect—"

"I take full responsibility," I say. "I lost control."

"Hugo, no. That was my favorite thing about it. I was right there with you. A thousand percent out of control with you." She buttons her shirt. "Don't forget, I instigated it."

I cup her cheek. "You get to talk about pineapple without a man losing his mind with lust."

"What's the point of talking about pineapple if a man doesn't lose his mind with lust?"

"You deserve better."

She gives me a witchy look. "Umm...not interested in that option."

Stella, so fucking contrary.

I try to collect myself. It was the hottest experience of my life. I was so full of lust, but we're at work. In an elevator. Stella deserves better than a quickie in some elevator. She deserves better than a man who can't uphold his code of honor.

She's rooting through her purse—the kind of giant everything purse she's carried since she was old enough to have purses. She's got wipes and napkins. She holds out a bag. "Put your condom in here. Oh my god, can this elevator smell more like sex? Is that even possible?"

I put the condom in the bag and pocket it. I'll deal with it myself.

She pulls out a small bottle and sprays the air with something that smells like lavender, and then we kneel down and start gathering the papers that are all over the floor.

I hand her a stack. She puts them in order, and I hand up some more. When we're done, I stand up and pull her up, not that she needs it, but I can't seem to stop touching her.

And I look into her eyes.

And that's when it hits me. A better way to get around the obstacle I'd identified in my QuantumQuilt equation.

"What's wrong, Hugo? Do I have something on my face? A carbuncle, perhaps? A bubo?"

"Hold on." I pull a small notepad from my pants pocket, take out the pencil I keep in the spiral part, and start to scribble. "Gotta get this down."

From my peripheral vision, I see her stiffen and frown, almost as if she's recoiling from the sight of me scribbling.

"I'm sorry, was all of our blisteringly hot sex keeping you from your work?" She sounds wounded. Angry.

"Hold on. This is crucial." I pocket the notebook and hit the button to start the elevator up again. I wouldn't call it a breakthrough, but an important piece has fallen into place.

I cup her cheeks. "You are amazing."

"Oh my god!" She pushes me away. "Are you saying that because you just now got a good idea?"

"No—I mean, I did get a good idea but—"

"Don't even, Roboto!" She hits the button for her floor even though I'd already selected it. "Thank you for reminding me why this is all wrong." The elevator car chunks slowly into place.

"Stella—you were amazing before I got the idea. What happened here was amazing, and we need to discuss—we're not done here."

"Follow me at your own pineapple risk." She marches out.

The courier desk girl—Tinley or Linley or something—is

there, and Stella grabs her arm and says something I can't hear, and they laugh. People crowd into the elevator next to me.

We're not done. I don't care what she says. If nothing else, I need to explain to her why I wrote the letter—as soon as I warn Cooper. It's time. What happens in poker stays in poker, but this has gone too far. I'll warn Cooper and tell her the truth.

I return to my whiteboard and make significant progress using the idea I got in the elevator. How is this possible? I've never been more distracted, more all over the map with emotions, and in spite of that, I'm making headway.

Or is it because of it that I'm making headway? Twice I've made breakthroughs.

I stroll to the window to look down at the street, shocked at the irony of it.

All this time I've been seeking out women who are as busy and driven as me, women who are content with quick hookups, women whose presence in my life doesn't create even the faintest ripple, lest my work get affected.

And then Stella cannonballs into my life, and my work is better than ever.

Is it possible the distraction of her is a good thing? Or is it the fact that I'm happy when she's around? Or am I happier because of the work progress? I'm trying to remember when this happiness began, but who the hell cares?

I'm happy with Stella in my life, and already I want to see her again. For the first time in my life, I might be rethinking a code. Is there a time and place where that's the right thing to do? I find these thoughts scary, destabilizing—but also a little exciting.

Because why is she off-limits? Why does the code exist in the first place? She's not underage. And yes, I gave my word to Charlie, but that was then. We're adults now.

This code of mine is like that equation remnant—an artifact from the past that no longer serves, except as a useless obstacle.

People rush back and forth on the street below, streaming around an illegally parked delivery van. I used to judge people who let their heart influence their logic, who create rational-sounding reasons to do things that they're going to do no matter what.

And here I'm doing it.

I need to see her again. Soon. And again, and again.

And I need to tell her about the letter, too. I'll make her see why I wrote it—she'll understand, and it'll change everything.

CHAPTER 26

STELLA

What just happened was wrong, but not because he lost control and then went full math nerd.

The problem is that sex with Hugo was transcendent. As in, the best ever.

Being with him in that place hidden between floors, out of time, out of sight, this man I've adored for as long as I can remember.

Transcendent.

As in, sex with him was twenty thousand on a scale of one to ten. More than that. He was out of control—fuck yes—and it was the best thing ever.

It feels dangerous, how much I loved being with him.

Also, the quick orgasm? My whole identity as a person who doesn't come from screwing alone without a lot of machinations had to be reversed by Mr. Roboto? The one man I most need to stay away from?

Also wrong.

I lured him in and I'm paying the price.

He's right—I do need more self-control.

I also need for a hot poker to be shoved into the memory section of my brain so that I can forget how awesome sex with him was, so that I can go back to sex with normal guys and think it's good.

And then he drops everything—us, the hotness, our connection—and starts scribbling math shit. I'd be offended if I wasn't so grateful that he did that, because it was the best possible reminder of who he is—a perfectionist who only cares about his perfect pursuit of perfect greatness.

That evening I emerge onto the bustling sidewalk overseeing my usual good-versus-evil dinner plan thought-war in my head when Hugo peels off the wall and falls into step next to me.

"Want a ride?" he asks.

"No thanks." Wall Street Station's two blocks up.

"You sure? The car's just a text away. I'm calling it either way."

"Not interested," I say.

"You want to grab dinner later tonight?"

I slow my steps and steal a glance at him. "Grab dinner? As in, go on a date?"

"Let's talk about what's happening here. I have things I need to tell you, and we need to eat. Name the time. I'll pick you up. Why not?"

"Why not? Because I'm not dating you."

"It's just dinner."

"Dinner is a date, and that is not happening," I inform him as we head up William Street, gray stone buildings like cliff faces on either side of us. "Last I checked, you screwed up my dream job. And then we banged in the elevator, which immediately inspired you to start scrawling math on a piece of paper. And you think I'm reckless and unruly and I refuse to follow orders, statements that you seem a hundred percent on."

"Look, I'm going to explain about the letter once I clear something on my end, but Stella, those things I said? Yes, I stand behind them."

"Oh wow, thanks!"

"You *are* reckless," he says. "You have original ideas and the willingness to try big things, even if failure is all but guaranteed. It's a superpower in business, and I think you know that. You're unruly, always ready to go left when everybody else says to go right if that's what it takes. You will not be managed. You eat cheese balls with a damn spoon."

The way he says all this, it's like he suddenly thinks these are good things.

We stop at a light. Up ahead, the windows of a skyscraper reflect the last gasps of the setting sun, a warm grid of light set into cold stone.

"And I recall incorrigible..." I say.

"Yes. For example, remember when you played sax in band, and you would honk out random notes?"

I try not to smile. It shouldn't still be funny. "Well...my friend and I would dare each other."

"But you were the only one who did it. And it was fucking hilarious."

I pull the belt around my coat, hoping he doesn't notice my hands trembling. "So you want me to believe that these are traits you suddenly admire? This from the man who can't bear to look at a Chia Pet, what with the sproutalicious hairdo?"

"I deeply admire those traits."

"Well, thank you, but it was still a pretty massive dick move to write them in a letter to a prospective boss. Not the sign of affection you seem to think it was."

"That's the point here. I want you to let me explain about the letter and for us to work on a plan to make it right. I can't explain right now, but over dinner I'll be able to."

"Why can't you tell me now?"

"Because I can't."

The mob is moving again, and we move along with it. I *would* like a ride, and to eat dinner together, and of course, I desperately want to know what his supposed explanation is. But I also know the danger of this.

"Tell me or don't, Hugo, but dinner's a date. I won't date you. Anyway, I thought I was the most distracting woman alive. What happened to that?"

"You're a breath of fresh air."

I can't help but think he's saying that because of the math breakthrough. "I'm not your fresh air, and I'm not your muse, either."

"Of course not," Hugo says. "But before you officially say no, you need to understand that the restaurant I'll take you to will knock your socks off. It's as if it was made for you—you won't believe there's a restaurant like that."

"What's the restaurant?"

"You'll see."

"Stop making me curious and then I have to go out on a date with you to get my answers. It's a no go. Also, don't forget about Charlie! Hello! If we went out to dinner? Would he be mad or what? I'm going to recommend not telling him."

"Charlie can deal with it."

My pulse skitters. Hugo always cares about Charlie's opinions.

An evil little voice inside me whispers, *Why not have dinner? And he has something to tell you about the letter. Maybe hear him out? And then enjoy more out-of-control sexerations? And what the hell is this restaurant?*

"So we won't call it dinner," he says. "How about if we call it payment for the pineapple image file?"

"You know I'd never show anyone that picture," I say. "I'll give it to you if you want."

We stop across from the station entrance amidst a crush of people all gunning for the trains. It's going to be a mob scene down there—no way will I get a seat.

Hugo settles a hand on my arm. "How about this—you give me the image and I'll give you a gift in return. A gift that you'll love. I already know what it is—I already picked it out."

I turn to him. "A gift?"

"A gift that I picked out for you."

This gets my attention, by which I mean kicks up my girlhood obsession with Hugo giving me a gift, Hugo taking the time to consider me so deeply that he'd intuit what I most want. Like Brenda's galena. Like the fractal sculpture he got for my mom or Charlie's tricorder.

My pulse races. The perfect gift. Hugo's weird superpower—turned lovingly on me.

"You picked out a gift for me?" I ask.

"I did."

"What is it?"

"Nice try, Sparky." He smiles—it's a big, genuine smile, complete with tiny crinkles at the sides of his eyes. It's a good gift —that's what the smile is telling me. I want it so badly, I can barely think.

"You're free to give me a gift," I say. "But I'm not dating you."

CHAPTER 27

HUGO

Stella's curiosity is boundless—especially when it comes to gifts and surprises.

"If you want it, you have to come with me to pick it up," I tell her.

She furrows her brow, lips pursed under her button nose. I can see the gears working, like she's trying to solve some equation.

"You want your gift or not? Those are my terms."

The light changes and I pull her to a protected area, out of the stream of people heading for the subway entrance. Stella still doesn't know how to move in the crowds.

"You sure you don't want a ride?"

"I'm sure." She regards me suspiciously. "So this gift—is it some sort of food served on a plate? And we sit down to eat it?"

"It's an object that's in a store. I spotted it a long time ago, and I knew it was the absolute perfect thing for you."

"What kind of store?"

"You'll see."

She rolls her eyes, trying hard to feign disinterest. But this is the girl who snuck down to the living room in the middle of the night and unwrapped her Christmas presents—and a few that weren't for her—and then carefully taped them back up. Not once but several years running. She'll crumble.

"I'll pick you up at seven."

"It's too much like a date."

"You don't want your gift? Could I be hearing this right?"

"Why do I have to be along to pick it up?"

"Because those are my terms."

She narrows her eyes. "I'll meet you at the store," she tries.

"I'll pick you up at seven."

I make the call when I get home from work. Cooper picks up right away. The group of us from the Tuesday night game don't call each other for no reason.

"Jones. What's up?"

"Remember how a few weeks ago I told you that a family friend had just gotten a job at Zevin Media? You mentioned that business about Bennett Zevin being a scumbag and the assault charges and the secret settlements, remember?"

"Of course," he says. "The man is a menace. Did you find a way to get your friend to change her mind?"

"Not exactly." I tell him about the letter, and how the whole thing went off the rails.

"Goddamn," he says. "You couldn't have just told her?"

"I know. I wasn't thinking straight. I imagined her at the mercy of this guy...in retrospect, yes, telling her would have been best. She's not much for heeding warnings, but still. It was a bad move, and she's upset—"

He's laughing. "You're into her, and you went and tanked her job prospects. And now she's pissed off."

"That's about right," I admit. "I know what's said at the card table stays at the card table, but I want to tell her why I did what I did. I want her to know."

"Are you asking me for permission to tell her?"

"Not really. I'll tell her either way. This is more of a warning."

Cooper's laughing. "Hugo Jones, are you trashing our code of silence for a girl?"

"She's important to me," I say.

"Tell her," Cooper says.

She's waiting under the bright green entryway canopy that stretches out from her building, talking to the doorman when we pull up. She looks beautiful and badass in a large blazer over a miniskirt and blue cowboy boots. This outfit is pure Stella.

I'm looking forward to telling her why I wrote that letter. She'll see that I did it to protect her.

I get out. "Stella!" I open the door, because I'm not the kind of man who lets his driver get the door for guests.

She strolls up in full amusement mode. "You ride around in a limo?"

"It's not a limo, it's a town car."

We settle in.

"Not a limo? Umm..." Her sweeping gesture takes it all in. The leather seats. The privacy panel. The beverage bar. "Walks like a limo, has a driver in a cap like a limo..."

"Limos are elongated luxury vehicles for events and the ultra-wealthy. A town car is designed for executive transportation. It's efficient."

"Whatever you say, Mr. Billionaire."

The billionaire thing. Of course she'd have heard. "Money's nothing but electronic signals. A cloud of ones and zeros."

Stella snorts. "Tell it to the starving people."

"I know, it's a bit much," I say. "I give it away, but it just builds up again."

"How annoying!" she teases. "And yet you endure the hardship!"

I catch her hand in mine. Everything's fun with her. "I don't give a shit about the money."

She grins. "Just the math, ma'am."

"Something like that."

She puts her hand to the side of her mouth for a big fake stage whisper. "Pssst: you're riding in a limo."

"Trust me, I'd be riding in cabs and Ubers, but Wulfric's intent that I take this thing."

"He makes you ride in it?"

"He doesn't make me. He puts it at my disposal day and night. It would be ridiculous not to use it."

"He's protecting his golden goose," she says. "He doesn't want you in the subway or even a cab. So that you keep laying those golden eggs."

"Exactly."

"You're just laying them all over, aren't you, Hugo?"

I give her a hard look, but that only goads her on.

"Big piles of golden eggs. And Wulfric eats them up with a spoon. I hear some of them are massive!"

"Be serious, Stella. I need to tell you something." I check to make sure the privacy divider's all the way closed.

She looks concerned. "Do you have to lay an egg right now?"

"I need to tell you why I wrote that letter."

She regards me warily, but at least she stops with the egg business.

"I play cards every Tuesday night with a group of guys who

tend to be pretty well connected in terms of knowing things, let's just say. I mentioned that I was working on a letter of recommendation for a family friend who was going for a job at Zevin Media, and one of them told me something extremely disturbing about Bennett Zevin, your prospective boss. He's been accused of sexual harassment."

She blinks, not looking entirely surprised. "And?"

"There's even been an assault charge out there that got settled out of court. Sexual assault," I clarify.

"Uh-huh."

"There are people who consider him dangerous, Stella, but I wasn't at liberty to tell you—what's said at the card table stays at the card table. But I knew you'd gotten several offers. I thought if this one was off the table, you'd take one with a boss who would respect you."

She takes a deep breath. "And that's why you wrote the letter?"

"Yes! I didn't mean for it to be publicized the way that it was. I'm absolutely livid about that, but in any case—"

"You had to save me," she says. "From big bad Bennett Zevin."

"Well, yes," I say. "I couldn't tell you what I knew because of this ethos in our group that what's said at the card table stays at the card table, but I had to do something."

CHAPTER 28

STELLA

Hugo clearly expects some kind of gratitude.

"Did it ever occur to you, Hugo, that I might have done my research and been aware of this information?"

He looks stunned. "But it's not public knowledge."

"Yeah, well, women pass this sort of thing on. They warn each other—it's how we survive out there. So yes, I did my research, and guess what? I still wanted to work there. I had a strategy."

"But, assault charges, Stella—not inappropriate jokes, not a hostile atmosphere, but outright assault. The man's dangerous. Surely there are other jobs just as good—"

"Newsflash—if I ruled out all the companies that might have a lecherous freak on the leadership team, my list would be cut by half. I wanted that job, Hugo. I wanted it a lot. I'm not the helpless little sister, bumbling through life like a doofus!"

"I know! But when I imagined it...this guy..." He gazes into the middle distance with this fierce, primal look, like he wants to set the world on fire.

"Well, I had it under control," I say.

"A man like that," he growls. "Imagining this guy anywhere near you, I couldn't think straight. My judgment got clouded with this irrational, counterproductive impulse…"

An irrational, counterproductive impulse—meaning a caveman impulse, I realize. Leave it to Hugo to describe a caveman impulse as irrational and counterproductive.

Yeah, it's hot, but having my dream job would be way hotter.

"Again, I had it under control," I say. "I wanted that job, and you had no right to take matters into your own hands like that. If they came to me and offered me that job today, I would definitely still take it. And it would have been amazing, and I would have handled it."

"Why not shoot higher?" he says. "Go for what you would truly want instead of a situation to handle, to endure."

"Like, hold out for the perfect job?"

"Yes! Exactly!"

"I'll tell you why not—because the perfect job doesn't exist. You can't reject something because it's not perfect. Haven't you ever heard that the perfect is the enemy of the good?"

"I hate that phrase."

"Of course you hate that phrase. You're on the side of perfect. You think that should be everyone's goal."

"Everyone should be on the side of perfect; otherwise you're settling. And yes, it's a worthy goal."

"Maybe you live in a world where the jobs are perfect, Hugo, and the homes are perfect and the data model is perfect and all the numbers line up, but I don't live in that world. I don't ever want to live in that world."

He furrows his brow. I can see it's finally sinking in. "You looked at the risk and you decided to manage it."

"Yeah, and I get that you were trying to help, but you cost me that job and a bunch of other ones, too."

"I'm sorry," he says. "Of course you would have investigated it. You know your own business. You're an accomplished professional who knows how to navigate this world."

I gaze out the window, grateful for this. Unsure what to do with it.

"I'm working on a way to fix it. I'll reach out to my poker club. It's an amazing network—"

"No! You have to let me manage this on my own. I have my own network. I just don't understand—why not warn me?"

"If I had thought about it for more than two seconds or used my frontal lobe instead of my lizard brain, I would've."

I try not to think too hard about the idea that I bring out his lizard brain. I resist seeing it as exciting or tantalizing. We're doing this one errand and it's over.

I grab a fizzy water from the beverage area, and pop the cap, replaying the things my therapists have told me about rigid, perfectionistic, emotionally unavailable men. I also flash on our little incident in the elevator where he was suddenly scrawling math formulas, seconds after we screwed.

"This had better be a great fucking gift."

He gives me one of his intense Hugo looks, gray eyes focused fiercely on me. "You have no idea."

I sniff like I'm so above it all, but I'm so not. I'm as infatuated as I've ever been, and I'm sinking deeper into this illusion that he could feel the same way. And now I'm in this limo with him, and he's going to turn his amazing gift-giving powers on me. He's been thinking about me, and he chose the ultimate perfect gift for me. He spotted it *long ago*! After so many years of dreaming it, it's actually coming true!

Hugo is going to give me the perfect gift.

I turn away from him like I'm studying the buildings along the Hudson River—that's how hard I'm grinning.

This is how I protect my heart? *This* is my strategy?

I had a poster of Zac Hanson from the Hanson Brothers on my bedroom wall when I was twelve. Zac was dreamy, and I sometimes took the poster down and draped it over myself and pretended Zac was kissing me.

This fakery that I'm doing right now, going through these motions as though Hugo is my boyfriend or something, letting him get me his gift and all that, is a dangerous version of the Zac Hanson poster.

The devil on my shoulder is like, "Is it so bad to let him give you a magical gift? And hey, why not grab a bite after? You have to eat sometime!"

The angel on my shoulder is like, "Have fun getting your heart stabbed repeatedly in the basement or getting turned into a human centipede! But don't say I didn't warn you."

CHAPTER 29

HUGO

I help her from the car. Our hands touch. Our eyes lock. Electricity sizzles between us.

And as soon as she's on the sidewalk, she shoves her hands into her pockets, as if to ward off our connection.

I need to repair this somehow, to make up for the letter. I'm used to calming chaos, managing household disasters of every kind. I was doing it from a very early age.

Or is it more than the letter? And if so, what? And why won't she tell me?

Well, I'm a quant. I work out the most complex problems on the planet. I can figure out why she's so against the two of us going on a date.

"My gift is at Carruthers?" she asks.

"Yes."

Carruthers is a cavernous old warehouse deep in Brooklyn full of vintage furnishings and housewares and knickknacks.

"This is a place you come to?"

"Sometimes."

The owner, Felix, nods at me from behind the jewelry counter as we pass. I nod back. He's busy with a customer—probably for the best. Felix loves to talk.

"You know the clerk?"

"He's the owner. This way." We head deep into the maze of aisles, circling a midcentury housewares display and heading down an aisle full of art deco figurines that have very little utility in everyday life.

She stops here and there and examines whatever catches her eye. Sometimes she gives me a sly look as if to say, *Is this my gift?* I give her a stern look back and shake my head. There are specific looks of mine that she seems to like, and I'm not above abusing them.

"Are you going to give me a hint as to the general area where it is?" she asks.

"Nope."

She comes to me, all fake anger. "*You're* incorrigible."

Heat blooms between us. Her eyes drop to my lips, and I think she's going to kiss me, but then she seems to think better of it. She spins around and continues, stopping only to examine a tiny bowl—so tiny as to be completely useless. "Look at the work on this."

"I know. People used to put a ridiculous amount of effort into making useless things elaborate."

"It's called beauty, Hugo. Some people like beauty."

"Uh-huh," I say.

She turns and walks backwards. "Why do you come here?"

"Not everything here is ridiculous."

"Huh."

We head around a corner into a tall thicket of shelves. She touches random bright things, sometimes picking them up and turning them—examining the way the light changes, no doubt. She picks up a bird statuette that's also a vase. "Is it this?"

I take it from her fingertips and set it back, never letting my gaze stray from her eyes. "Nope."

Just four hours ago we were in that elevator, and I want her again. I wanted her again the second I wasn't touching her anymore. This irresistible need that I have for her—I don't know what to do with it.

She pauses, studying my eyes. She seems to rouse herself and continues on. She picks up a blue glass vase and turns to me. "This?"

I lift it from her fingers and set it aside. "Do better."

She comes near, lips a hair's breadth from mine. "Is my gift of legend within visual range?"

"No hints."

"So it's not, then?"

I cradle her cheeks and kiss her, right there between the dusty rows of shelving that seem to go for miles. "No."

She slides her hands around my back and presses into me. "Evil," she whispers into the next kiss. "Have we passed the area where it is yet? Will you at least tell me that?"

"We have not passed it."

"Then how do you know it hasn't been sold?"

"Because nobody but you would think it was worth the price."

Her smile brightens the whole gloomy place. We continue on.

I've thought about buying it for her a few times over the years, but giving a strange and extravagant gift to my best friend's little sister? A woman I haven't seen in a decade? Who does that?

I'll be buying it now.

"I'm still mad at you, you know," she says.

"The letter?"

She narrows her eyes at me and picks up a glass asparagus. "You better not be getting me this."

"Please."

A few minutes later, she finds a ceramic owl clock. "This?"

I groan. "What do you take me for? That is not your kind of owl at all. Too realistic."

"Right? Everybody gets me owl stuff. If it has an owl motif, people think I want it, but it's not true."

I pick up a big-eyed seventies owl. "This is more in the ballpark...if it was a couple of clicks more ridiculous."

She looks at me, amazed. "I know you think you're deeply and hugely impressing me right now, but don't think that'll get me to change my mind about dating you. Or forget what you did to my dream job."

"Why won't you let me fix it?"

"Why won't you accept that I asked you not to try to fix it?"

I move close, my lips a hair's breadth from hers. "You are impossible."

"So I hear."

"Mr. Jones!" It's the owner, Felix, calling me over.

I sigh. "He probably has something to show me. Keep trying to find your gift. You'll fail. And when I finally give it to you, you'll be speechless. And I'll take advantage of you in some outrageous way."

Again the eye flare. Will I ever get sick of that goddamn eye flare?

CHAPTER 30

STELLA

Hugo's up at the counter with the owner, holding some glass orb thing up to the light. Is that the one thing he doesn't find ridiculous?

I drift nearer, to a spot where I can better see the two of them without eavesdropping or interrupting. I love knowing that he goes to this place, that he knows this guy. It's like seeing into his secret life.

What is this thing he's admiring and scrutinizing so hard?

I can't stop wondering about the rest of his life. Mom says he lives in a nice condo, but what is it like? What does he have on the walls? I'd imagine geometric things, but maybe that's wrong. What does he do in his spare time? Keeping my distance from him is a double-edged sword, because I'm burning with curiosity about him.

He says something to the man. The man pulls out his phone, pokes at his screen, and then shows it to Hugo. It all seems very serious, but that's Hugo. So serious. So intense.

What if? What if I said yes to dinner? What if we were together? What if he was mine?

He turns as if he feels me watching.

I grin, and before I can stop myself, I'm going to him. "Whatcha got there?"

"It's a paperweight," he says.

"A signed Gerhard Schechinger clear glass 'torus' paperweight," the man clarifies. Hugo introduces him as Felix.

"But you hardly ever use paper," I point out.

"I collect these." Hugo hands it to me.

It's a clear glass orb, and inside there's a bubble in the shape of a stretched-out donut. I hold it up the way he did.

"It's all about the bubble in there," he says.

I turn it around. "Is there something special about it?"

"Imagine if you drew a dot on one part of the donut, and then a dot on another part, and then you twist and stretch the donut so that the dots meet. It's sort of a thought experiment that unlocks the connections across shapes and spaces."

I hand it back. "So you have these at home, and you take them out and look at the bubbles?"

"Yes." Hugo gazes into it like a man on fire. Dots on a twisted donut. I love how into it he is.

"So is that your favorite shape?"

"Favorite three-dimensional shape, yes."

The rush of pleasure I feel right then makes every atom in my body happy, and I so want to kiss him. "Favorite *three-dimensional* shape," I tease. "But not your favorite two-dimensional shape."

"Certainly not."

"Well, it's beautiful," I say, but really, I mean him—he's beautiful.

He's telling me more things about the donut bubble. Something about "tori" and shapes with holes and the light they shed on math whichimabobs.

Out of nowhere I get this memory of Hugo's doodles turning up around the house. Interconnected triangles. "Your fave two-dimensional shape. Could it be the triangle?"

He looks at me, stunned. "How'd you know?"

"A little thing called visual recollection."

His eyes sparkle. "Touché." He goes back to his inspection.

So, so Hugo-ish. And here we are. And he has a gift for me. I'm so happy in this moment, my heart might just pound right out of my chest. And I'm thinking maybe this thing with the two of us is worth taking a chance on. Maybe things can be different this time.

"So are you buying it?" I ask him.

"No. It's nice, but there's a surface imperfection."

"What surface imperfection?" Felix demands.

Hugo scowls. "Come on." The way he says it, you'd think Felix tried to pass off an orb with a blob of poop on it.

"There's no surface imperfection," Felix says.

"Not only is there a surface imperfection, but it's glaringly obvious." Hugo shows him the alleged imperfection.

A magnifying glass comes out. They proceed to argue. Felix feels it's nearly imperceptible, but Hugo finds it offensive, and he cannot imagine buying it. No, not for any price. This flawed little thing disgusts him.

Felix turns to me. "Only the best for Hugo. He's my toughest customer."

"Hugo craves perfection." When I say it, it probably sounds like a compliment and not the most devastatingly true fact of the millennium. This whole incident—it's like a sign from the universe done in flashing pink neon: *Stella Woodward: what the hell are you thinking?* I'm feeling queasy.

Hugo hates flaws, and he sees them all—eventually. And how they disgust him!

My heart pounds wildly, but not in that beautiful, Hugo-loving way anymore.

He's right about one thing: I'm definitely reckless. Shopping with him, having sex with him, letting him buy me a gift.

It's as fake as kissing the Zac Hanson poster, but so much worse, because instead of ending up with soggy paper bits on my lips and a poster with a hole in it, and then my friends come over and stare at Zac's mangled lips and feel afraid to ask why I would tear a hole there, it's my heart on the line!

I'm being reckless with my very own heart. I can't be falling for him. I can't do this again. I can't go through it again.

"I have to go," I say to him.

"But...your gift—"

"Don't get it for me—you can't get it. I won't accept it." I mumble something about getting air and head out of the store, out to the sidewalk.

It's already dusk. The days are getting shorter. I button my jacket all the way up to the top and lean against the wall.

Deep breaths. In. Out.

I know better than to fall for Hugo, but then I get around him and I forget.

If only I could pin a picture of Jonathan to his shirt. It would be like a warning sign on a pack of cigarettes: Remember these rabid perfectionists? Remember what happened when they started fixating on your flaws? You really want to ten-x that feeling?

Or I could give him one of Jonathan's sweaters that smells of his stupid signature cologne, Obsidian Valor, and whenever I was near Hugo, I would remember.

They say it's better to have loved and lost than never to have loved at all, but I don't think that saying is meant for a situation like mine. I feel that *those who don't learn from the past are doomed to repeat it* is more appropriate for me.

The door to the shop *clunks* open. Footsteps approach my place of doleful leaning. "What's going on?"

"I don't want you to give me a present anymore."

"But you're going to love it."

"You know who gives presents to each other? People who are dating. We are not dating."

He comes and leans next to me. "Let me give you this thing, Sparky."

Of course he uses my nickname. He pretends not to know people, not to know their hearts, but he's playing mine like a banjo. "You giving me things is too much like dating."

"What is so wrong with dating?"

"I'll tell you what's so wrong with it: I'm that orb. And it looks good to you at first, and you think you like it, but when you take a good hard look, the flaw is just too much."

"The two situations are not at all analogous. This is us, Stella."

"They're totally analogous. You see me as reckless and unruly, and I get that you think you are liking those things for the moment—I'm a refreshing break from the stress of your data model equations. I'm an amusing honk in the middle of your perfect symphony, a distraction that deserves further exploration, and you got an amazing math idea after we banged, but you know deep down that we don't fit. You can't understand why I'd settle for a job with a shitty boss, or how I could like the art of Salvador Dali or leave my shoes untied or a million other things. I will never be thirty-six point whatever improvement in your life. I won't even be one percent. I'll be negative four."

"I don't care if you're negative a hundred."

"There's a large chart in your office that says different."

"To hell with the chart. We're good together. I know you know it. I know you see it. I know you."

"You know me from the outside looking in."

"Disagree," he says.

"I'm sorry. I know how this song ends. The song of us dating."

"How can you know how it ends when we haven't written it yet?"

"Because I've sung it a few times before."

"Are we talking about that asshole in Madison? That Jonathan character?"

"How do you know about Jonathan?"

"Charlie told me. And I'll remind you that I am most certainly not Jonathan."

Miserably, I gaze out at the scaffolding of the building across the street. Two stories of chock-a-block wood and metal against grand old bank.

"I know you're not those guys." *You're so much more. More perfect. More dangerous.*

"Well?"

"Hugo, this is my decision. You can't argue somebody into being in a relationship. I've told you I won't date you. This is what I've told you."

He makes his rumble of frustration.

I wrap my arms around myself. It's hard not to kiss him right now. I'd kiss him and then I'd say, "Never mind! Go get my gift and let's eat!"

I could still do that.

Maybe I need to quit this job. Maybe Mia's Meow Squad place where she used to work has more hours for me. Or I could get something in a restaurant. I could be more aggressive about landing freelance jobs.

The idea of not seeing Hugo, though—I hate it. I can't not see him.

"Where does that leave us? Banging in the elevator?" Hugo says. "Secretly groping each other in the office like fugitives?"

I sigh. Some of the most exciting experiences of my life.

"Some lurid and tawdry, no-strings office affair?" he continues. "That can't be what you want."

Wait.

I narrow my eyes, pondering. *A no-strings office affair.*

Could that work? What if we don't get involved in each other's lives or go to each other's homes, is it possible that will prevent us from progressing to the disgust-at-Stella's-glaring-imperfections stage? It's hard to be annoyed at a person's flaws when she's riding your face or sucking your cock.

No strings. Lurid and tawdry. Is that possible with us?

But why wouldn't it be? Why throw the baby out with the bathwater?

The more I think about it, the more I like this idea. Though sometimes I lie to myself when I really, really want something that isn't good for me. Am I doing that now? I study the building across the street, pondering hard.

"A lurid and tawdry, no-strings office affair."

"What about it?"

"I'd be up for that."

"What are you talking about?"

"A lurid and tawdry, no-strings office, no-life-details affair. Yes, please."

"Stella, no. You deserve better. We deserve better."

"That's how far I can go. That's what I want. Isn't that your preferred style of dating anyway?"

"Not with you!"

I press a finger to his lips. "But if it were your only option?"

He gives me a stern look, thoughts churning behind dark gray eyes. He doesn't say what he's thinking, but I'm guessing the idea of making me relent is in there somewhere.

CHAPTER 31

STELLA

Mom picks up a silk scarf from a display table and presses it to her cheek. She's in town for a short stopover before she flies out of JFK for the wedding of a school friend in Ireland.

"It goes with your dress!" Kelsey says brightly.

"I'd like it better in a lighter color," Mom says. "And smaller."

The three of us are at Macy's because Mom has a gift certificate to spend. She's been trying to buy us stuff with it—such a Mom move!—but we refuse.

"You will use it for yourself, and if you buy something for anyone other than yourself, I'll personally rip it to shreds and toss it over Fifth Avenue like confetti!"

"Money down the drain and littering..." She gives me her disappointed face. My mom, the most literal person ever.

"I'm just saying to use it for yourself," I say. "I wouldn't actually rip it up."

Kelsey gives me a sympathetic smile. I've explained to her how my entire family thinks I'm an irresponsible doofus. She had a hard time believing it, which made me feel awesome, but it's even more validating that she's able to see it now.

We've been eating our way through Manhattan, and Kelsey got us front-row tickets to the Broadway musical she's in —*Anything Goes*. Afterwards we'll stop for champagne at the Plaza, a fun, splurgy treat for Mom so that she can have the whole deluxe New York experience.

I find a brown T-shirt with a chipmunk picture on the pocket. "I would've worn this in my old life. In my actual chosen field of employment."

"You'll get back in your field," Mom says brightly. She apologized again about the letter, which I appreciated. She's trying.

"I do miss it," I confess. "I miss the brainstorming. I miss the arguing, the testing, the difficulty of making something effective and awesome that the client will actually sign on to."

"I'll buy it for you with my gift certificate," she offers. "As incentive."

"I don't need an incentive." I list off the agencies I've applied to. I list off the additional letters of recommendation I've marshalled. I'm probably overdoing it—maybe I need to stop being so reactive. "I feel pretty good about getting something on my own steam, that's all."

"Of course you will!" she says.

I plaster on a confident smile, telling myself to take that at face value. "And this'll be a prize for when I land that amazing something."

Kelsey comes up with giant neon-blue earrings that have silver sparkles and dangly shimmering things. She holds them up to her ears. "What do you think? With this top? Right?"

I smile. Neon pink, neon blue, and sparkles everywhere— that's so Kelsey. "A hundred percent."

"Oh, Kelsey," Mom says. "You're so pretty, you don't need to wear such loud things. They just distract from your beauty."

"But I like wearing loud things," Kelsey says, unaffected. "I think bright things look good on me."

"They look great on you!" I say.

Mom's face says she disagrees, but I love Kelsey's style—the bold things she wears go perfectly with her big laugh and outsized personality. Everything about her is awesome.

If she knew Mom a little bit better, she'd have realized that the pretty comment Mom made was also aimed at Kelsey's makeup—I could tell from the moment I introduced them that mom thinks Kelsey's makeup is overdone. It's not that Mom's trying to be mean, she just thinks her way is best on every level.

Kelsey spots a funky dress. "For when Hugo takes you to the restaurant that is made for you."

Mom perks up. "What's this?"

"Something that's not happening, that's what it is," I say. I told Kelsey about Hugo's offer and she's been going crazy trying to figure out what restaurant he could possibly have in mind.

"Hugo wanted to take Stella on a date, and she'll have none of it," Kelsey says.

Mom's laser beam of a gaze is now boring into my face. "Hugo wanted to take you on a date?!"

"I know, right? Has he lost his mind?" I joke.

"No, I'm sure lots of boys want to take you out. It's just that you and Hugo are so different." Mom pauses here. "Though you two always did have fun together...the rare times you'd stop sparring."

"Yeah, those rare moments between the long stretches of him hating me."

"Actually, there *were* times when I wondered if he had eyes for you," she says.

"Well, it's not happening." I don't tell her about our exciting plans to meet secretly at Hotel Luxe later this week.

"You and Hugo." Mom is pondering this hard.

"Not to mention that Charlie would go cuckoo for Cocoa Puffs." I grab a pair of maroon cowboy boots. "I wonder if they have these in my size."

"Oh, it's true. Smoke—out of his ears. Even now—" Mom looks at me alarmed. "He doesn't know about Hugo wanting a date, does he?"

"Are you kidding?" I say. "He'd hop a plane so fast. He'd probably break his hand banging down Hugo's door, and then he'd break the other hand punching his face."

"Wait—why would your brother be so against it?" Kelsey asks.

Mom looks baffled, as though she'd never thought about it before. "Charlie's very protective over Stella," Mom decides. "When Stella jumps into something, she goes feet first."

I roll my eyes. So much for Mom trying to see me as a capable adult.

"She doesn't stop to comb through options," Mom continues. "That is the trust that she has."

I do nostril dragon at Kelsey, because apparently I've regressed in age by fifteen years at least.

Kelsey's frowning now. "I don't know about that—I have known Stella to be very thoughtful about things. Very sharp and shrewd. And she gives great advice!"

I could kiss her.

"And when she loves, she gives her whole heart," Mom adds.

"It really is amazing I've managed to stay alive for so long," I say.

"You have a generous heart," Mom clarifies.

I turn back to my boots.

"Here's what I don't get," Kelsey says. "If Hugo is such a good friend of Charlie's, why wouldn't he be happy for Hugo and Stella to date? It's not as if they're kids anymore."

It's an excellent point—why *is* Charlie so rabid about it? I always went with a combo of him being a jerk and doing a big brother thing.

"Charlie can be a little sensitive when it comes to Hugo," Mom says. "And he knows that Hugo is not like other boys. Hugo has always been more interested in the life of the mind. A relationship would be low on his hierarchy of priorities. Hugo is uncompromising in his quest for great things—a hard-driving and rigid boy with no time for romance."

Nostril dragon comes back out, and Kelsey looks away, working hard not to laugh. It's official, shopping with my mom has transformed me into a teenager.

A clerk comes by, and Mom shows him the scarf and asks for the same scarf created as an entirely different product with completely different features. He brings Mom to another area of scarves that might suit her.

Kelsey turns to me. "I don't care what your mom and brother say. You need to give that man a chance."

I spin a rack of earrings. "I am giving him a chance. In bed. At Hotel Luxe." I get excited and nervous every time I think about us meeting like sexy secret agents. I've already picked out my underwear for it.

"But didn't you hear your mom? Maybe he always had eyes for you! Could he have loved you all along?"

"Highly doubtful." I spin another rack. I've explained this all to Kelsey in excruciating detail, how men like Hugo start off loving my sunshiny ways. So refreshing! Then comes the part where they shut me out because I'm not a serious person, just this shiny and slightly distracting object. And finally, the barely concealed disgust.

"I've had more than enough of the not-measuring-up shit for one lifetime. It's a thing with me, Kelsey. It just is."

"I get that it's happened historically, but it doesn't mean it'll aways happen. Maybe *guys like Hugo* turn out to be shit boyfriends because they're not Hugo."

I snort. "That's like saying, if you're allergic to the peanuts in peanut brickle ice cream, have I ever got a delicious treat for you! Here's an entire bag of peanuts. Enjoy!"

"Poor Hugo," Kelsey says. "Such a fox, so bananas for you."

I examine a pair of silver hoops. "I run a hard bargain." I put the hoops back. "A lurid and tawdry office affair, that's the only affair for me!" It's hard to keep from smiling when I say that, though. I love that he used the word tawdry—it's so old-fashioned.

I do that a lot lately—think about things he said and get a warm glow.

An hour later, we're down on the men's floor where Mom's hunting for a wallet for Dad, much to my exasperation, when I catch the scent of Jonathan's peppery bergamot cologne.

"You smell that?" I clutch Kelsey's arm. "That's Jonathan's cologne. The smell of heartbreak."

"Very masculine," Kelsey says.

I'm looking around to figure out who's wearing the offending scent when I see the display—a circular table piled high with the telltale black boxes of cologne under a black-and-white photo of a hot model gazing into the distance in a hot and manly way.

I beeline to it, slide my finger over the tops of the boxes. It's like a sign. *Stay strong, Stella!*

Kelsey comes up. "Just can't get enough of the smell of heartbreak?"

I pick up the box. "What if I got this for Hugo?"

"And you would do that why?"

"It would be like sticking a warning label on him. Known to cause heartbreak. Beware."

"Stella, oh my god, you can't."

A salesperson comes up. She wears an excited expression and

a nametag that says Florence. "Did you see the special we're running right now? You get a Jack Hermann overnight bag with each and every Obsidian Valor purchase."

"See?" I say. "A cute overnight bag. It's a sign."

Kelsey widens her eyes. "You really want him to walk around smelling like heartbreak and devastation? This is what you want?"

"Hmm..." Florence tilts her head. "I think of this scent as more like bold sophistication."

"Nose of the beholder," Kelsey says.

"I think of it as heartbreak, and I want him to smell like that," I say. "Heartbreak and devastation and agony. A man who cuts you to shreds until your self-esteem is zero."

Florence looks concerned. "I could show you some other colognes."

Kelsey grabs my arm. "Dude."

"You're right," I say, putting the box back.

I thank Florence for her help, and we get out of there.

CHAPTER 32

HUGO

Hotel Luxe is an upscale boutique hotel in the Financial District and my preferred no-strings hookup place. A tagline on its understated sign promises it's "a hidden gem of tranquility and opulence."

There is a certain serenity to the place, I suppose; the lobby is full of rich velvet furnishings done up in deep gem tones, all bathed by dim pools of light that make it hard to read anything that's not on a screen.

Elegant. Discreet.

I came here weekly over this past summer with Susan, a bond analyst who is only ever free over a four-hour window on Saturday nights. This is also where I occasionally meet Laurel, a data security thought leader with a hotel room thing.

Purely utilitarian, no-strings affairs like these work when people are on the same page, and Susan and Laurel and I are definitely on the same page—we prefer fucking without the dates, without the conversations.

I stop at the concierge and do an expedited check-in, leaving a keycard for Stella to pick up, then I head down the plush hallway to 510, my favorite suite.

Meeting Stella here doesn't feel right—not at all.

But I have to see her, and this is what she asked for. I'm done deciding what's good for Stella. What's good for Stella is officially up to Stella.

She doesn't want gifts and dinner dates. As a man who prefers utilitarian relationships and absolutely cannot be distracted, I have to prefer that. When you think about it logically, it makes sense to do the no-strings thing.

Stella Woodward, the voice of logic and reason. A distracting person who helps me work. What is the world coming to?

I stroll into the room and adjust the heating, hoping she'll be on time. I haven't seen her for one full day, and it's too long. Being with her feels like home—not just because of our history. It's more. Being with her is beyond anything.

Beyond anything is the fuzzy sort of phrase I wouldn't have used even a month ago, but there it is.

Stella arrives seven minutes late. She closes the door and stands there. "This is your idea of tawdry? It's a five-star hotel!"

I back her up against the door and kiss her. "The things I'm about to do to you are going to be so tawdry, this place will feel like a raunchy sex palace by the time you walk out of here."

She smiles. "That is pretty tawdry."

I slide her shirt aside, baring her shoulder, kissing her soft skin, dragging my lip up the satiny smoothness of her red bra strap.

"You'll change the fabric of reality with your dirty ways?"

"The fucking fabric of reality, baby." I kiss her neck.

"All of the elegant people out there will be transformed into gross men in overcoats?"

"Are you almost done with the comedy routine?" I growl.

"Dear Diary, I walked into an upscale hotel to meet him, and the sex was so tawdry that when I walked out, the hallway lighting had transformed from elegant sconces to flashing neon triple-X signs. A red-letter day, indeed!"

I stop kissing her.

"What?"

I take her hands and pin them to the door, hands up on either side of her head, waiting for her to be serious. She wanted a tawdry fuck, and tawdry fucks aren't joke fests.

She raises her gaze to mine.

I wait for her to understand that I can hold her here for as long as I want. I *will* hold her here.

Her chest rises and falls, breath coming fast, watching me with those big brown eyes I could lose myself in, though brown isn't at all sufficient to describe the color of her eyes—it's more like chestnut and mocha, crackled through with burnt honey. Her eyes are deep. Endless. Full of soul and dimensionality.

"Hugo." She's breathing harder. "The comedy part is over."

I'm so hard, I can barely think. "Are you quite sure?"

"Maybe."

I release her hands and kiss her and then I pull away. "Unbutton the next button of your shirt."

She looks uncertain.

"Do it, or do I have to do it for you?"

She complies.

"Do the next one, Stella. Take it all the way off."

I watch her unbutton her shirt. A red lacy bra comes into view. Did she pick that out for me? I watch her wriggle out of her shirt.

"Bra, now," I say softly. "Hot as it is."

She removes it and drops it to the floor. "Skirt now."

"Not the panties first?"

I growl and go to her.

"No way! No ripping! Not these ones." She wriggles out of her skirt and panties, and stands there, completely naked. She puts her arms around me. "Say the thing again."

"What thing?"

"You know."

I take hold of her hair and bare her neck like a vampire. "Relent to me," I growl, planting kisses up the silken side.

She gasps, hands roaming all over my shirt. "Relent in what sense?"

"What?"

"Relent. What does it mean?"

"It doesn't matter." Nothing matters. There's only touching her. Tasting her.

"You have to tell me what it means in your mind."

I growl.

"Tell me," she gasps. "It's hot and I need you to tell me."

"It's a term I'll use in conjunction with a certain data mapping concept. Forget it."

"Tell me how you use it."

I kiss down her belly. "I might say something like, through successive iterations…" I kiss lower. "The rules relent to accommodate the evolving objectives." I kiss her mound.

"I was right—it is a nerdy way of saying submit."

"Yes."

Stella is panting. "Say it again.'"

I pick her up and carry her to the chair. "Loop your legs over the arms."

She does as I say, watching me, amazed. "Bossy."

I take her hands and place them on the arms. "I am going to lick your pussy and fuck you with my fingers and you are going to keep your hands right there until I'm good and done with you."

Her eyes flare wide. I don't wait for her to answer. I can't wait. I kneel, and swipe my fingers down her sex, wet and perfect.

l swipe my tongue clear up her slit.

She shudders.

"Relent to me." I do it again and again, pushing my finger deep into her and hooking it just so until her orgasm shatters over her, and then I'm inside her, deep inside her, weird chair angle be damned.

CHAPTER 33

STELLA

We end up in the shower where I'm about to give him the world's best blow job, or that's my goal, anyway.

I grip his cock at the root and kiss the side of it.

He groans. He likes his cock gripped during blow jobs—that much I've noticed.

I look up. "I'm gonna suck the bejesus out of you. But first…" I kiss the other side. "Do you prefer the gripping thing I did yesterday? Or a gripping-plus-sliding thing…"

"It doesn't matter."

"Tell me." I put my lips over the tip. "Telllll me."

He groans. "If it's in your mouth, I'm good."

"Come on! This is no time to stop being precise."

He groans.

I want it to be good. I want him to love it.

"I'm gonna torture it out of you otherwise." I lick up the side. "I'll horribly torture you."

"Grip it."

"There we go." I grip it and make him rate the hardness of my grip. When I get the data I need, I give him a good hard suck.

He groans again and grabs my hair, twisting it pleasingly.

Yesterday I told him I like him extra growly when I give a blow job, like as caveman as possible, and he's really going for it, mercilessly fisting my hair and a little bit pushing my head like a barbarian warlord. Those were my specific instructions.

He makes this very Hugo sound when he comes. The bear sound.

Lying in bed afterwards, I slide my finger down the outer edge of his arm, tracing a line over the contours of his arm muscles, glistening with sweat. I want to say something about the bear sound and how much I love it, but I'm afraid he won't do it ever again, so I stay quiet about it.

"What?" he says.

"This," I whisper.

"Yes," he says.

Back in my most intense Hugo-crush era, I would imagine what it was like to be with him, and those ideas I had were nothing compared to the reality of him.

It's not just the sex, but it's his idiosyncrasies—how ticklish he is on the backs of his thighs. The warm, solid feeling of his chest when I lay my head there. The long, low growl he makes when he comes, like a brutish bear. The cute birthmark on his right butt cheek that he didn't even know about.

My stomach rumbles. Hugo kisses me there. "We need to get you some food," he mumbles.

"Hey, why does everyone think you're allergic to pineapple?" I ask.

He kisses me. "I thought this was a no-strings, no-life-details affair."

I shove my fingers into his thick, dark hair. "I'm gonna make you tell me."

"Doubtful."

I frown. It's driving me a little bonkers—why would he tell people that? It's so unlike him to lie, and this is a whopper. But he's right. That was my rule.

My stomach rumbles again.

"The cabinet next to the mini fridge usually has a good selection of energy bars," he says. "I'd recommend the almond dark chocolate."

I laugh. "What, are you a connoisseur of hotel snack selections? Right down to the types of energy bars? How would you know..." The question dies on my lips.

He brings other women here.

He seems to realize what he's just revealed. "Or we could grab sandwiches on the way back," he says quickly. "Maybe call ahead to that Italian deli."

"I'm good." I climb out of bed, grab my purse, and snatch up my clothes, which I seem to have thrown everywhere.

I practically sprint into the bathroom without so much as a backwards glance lest he give me some insider tips on the merits of various Hotel Luxe-supplied toiletries, which he probably could, being that he brings his women here.

What did I expect? It's not like he's a monk. Of course he would do hotel quickies.

I brush my hair in the mirror.

You wanted an impersonal, tawdry, no-strings affair, and you got it, I tell myself. *You are avoiding the horror show of the heart. You are staying upstairs where there's popcorn and light. Be happy, goddamnit!*

I tell myself that bringing me to a place where he brings other women is the perfect bat signal to my subconscious—*don't get any big ideas, because this thing is sex only.*

I put on lipstick, rolling on with my pep talk. It's good for this to be clarified, because Hugo has the power to break my heart in a way that makes my Jonathan heartbreak look like a skip daisy patch.

And I definitely don't grab one of the energy bars.

CHAPTER 34

STELLA

One of the lesser-known downsides to being a teen or preteen girl and having a crush on your brother's best friend is that your crush is frequently hanging around in the place where you live your life.

This might seem like a good thing, and in some ways it was because I got to see Hugo a lot, but I'd find myself putting way too much thought into what I might wear for something as low-key as lying on the couch in front of the TV, because what if Hugo came around? And then there was the temptation to wear makeup twenty-four seven—including foundation, a temptation that I gave into a lot. Not great for the skin, let's just say.

But I wanted Hugo to think I was pretty. I might not have been able to contain myself when he was around, but at least I could look nice, and maybe he could think of me as more than a pesky scamp of a sister.

Sometimes I imagined he did see me as more. There were times during the more boisterous dinner table discussions—by which I mean I was being boisterous, and everyone was probably wishing I'd zip it—that I'd look over and imagine that he was on board with my fanciful ideas.

Or was he, too, wishing I'd zip it?

Or I'd be ready to go out, all dressed up, waiting by the front door for my girlfriends to pick me up, and I'd look across the foyer and catch his eye from where he usually sat at the kitchen table, and I'd imagine we were having a moment, or maybe a millisecond, but then he'd smile politely and turn back to Charlie or look back down at his phone. And I'd want to think he was looking at me with admiration, but it could've also been him wondering why my friends were always so late.

There was one time when I was waiting for my friends that he walked through on his way upstairs and stopped short, clearly surprised I was there. "Wow," he blurted, "you really look nice!"

It was an unexpected thing for him to say, and I had the thought that it caught us both off guard.

I don't remember how I replied—probably stammered senselessly.

And he was about to say something more—I braced myself for whatever horrible punchline was about to come, but then Charlie walked up, and they both bounded up the stairs, and I never got to hear it.

The incident became a kind of litmus test for my teen self-esteem at any given moment; when I was feeling good about myself, I could almost believe that Hugo really meant what he'd said, because it had seemed to have been an unfiltered reaction, right?

When I was feeling down, I'd feel sure that he'd been just about to deliver the zinger of the century. Like, yeah, you look nice...in a sad little mall-rat way.

I thought about it a lot. So much thought for one random

little moment in time that he probably forgot. So much wondering.

We're a week into our Luxe rendezvous when I get the answer on it.

By this time in our illicit affair, we've taken to ordering room service and eating it quickly before parting—usually sandwiches —swiss roast beef for Hugo and a veggie delight with no onions for me. I've flexed on the issue of sharing a meal enough to do post-sex room service.

So I'm sitting up in bed next to Hugo, half under the covers, plate balanced on my lap, when I think to ask him.

"Do you remember this one time I was going out with my friends, and I was standing at the door waiting, and you came from somewhere and nearly ran me over. I think you thought I was gone. And you told me I looked nice. Out of the blue."

"Waiting for your friends at the bottom of the stairs?"

"Why am I even asking you? Why would you remember a two-second encounter from fifteen years ago? And why am I asking? That's not what we're doing here."

"Hey." He sets his bag of chips on my side because I always steal them anyway, and he looks me in the eye and he says, "Do I remember that night you were standing there wearing that blue sequin tube top and blue flowered skirt? And you're all smiles, frothing over with excitement? In those platform boots you always wore? And your hair shiny like a mirror? Are you asking me if I meant it when I said you looked nice?"

Shivers go over me. I'm stupidly excited for how much that sounds like a yes. "I shouldn't have asked. You shouldn't—"

"Damn right I meant it." His voice is low like his orgasm bear growl. "Damn right."

"Oh," I whisper.

"And just for the record, that time when you kissed me, when you thought I was the other kid?"

"Yeah?" I say.

"It nearly broke me."

"Me too," I say.

I get out of there soon after, because we're going way too close to the line, if not outright crossing it.

CHAPTER 35

HUGO

I meet Stella at Hotel Luxe three or four times a week, sometimes at lunch; sometimes after work.

In spite of her dedication to us keeping each other at arm's length, I'm learning a lot about her. Not just her as a sexual being, though as a sexual being she's fucking magnificent—but also her likes and her dislikes, her sounds, her scents, her moods, the way she reacts to sirens out on the street—she's still not used to Manhattan's decibel level—and to workplace dramas; work being one of the topics of conversation she hasn't deemed too personal.

Meanwhile, my data model is going disastrously. Those breakthroughs took me further than I was, but I'm starting to question the viability of the project itself. The goals. The premise.

Usually when work is going shitty, my mood is bad. But somehow, in spite of the fact that I'm now questioning the foundations of my project, which is a complete disaster, and daily failures in front of my whiteboards, the world seems...bright.

I'm just happy.

Do I want us to be together like a real couple? Does it torment me that she doesn't want that? Yes, it definitely does. But in the las week or so, I've decided that what we've got is good. Humans are hardwired to be communal animals in addition to being sexual animals, after all. So of course this thing with Stella would be biologically satisfying to me as the higher-order mammal that I am, producing feelings of well-being that could be mistaken for happiness.

Or maybe this simply is what constitutes happiness.

But then we're at Hotel Luxe one day after work, and Stella comes out of the bathroom, all wrapped up in a fluffy Hotel Luxe bathrobe, hair wet from showering, and she holds up a tiny bottle, eyes sparkling with delight.

"Have you seen this, Hugo? The hotel hair conditioner is named Pure Essence Platinum Silk Mane Radiance Elixir! Just two of those words would've been fine, but they had to name it all seven! Just for their hotel hair conditioner! Did they have a brainstorming session and decide everybody's idea should be included in one giant name?"

She's just laughing. She brings it over so that I can read it for myself. It's just the sort of thing she always thinks is funny.

I take the bottle and read it aloud. "Pure Essence Platinum Silk Mane Radiance Elixir!" I look up, and she's grinning at me—that's how delighted she is.

And I think that my heart might explode.

And it's here that it hits me: I love her.

I actually love this woman.

All those years of holding back my emotions around Stella. All those years of battling the supposed annoyance and torment and distraction of Stella's existence.

It wasn't any of those things.

It was love.

All along it was love. I loved her back then. I love her now.

I love her so much, it's incomprehensible.

I love this woman.

All this love that I keep stuffed down, clamped down. I didn't let myself know.

She takes back the little bottle. "Right? Is more the new less or something like that?"

She gives the bottle a humorous frown.

I don't know the answer to her question. All I know is that I love her, and that I'll always want more from her. More and more and more.

CHAPTER 36

STELLA

There's something up with Hugo. His scowl is missing, but it's not just that. There's a sort of lightness to him.

"Do I have a carbuncle—"

"Stop." He takes the small bottle from my hands and puts it on the hotel room dresser. He wears this wonderous expression I've never seen, and the light in the hotel room seems different, like something weird and serious is happening. He cups my cheeks—gently—like my face is a fragile and truly enigmatic bird. "I love you, Stella."

I blink.

My heart swoops.

Hugo loves me? He loves me? *Swoop!*

Noooooo—no swooping!

I take hold of his wrists and remove his hands. "Hugo—no—"

"I love you," he says, like it's this stunning discovery he's just made.

"Be serious, Hugo."

"I'm in love with you. I am."

Fear wells up inside me as the wounds from my past flare back to life. "Dude. We just had sex, and suddenly you're in love with me? Do you know what a cliché that is?"

"This is the real deal—I know you feel it, too. Tell me you don't feel something."

Of course I feel something: ecstasy with a side of pure terror.

I've been down this road—and crashed. There's a tragic wreck still there at the end of this road, all twisted metal and broken limbs and a crushed heart. Sirens are wailing.

The only difference is that my joy is more extreme this time. What is it that they say? The higher you go, the harder you crash?

"You can't say it, can you?" he presses. "You can't say that there's nothing here because you feel something, too—I know you do."

"Yes, I feel something. It's called the thrill of the forbidden."

He shakes his head. "It's more."

"I'm your best friend's little sister. We've been off-limits to each other for years. Forbidden fruit is always delicious, but you can't live on it. Forbidden fruit can't sustain you. In fact, forbidden fruit is what kills people."

"I love you. You don't have to say it back, but you can't change how I feel. How I've always felt."

"Okay, Mr. Oxy-dopamine—"

"Don't—"

I pull the bathrobe tightly around myself. "You and your pleasure hormones are on a serious joyride today."

Hugo's having none of it. "All these years... I spent the energy of five nuclear reactors not letting myself know how much I love you. You have no idea how hard it was to be in the same room as you. How hard I tried to push you out of my mind. It was always you—always. I'm done walling off that feeling."

His words are a sparkly fire hose of happiness. But firehoses like that always start sparkly, only to end up toxic and sludgy. He doesn't know. He hasn't been down the road like I have.

I touch his lips because I'm a bandit, taking what I want before retreating to safety. "I'm just the off-limits little sister. You'll see that I'm right."

He comes to me. "The things that I would tell myself, the promises that I would make myself, over and over. Only assholes look at their best friend's little sister. What would Charlie think. What would your parents think, having taken me under their wing like they did. The codes of honor I set for myself, burned into my own brain. I've made a lot of codes for myself, Stella. Do you know how many codes I've broken in my life?"

My voice is a shaky whisper. "No."

"Take a guess."

"I don't want to guess."

"One. I've broken one code in my life—it's the code to stay away from you." He gives me a hard look. "And I'd break it again. This is the real thing. And the code about not telling what gets said at the poker table? I would've broken it if I hadn't gotten permission. I'll do what it takes—I will."

He sounds so sure.

Hugo thinks he loves me and my recklessness, my unruliness.

My Hugo-lites loved that sort of thing about me, too, until the day-to-day reality of me became too much, until they saw flaws they could not unsee, followed by cutting me out of everything important, and then the gut-wrenching disgust.

"I know you *think* it's real." I grab my phone. With shaking hands, I put in our usual order at the deli.

"I know it's real."

"Look who's unruly now," I say. It sounds like a joke, but it's not. Hugo's breaking the rules, and he has to stop. I put the phone aside and look him straight in the eyes. "Play by the rules or this game is over."

CHAPTER 37

HUGO

It's a dark, cold Sunday night, the kind where the wind whips down the streets with an aggression that makes it seem alive.

Stella's been doing her best to pretend this thing isn't real, but I'm done with that. What's more, I haven't seen her since Friday, and I don't want to wait for Monday lunch.

So I text her.

> Me: I'm coming over. Be ready for me.

> Stella: What? You can't. No-strings. Remember? TAWDRY.

> Me: People in no-strings office affairs can see each other outside of the office. It's known as a booty call.

> Stella: You're not coming over.

> Me: Fine. Come over here.

> Stella: We can't see each other's places. That's boyfriend-girlfriend stuff. We have established this.

My groan of frustration echoes across my living room. I need to see her, and I'm not taking her to Hotel Luxe.

> Stella: Patience and self-control pleez.

I know Stella well enough to know that this message is aimed as much at herself as it is at me.

> Me: I'm picking you up in twenty. You won't see my place. We don't even have to talk. How about that?

Dots appear. Disappear.

> Me: Dirty, dirty fucking. I will make you relent so hard.

Dots appear. Disappear.
I decide to sweeten the pot.

> Me: Wear something you're not attached to.

> Stella: Hmmmmm.

I smile. The last time I ripped something was at Hotel Luxe one morning before work. I was out of control in a way I found troublingly primitive, but Stella loved it.

> Me: Be out on the street in thirty minutes.

> Stella: So...is this a hotel situation?

> Me: See you in twenty-nine.

I pocket my phone.

Stella loves surprises. I'm still surprised that she turned down the gift and my offer to take her to the one restaurant that she would love the most, but she'll go for this.

In data modeling, you start with the one thing you are sure about—this is known as the primary entity. From there, you expand out by making and testing observations. Little by little, you add related entities. You keep iterating and expanding until the model covers the entire system.

She slides into the car wearing a winter scarf and hat, rosy-cheeked from the whipping wind. She sets her giant everything purse on her lap. "Back in the golden egg mobile."

I take hold of her scarf and pull her in for a kiss. I love her. I love us together.

"Where are we going?" she asks.

"Does it matter? We'll be fucking. You won't see my place. Those are your conditions, are they not?"

Warily, she studies my face. "A rent-by-the-hour hotel?"

"You know everything you need to know. Or do we have to review our text exchange?"

Her eyes sparkle. She likes this, and it does something to me, giving her things she likes. She moves near and settles her hand onto my thigh. "Are we staying in here?"

"Please."

"So you're not telling me?"

"You know everything you need to know." I run my fingers through her silky hair, arranging one side to lie flat in front of her shoulder in a way that matches the other side of her hair.

We turn onto a street where they've strung up the holiday lights. I usually find it annoying when the holiday lights go up before Thanksgiving, but this year the lights are warm and festive. And the festive holiday displays in the windows. Somehow my store of goodwill is larger than normal. A Stella effect.

My driver pulls up in the circular driveway in front of my building. I help her out and she gazes up at the elegant facade. "Fancy! If I'd've known we were coming someplace like this, I would've worn better underwear."

"Come on." I take her hand and lead her up the walk.

"This looks residential."

Vern, the doorman, opens the door for us. "Good evening, Mr. Jones."

"Evening, Vern." I lead her across the luxurious lobby to the elevator.

"He knows you?" Stella spins around. "You take women here?"

"Never."

"Wait! This had better not be your place. You said it wouldn't be your place."

The door opens. I guide her in and hit the button for my penthouse. "I said you wouldn't see my place."

"Is this or is this not where you live?"

"Turn around."

She refuses, of course, inspecting my face. "Why should I?"

I pitch my voice as low as it'll go. "Turn. Around."

"Oh, so it's gonna be that kind of fuck, is it? F-minus for romance."

I wait.

A hint of a smile appears in her eyes. She'll turn around. It's outrageous, but she'll comply. Stella can't resist a dare, as evidenced by her short career as a saxophone player in band where she probably got a D in music, but she killed it all the same.

"We better not be heading to your place."

I whip a blindfold from my pocket. "You won't know the difference."

Her eyes widen.

"You'll see nothing. You'll only feel the exquisite things that I do to you. You won't know where you are, and you won't care. I'll make sure of it."

CHAPTER 38

STELLA

He stands there in the dim light of the elevator, blindfold dangling from his fingers, voice low and gravelly. "I'll make sure of it."

Shivers skitter over my skin. Hugo doing a sexy blindfold thing? Works for me!

He turns me by the shoulders as the elevator glides upwards and ties the blindfold onto my head, fingers working busily at the back of my hair.

I touch the wall and the flat metal railing. I find my way back around and grab on to Hugo's coat, turning my head this way and that, trying to get my bearings. This is no half-assed blindfold; it's a top-tier, CIA-level, comprehensive blindfold. No light gets through. No dim shapes. Nothing.

"I'm wearing this the whole time?"

One deft finger traces a path down the side of my neck.

Nothing more. Just the finger.

My heart galumphs.

He's a silent and imposing presence there in the elevator. When there's nothing to say, Hugo says nothing. He's a gryphon atop an ancient building, full of foreboding and gravitas.

And he loves me—he said so. That's still there. It was with us in the limo, it's here in the elevator. He says he loves me, and it's wonderful and terrible, like a blazing fire, and I know not to get too near. But there it is, blazing. And I can't seem to turn away.

"It feels a little like cheating," I say. "I mean, you're still taking me to your place. I'll be able to smell it and feel it."

Hot fingers touch the bottom of my chin. He tilts up my head and kisses me.

"Somebody might get on the elevator at any moment," I whisper. "What will they think of you taking a blindfolded woman to your home?"

"I'll kick the shit out of them," he grumbles, kissing my neck.

I grin. It's so unlike Hugo to be all dark and sexy, but I like it, and I like how it's heightened by the excitingly helpless feeling from the blindfold.

"I'll kick the shit out of anybody who comes near you," he says.

I smile as he nips my ear.

The way he touches me, the way he kisses me—I'd know it was him even if I couldn't hear his voice.

A bell dings. Strong arms scoop me up, purse and all.

"Oh my god!" I stab what is probably his cheek with my finger before I successfully loop an arm around his neck. He carries me down the hall, or what I assume is the hall.

I hear keypad beeps, and then we're on the move again. He turns me this way and that, taking care that I don't hit walls and corners, maybe. Are we in his place?

I'm airborne for a split second before landing on something soft. "Unbutton your coat," he growls.

I unbutton my coat and work it off.

The coat is whisked away. "Hands up."

I comply. He pulls off the long, shapeless sweater I've worn, revealing the lacy slip-sheath-garment thingy that I got at a vintage store for a buck. It was going to be a zombie bridal veil until I decided to be a sexy witch at the last minute.

Anyway, whatever you want to call that lacy sheath thingy, it's definitely an effective Hugo exciter, judging from the guttural curse that comes from his mouth. "This outfit," he rumbles, touching and owning every part of my lace-clad body.

I never know where his fingers will be next. I like it.

He was joking in the elevator with the bit about kicking the shit out of anybody who comes near me, but I don't need to pull off the blindfold to know that primal Hugo is in charge right now —I can tell by the way he touches me. Primal Hugo is wild and dangerously into me and the opposite of smooth, and I am here for it.

"God, Stella!" Warm lips close over my breast. "What. What."

My boobs are nothing special, but to Hugo right now, they are.

"One of the top boob wonders in the known world, that's what," I joke.

Teeth graze over my lace-covered nipple. "Damn right."

I turn my head, taking in the fresh scent of his sheets and the quality feel of them on my cheek as he kisses down my belly. They're probably some of the best sheets on the market—not a luxury brand with a big name, but a quiet top-shelf brand. Hugo is the ultimate substance-over-style man.

He kisses down my thigh.

It's nice to be in his room surrounded by things that he chose for himself. And even though I can't see his bedroom, I'd bet that it's both attractive yet highly practical, probably designed to reflect the latest sleep environment science. Hugo is also a practicality-and-science-over-trends man.

He trails his hand down the front of the lace…lovingly. "God, you're hot. So, so, so hot."

I shove my hands into his hair, enjoying the feel of him, though it's driving me a little bit bonkers that I can't see his décor. I'd at least like to know what he has on his walls. After entertaining a few options, I decide that it would be photographs of math things—don't guys like him geek out on seashells for Fibonacci reasons? Or maybe a photo of a stairway or a bridge that is attractive to him on the basis of geometry.

He's pushing the sheath up over my hips. He shoves apart my legs. I groan as warm breath heats my sex. Yezzzzzzz!

Teeth graze over my tender bits, and I nearly explode with excitement.

"Fuck!" I say.

Massive hands grip my thighs as if there's a need to hold my legs spread. As if I might try to wiggle away, which, for the record, I would not do, but I like that he's gripping me there like I'm his sexy blindfolded prisoner.

I gasp as rough whiskers graze my tender lady bits, and then he takes a big lick, and I nearly die from an overload of pleasure. And then he's doing wicked tongue things.

I reach up with one hand and grope the headboard, pleased to find it's made of squarish wooden bars, like mission furniture. Having created furniture ads at the beginning of my career, I happen to know that mission furniture is prized for its strong, straightforward pieces where even the joinery is visible—as opposed to being ornately disguised, like it would've been in the Victorian era that preceded it.

It pleases me to no end that Hugo goes for mission furnishings. And naturally the tie-Stella-up possibilities haven't escaped my mind.

He hoists my thighs up on his shoulders, licking ferociously.

With my other hand I grip his hair, whimpering with pleasure from the wicked things he is doing with his tongue.

But then I'm back to the walls.

I'm now thinking that mathematically significant photos are too obvious for Hugo.

I could see him going for off-brand, like photos of old-timey piano players. Or sailboats. Or maybe he's put up heavily textured woven things for a hushed feeling. Or would he be displaying his glass orb collection? Or nerd things? He and my brother were *Star Trek* guys. I'm suddenly imagining a life-sized replica of Captain Kirk. Or maybe the USS Enterprise.

"Hey!" He settles my hips back down onto the bed and crawls up over me. "Where'd you go?"

"I'm here!" I insist, because this is a sex-only liaison where we're not supposed to be digging into the details of each other's lives.

I instruct my inquiring mind to think only of his sexy body. I fumble around and find his shirt buttons, open the buttons, and press my palms to the solid plane of his chest, exploring the contours of his muscles.

"Mmm."

Down, down, down I slide my hand, down under his waist-band and down under his underwear, grasping his rock-hard cock.

He rumbles his approval, but mostly he's kissing my lace-covered self in a worshipful way like I'm the lost treasure of Camelot.

Where did primal Hugo go?

Gentle, sweet kisses. "So...fucking...beautiful. And this thing on you..."

"Just as a reminder, you said to wear something I don't care about, and I did."

"So hot."

"So if you needed to rip it off…"

"It looks nice."

"Nice to rip."

He brushes a kiss over my neck, and I melt. "Nice to love."

Another gentle kiss.

"But just FYI, this garment was destined for life as a torn zombie veil. So honestly…" I start undoing his pants. "And you're losing these, mister."

"Stella, Stella, Stella." This in a voice suffused with adoration.

A smile takes over my entire face—I probably look goofy, but I can't help it. I'm sinking into some very extreme happiness here in Hugo's nest, and he's saying my name over and over, and it makes me feel ten feet tall. Or ten feet long, being that I'm horizontal.

Even if there's a life-sized Captain Kirk watching us from the corner, I want to live here in his bed.

I smooth my hands over his muscular shoulders, and I get this forbidden flash of us spending a weekend snuggled in the covers. We would read and play games and confess Chia-Pet-hiding-type secrets of yore, and of course make love.

Maybe order takeout. Hugo was always partial to anything with curry…

I give up on the pants because my arms are not four feet long. A rustle of fabric and the clink of a belt buckle tell me that he's probably pulling them off the rest of the way. He falls to kissing me some more, like I'm the most precious being on the planet.

"Hey! Don't forget—lurid. Tawdry."

"You're wearing a blindfold. I'm gonna fuck you soon. That's lurid and tawdry."

"No it's not!" I say. "Here I am in your home, and you're acting like I'm precious and you cherish me. All signs point to the opposite of lurid and tawdry."

"I do cherish you. These things aren't mutually exclusive."

"Disagree," I say.

He makes a sound that shows he disagrees with my disagreement.

"Okay," I say, "get out your phone and look up tawdry and lurid."

"Now?" he says.

"I was promised tawdry and lurid," I remind him. "Look it up."

"You gotta be kidding."

"We can go no further until we have this settled."

He grumbles and shifts, and I know he's getting his phone. Hugo is all about codes and promises and the letter of the law.

Silence.

I reach into the darkness and find his thigh. "Read it," I say.

"Tawdry," he says. "Cheap and tasteless."

"Okay, then," I say. "And lurid?"

"Horrible in fierceness or savagery. Marked by sensationalism."

"Aha. Somebody refuses to follow orders."

"It's not how I feel, Stella. I won't act like you're just a warm body for my consumption. It's you."

It's you.

And just like that, Lord help me, lurid and tawdry isn't where I am, either.

I reach up to him, fumbling for his hand. When I find it, I curl my fingers around his. It's a sweet connection that is way more dangerous than primal Hugo or playacting Hugo.

I go up on my knees and straddle his lap. I don't have a plan anymore. I just want to kiss him. I don't have the strength to be lurid and tawdry for the both of us.

He splays his fingers over the sides of my hips. I'm kissing him, moving slowly against him.

He urges me on. I shouldn't have come here. And I don't want it to stop. I'm pulling up his shirt trying to get him to take it off.

He does a quick assist; fabric brushes my bare skin and then I hear the soft plop of clothing landing somewhere.

I'm in his bed that smells like him. He's under me, shirtless, whispering things that I'm trying not to make sense of but that contain the word *beautiful*, and I'm losing sight of why I was ever resisting his love. I'm trying to remember, but I can't.

"Fuck it." I pull off the blindfold.

There he is, serious, surly Hugo, brows drawn in over gray eyes, like he's perplexed by the intensity of his cherishing me.

My heart thunders. We're watching each other, naked on every level. It's intimate in a nearly unbearable way that I would normally avoid, but this is Hugo. Everything is different with Hugo. I'm hungry for every last molecule of Hugo.

"Come here." I reach down and make contact with his condom-clad cock and urge him onto me.

His gaze burns into my soul.

He rumbles his utter pleasure.

"Right now," I whisper.

He doesn't need more urging than that. He pushes into me, and I gasp. The pleasure is intense. Exquisite.

"Too much?" he asks.

"Too perfect." I tilt my hips, moving over him, and we're in a zone of perfect sex ESP, working in the free flow that we do so well together, like a song we both know, and we've made it ours. He reaches up and traces my lips and I suck in his finger, keeping it in my mouth while I fuck him.

It's curiously hot. I make a sound to show I think it's hot.

"Keep it, then," he rumbles.

Yes, my guardrails for myself are twisted and wrecked, and I don't seem to care. I take his wrist and remove his finger from my mouth and urge him down to my clit.

"Right here," I say, positioning three fingers just so on my clit. "Make a triangle."

He makes a triangle for me to rub onto. He likes when I find ways for him to help me get off. I like that he likes it. We're looking into each other's eyes. I'm so connected to him. I'm glorying my brains out—emotionally, physically.

My orgasm shatters over me. I'm clutching him, hanging on, nose to his sweaty chest as I come. It's outrageous how hard I come, and I don't care.

Sometime after—ten seconds? ten minutes?—he comes with his orgasm bear growl. I want to kiss his very serious, pleasure-addled face, but I don't want to break his mojo, so I just watch him and adore him.

We collapse next to each other, puppy-pile-style, panting happily. It's so good, and I'm so into him. It's a little while until the fear creeps up—but creep up it does.

I head to his bathroom and clean up, trying to feel okay. I pause in the doorway on the way back and just look at him there in the bed.

"Is it shower time yet?" I ask.

He gets up and comes over and kisses me. "I do believe it is."

We shower together in a nonchaste way, because I can't resist him. We dry each other off and he goes into his closet to find me a shirt to wear. It's right there, while I'm waiting, that I spot the familiar black bottle of Obsidian Valor for men by Jack Hermann.

Noooo!

I tell myself it's not significant that he likes the same cologne as Jonathan. It's on a shelf with two other colognes, none of which he seems to wear.

He hands me a shirt and I put it on. "I have a new favorite three-dimensional shape," he announces, buttoning it up for me. "The fingertip triangle."

"What? No!" I hit his shoulder. "That's *my* favorite three-dimensional shape! You have the torus."

"I switched."

"Who's gonna tell the torus?" I ask.

He tucks a strand of hair behind my ear. "I'll tell the torus. I'll take care of all of it. I've got it."

For a second, I think he's talking about everything. He's saying *trust me*.

I want to. I really do. Maybe I can. I want to not be scared.

"This is good," he adds.

I smile and kiss him, and then I pull away and wander around.

Hugo's bedroom is all blues. There's one picture—a framed, black-and-white line drawing of a long-legged bird, bolder and more whimsical than true to life. Very unexpected. "Is that a stork?"

"An egret," he says, coming up behind me.

"Do you like egrets?"

"I liked that one. An artist was selling them on a picnic blanket in Washington Square Park. It spoke to me."

"Why?"

"I like that she drew it all in two bold lines, I suppose. It's not realistic like a true-to-life sketch or something. If you put a photo of an egret next to it, it wouldn't even be close, but there's something about it that seems so much like an egret. Maybe more than a photo, even. It's hard to explain."

I turn to him. "Are you saying you like how egret-y it is?"

"Egret-y isn't a word."

"Its ineffable egret-y-ness sold you?"

"Not a word."

I turn back to it, just eating it up. Here is art that Hugo chose for himself. He loved something essential in it, as though he sensed the soul of it. I suppose in his own way, Hugo is a seeker, peering through all of his numbers to get to some deep truth, though he'd be the last to admit it.

"I love that that's why you picked it," I say. "I love knowing it."

He kisses the top of my head. My heart is bongo-ing.

Clad in one of his shirts, I plod out to his living room where bright white walls with pristine crown molding soar to the ceiling, framing amazing views of the park. This is a pre-war building, but the openness of this space gives it a fresh feel. The wood floor is so dark it's nearly black, and there are square pillars where they probably took out the walls.

Simple, stylish pieces of furniture upholstered in complementary blues and yellows are clustered here and there. Did he consult a color wheel? That would be very him.

It's in the corner that I spot the wooden shelf of orbs. They glint in the light. His little treasures. I go to look and make him tell me more about why they're special to him. My heart does a little flip when I spot the card I got for him right there on the shelf with the orbs.

Again I wonder about the gift that he picked out for me. What could it be? It's driving me a bit crazy. But I resist relenting on that point. I have to draw some lines. Even though I'm so deep into Hugo's world, the warning bells are nothing but faint peeps, blending with the pigeon coos coming from the open window.

"So much for tawdry," I say.

"Tawdry is overrated," Hugo says.

I turn to him. "Don't think because I've seen your place that we're dating. It's not what I want, and I need you to respect that."

He nods. "I understand."

Was that too easy? Or is he coming around?

"Did you mean it before when you said you never take women here?"

"Never." He's wearing sweats and a super sexy black tee; he strolls across the place and around a sparkling white kitchen island. "Hungry?"

"Now you're going to feed me dinner? What part of not dating did you not understand?"

"It's not dinner if you eat it standing up. It's a snack when you eat it standing up." He pulls a circular white pan of something from the refrigerator and slides it into the oven.

"Is that so?"

"And we eat sandwiches at the Luxe." He sets out a knife and two large tomatoes. "Start slicing."

I grab a cutting board. There's a small bowl that looks like spices and parsley, maybe basil.

"What are we making?"

"A snack."

"So...you *cook*?"

"I have a chef in three times a week; she stocks the kitchen and does meal prep and all that. I just assemble. I share her with Wulfric."

I slide some slices to the side. "Wulfric lends you his chef. You are so his golden goose."

CHAPTER 39

HUGO

I grate Parmesan into a small bowl while Stella chops the vegetables. I'm pushing the envelope, I know. Making this into a real date. I don't care. It's time.

"Do you remember what happened to the golden goose?" I ask her.

She looks up, amused, surprised. People almost never think through the golden goose reference, at least not where it applies to me.

"That's right." I draw my finger across my throat. "The farmer killed him. And that goose hadn't even stopped laying eggs."

"Wulfric's not a fool," she says.

"No, he'll wait until the eggs are gone."

"How's it going? With the model, I mean. How are you feeling about it?"

I watch her chop the basil leaves into little bits, thinking about the question. People ask me about the model all the time—

when will it be done? How scalable will it be? What are the testing parameters?

But how do I feel about it? Nobody ever asks that.

She looks up when I don't answer for a while. "Is it going okay?"

"Not really," I say.

"Why not?"

"I have a vision for it that's proving challenging. I always knew it would be challenging, but..."

"Is it a big ambitious vision?" she asks. "Charlie says your first one was a massive disruption that reverberated through the markets."

"The first one made an impact, yes. And that's my goal for this one. I'm not planning on bringing my B-game like a hack." I tip the cheese into a bowl. "I'm not gonna go backwards."

"Is not making an impact really the same as going backwards?" she asks.

"To me it is."

"How about to Wulfric?"

"Wulfric will be happy no matter how much I move the ball forward." I toss the tomatoes into a bowl and start adding the spices.

"So...is this a perfectionist thing? Or a thing with your percentage-improvement whiteboard? You have to keep slogging onward and upward?"

"Somebody hates my self-improvement whiteboard."

"I do hate it."

"I'm not gonna do something derivative that's one sad little click off of what I've already done, that's all. Also, I know there's a way to upend the old model—I can feel it in the air, but I can't seem to get at it. Sometimes I wonder if the objective itself is the problem. I need to work it out before the presentation."

"So anything less than upending the old paradigm will be failure? And failure's not an option?"

"Not an option." I go around and kiss her.

She seems worried. It's worth worrying about, but it's mine to worry about, not hers.

She arranges the tomato slices in a neat row while I entertain her with funny stories about Wulfric frightening people. Wulfric making bonkers market moves that turn out to be genius. Wulfric buying an entire restaurant and firing the chef because he refused to delete pineapple from the menu.

"What happens when Wulfric finds out you're not allergic?"

"He can't," I say. "It's gone on too long."

"What would he do?"

"No idea," I say. "Uncharted territory I'd prefer not to chart." I take the pan out of the oven and check the temperature. Perfect. I slide it onto the burner.

"Wait, is that polenta?" she asks.

"Yeah. We're making baked tomato and parmesan polenta."

"Polenta is my favorite meal, and you know it. Hugo! It's not a snack when it's my favorite meal."

"You make a lot of rules." I toss the parm on top and set it back in the oven.

She fixes me with an accusatory gaze. Is she upset?

"You knew I'd take off the blindfold eventually, didn't you? You had ingredients for this dish ready because you knew we'd cook together."

"One of my favorite qualities about you is your inability to resist temptation."

She narrows her eyes. "Pretty sure of ourselves, aren't we?"

"Want a drink? I have a nice red for this."

"And now he pulls out the wine," she says. "If there are gummy worms for dessert, I fucking swear to god—"

"No such luck," I say.

"I'll have water," she says stubbornly. "Because FYI, this isn't a date. And you're not playing fair."

She's right. I'm not playing fair. I want us to date. That's my objective, and I plan to be merciless about it.

I grab us sparkling waters, wondering whether I can get the chef to make gummy worm ice cream. Chewy things in ice cream would be awful, but maybe she could freeze-dry them or just incorporate the tart flavor.

"Don't pretend you would whip up this little dinner if it was just you," she says, pouring her water into a glass. "I think you're bamboozling me."

She's right, of course. I did get the polenta for her. I chose the wine for her, too. "I think it's gonna be delicious."

She's silent for a long time, sliding her thumb along the condensation, creating a clear stripe.

Did I go too far in breaking her rules? Am I getting too cocky?

"You okay?" I ask.

"Was that Obsidian Valor I saw in your closet?" she asks.

"What? The cologne? Yeah. It was a gift. Why?"

"I think you should start wearing it," she says.

"You want me to start wearing cologne?" This is what's on her mind?

"Yes!" She disappears and returns with the little bottle.

"You like this one?"

"Notes of berries and bergamot—what's not to like?" She hands it to me.

I remove the cap and sniff. "I have no objection to bergamot, considering Captain Picard of the USS Enterprise drinks Earl Grey, a bergamot-flavored black tea."

"There you go!" she says brightly. "You should put it on. Just a little."

"Right now?"

"Yes!"

I dab a bit onto my wrists with the stopper top. "What am I gonna do with you?"

"Feed me polenta while wearing Obsidian Valor?"

I kiss her again, mind crowded with visions of taking her back to bed, but the oven bell rings, and as much as I want to go in for another round of fucking, I want to feed her, too. I want to care for her in every way. My feelings for her are obnoxiously primative.

I fix up plates with polenta and a gourmet coleslaw that features roasted grapes—and a sprig of parsley, because the chef extracted a plating promise from me for this meal.

"You even added parsley. Wow."

"Only the best for my lurid-and-tawdry-no-strings-office-affair fuckbuddy."

She smiles. She likes that. She comes around and kisses me. And sucks in the scent.

CHAPTER 40

STELLA

Viola is lording over Jane and me at my cubicle, harshly critiquing presentation materials that we put together for some C-suite bros to show to each other. Tinley comes up with a Post-it that she sticks on my shirt. "You're it."

I pull it off. It says, "Chia project noon."

Jane winces sympathetically.

Viola frowns. "What exactly is the chia project?"

"A thing Hugo Jones has me doing," I say.

A thing he has me doing at Hotel Luxe, but I don't say that part. Even though we mostly go to his place, we still sometimes visit the Luxe at lunchtime. It's like we're in a spy movie, and Hugo is the world's most grave and serious secret agent with the weight of the world on his shoulders.

Viola gets this weird look on her face. "The chia project? What does it mean?"

I mumble something about commodities.

Jane looks between her and me. Tinley seems to be suppressing a grin. Have people guessed our secret?

Finally Viola speaks. "You don't want to know what Hugo made me research this one time. Do. Not. Want to know." She fixes me with a hard stare and waits.

Okay, then. "What did he make you research?"

"Frozen orange juice consumption over the years," she says. "Sliced by state and age group. And then when I presented that, he asked for grapefruit consumption research. I had to retrace so many steps, because juice research. And he makes you feel like a criminal when you ask the smallest question."

I nod, looking extra concerned.

As soon as Viola leaves, a singsong voice drifts over the cubicle wall. "Hugh-dini likes youuuuuuu." Hesh.

"What? Stop!" I whisper.

Hesh pops his head over the cubicle wall, eyes narrowed. "He requests you constantly. He walks by twice as much."

"Hugh-dini doesn't like anybody," Jane says.

"He likes his ice-blonde Amazonian," Hesh says.

"Who's the ice-blonde Amazonian?" I arrange my pens, trying not to seem interested.

"Some hardbody high-performance trader he fucks," Hesh says.

"He doesn't like her," Jane says. "You saw them at the Christmas thing—they say two words and head off. Like they're sharing an Uber; not bodily fluids."

"Hugh-dini has bodily fluids?" Hesh says. "Since when is ice classified as a fluid?"

Jane turns to me. "He *is* asking for you a lot. Maybe you're... less bothersome to him?"

"But I do my best to be bothersome at *all* times."

Hesh snorts. "Maybe he wants you."

"Please, she's so not his type." Jane turns to me. "You're fun."

I give her a thank-you frowny smile.

"You are."

"Ice-blonde Amazonian," I say, hoping they'll add more details, which they do not.

~

I head to his office at lunchtime, telling myself not to ask about the Amazonian. No, no, no, no. We are not dating, we are fucking. He can have other fuckbuddies. He should have other fuckbuddies! That makes my heart safer, right?

I show up promptly at a little after noon and tell Brenda I'm here for chia research. She's got a lunch bag and seems to be on her way out, but she pauses, frowning. "Hugo's been doing a lot of chia research. Is there an agricultural or geopolitical angle to it?"

I wince inwardly, having forgotten that Brenda's favorite vegetable in all the world is the chia. "It's not really about chia."

"Hugo doesn't give things metaphorical names." Brenda stares down at her desk. "Well, whatever. I just...like to know."

"It's sort of a joke name."

Brenda sharpens her gaze, sensing subterfuge, because Hugo doesn't give joke names, either.

"You're late," Hugo booms at me, strolling in from the far side.

"If you need ancillary research on this thing, I've got space this afternoon," Brenda says.

"Just hold my calls." Hugo stalks back down the other way.

I follow, feeling shitty.

"Brenda's a little hurt," I say, closing the door, pleased to note that he's wearing the cautionary-tale cologne.

Hugo comes to me and cages me against the door. "Why should Brenda feel hurt?"

"Her favorite vegetable is chia. If you're doing a chia project, she wishes you would have involved her." I set to work on his belt buckle.

He presses against me and kisses my ear. "How do you know?"

I sigh and lay off the belt. "From the way she talked about it. Brenda admires the shit out of you. She would love to impress you. I think she wants you to treat her as a protégé."

"Brenda's an extremely capable, up-and-coming quant. She wants my name on her résumé, that's all. It's about my name, not about me." He undoes my top button.

"How can you be so clueless? She wants to work with you in a real way. She wants to understand how you think about all this gobbledygook."

"Skipping over the part where you call my whiteboard gobbledygook..." He kisses me and then pauses. "She did show me a data model that had promise. I wonder if she wanted commentary."

"Hugo." I grab his collar and look into his eyes. "Why do you think she took a job as your assistant?"

Hugo frowns. "This is why I don't get involved with people."

"But you knew her perfect gift. How is it possible that you know her perfect birthday gift but not why she's here in the first place and what she most wants from you?"

"I only know gifts."

"Knowing gifts is like knowing people. I mean, how did you know gifts?"

"It's a specific muscle that I deliberately developed for a specific reason."

"Really?"

"You're ruining sex," he grumbles, kissing my neck. "What happened to a no-strings, no-info tawdry affair? What happened to not asking each other personal questions?"

"You ruined it when you fed me polenta, and now you have to tell me."

"So you want to break that rule now?"

"I want you to tell me."

"It's not even interesting." He kisses my neck. "It was a childish scheme to repair my family."

I push him off me. "A scheme involving gift-giving skills?"

"If you're that desperate to ruin sex." He buckles his belt back up. "Early on, Mom and Dad would get perfect birthday gifts and Christmas gifts for each other and me. We made a big deal out of holidays as a family. Unlike you Woodwards with your gift cards."

I snort. Our family went the logical route on holidays. "Right? Why not just cash?"

"And at some point after we moved in, the money ran out, but the partying kept on."

I nod, amazed he's telling me about his family. Hugo's traditionally private about his parents.

He strolls to the window and looks out. "As soon as the money ran out, gifts became an afterthought if not completely forgotten. And of course, I was terrible at gift giving. I didn't know how my mom and dad did it. I can be oblivious to people." He pauses, silently scanning the city streets.

"You?"

"You know it's true. My parents moved us to cheaper places. They took whatever shit jobs they could get, and the drinking went through the roof. At some point, I got the idea that if I gave the perfect gifts like they used to give to me, they'd remember how happy we were. As if it was a problem of memory. As if they'd forgotten how to be a family. As if they'd be disconcerted by the contrast and realize how bad things had gotten and be inspired to go back to normal. Not my best feat of logic."

My heart twists as I picture scowly little Hugo, trying to

puzzle out how to put his family back together the way he might have puzzled out a geometry problem.

"It was the best you could do at the time."

He snorts. "Debatable. I took it on as a mystery that was assigned to me to solve, like Sherlock Holmes. I was a detective gathering gift clues. I worked at it, and it became a muscle. Like a weightlifter targeting a muscle."

"I was in awe of it, you know."

"You were?"

"God, you'd give my family a gift every year, and it would always be the best thing ever. Meanwhile, I'd be like, here's a lopsided sculpture made of coiled clay. You're welcome."

"They loved your gifts."

"Did you see any coiled-clay vases on display when you were last over there eating pineapple?" I ask.

He glances in the direction of Brenda's office. "Maybe I could pull her in on something. She mentioned a few areas of interest on her résumé."

"It doesn't have to be a perfect alignment," I say. "She wants to be around you and to soak in your way of seeing things."

"If you're going to do something, you should do it perfectly."

"I think the saying goes, if you're gonna do something, you should do it right.'"

"Yes, I know that's how it goes," he says with the maximum possible disdain.

"Yeah, alright, Mr. Perfect. I will admit that you do have a few things down perfectly. A few key things."

If he gets the joke, he doesn't show it; he's turned very serious, in fact. "I'm glad to know that about Brenda. I should've seen it. Thank you."

My heart swells. "Of course." It's so easy to think that Hugo doesn't care about people, that he doesn't give a shit about being better, like he's this icy wizard on the mountain. Even Charlie seemed to see him like that most of the time.

I feel really grateful that he's let me in. "Come here."

"I believe I am here."

I loop a finger into the button placket on his shirt and pull him close to me. "More here."

I kiss him. Things feel right with him. We can get back on shallow ground later.

A woman's voice sounds from the hallway. Footsteps coming our way.

Hugo swears softly, and for a split second, I wonder whether it's the ice-blonde Amazonian, but then I hear the snarled, muttered words of what could only be Wulfric.

The door bursts open.

"What the hell is this chia project?" A large man stalks in— Wulfric Pierce, I'm guessing—trailed by a woman with short black hair.

This would be Lola.

The men set to arguing, and Lola gives me a secret smile, a smile so fleeting that I think I might have imagined it. The next second, she's scratching notes onto an iPad.

She wears a smart black suit and big purple earrings, but what's most remarkable about her is the utterly serene expression on her face—shocking, considering that her boss is stalking around in front of the boards now, grumbling through gritted teeth like he can barely contain himself.

I'd expected Wulfric to look like a goblin, but this guy's no goblin--he's more like a Viking with white-blond hair and ice-blue eyes and powerful Nordic cheekbones set in a rugged-looking face, like he spent long hours in a deranged Russian boxing gym on his way to America.

Hugo pushes right back on Wulfric's grumbles of barely contained outrage at the data model scribblings. Hugo's all cool, confident math talk, delivered like it's so obvious. Which seems to annoy Wulfric further. He gets more ragey. Hugo talks more numbers, taking exactly zero shit.

They're evenly matched in their own weird ways, and it comes to me that they could go on for hours this way, like if Mothra and Godzilla joined a math club.

Wulfric suddenly turns his scary gaze to me. "And your role is…"

I stiffen. Is Wulfric Pierce talking to me? I didn't think he'd actually talk to me. I didn't think he'd even see me.

Hugo fixes Wulfric with a hard, hawkish gaze. "I won't have you questioning my people or micromanaging this operation."

Wulfric takes a step nearer to Hugo. "Is that so?"

"You want me to deliver?" Hugo asks.

"Oh, I want you to deliver…"

"Then you won't question my people or micromanage this operation."

They roll on in this vein, going for another round of menace at the math club.

Lola glances over yet again, her expression deadpan. I don't know whether she's trying to be funny, looking at me with that blank face while the two of them are doing alpha-male-testosterone hour, but it's completely hilarious, and this would be a terrible time to laugh.

Terrible, terrible, terrible.

But they are just so serious and alpha on each other…

I grab a pad of paper and start furiously writing nonsense, because my face is contorting with stifled laughter.

Finally Wulfric and Lola leave.

I collapse into Hugo's buddy chair. "Oh my god."

"Don't worry about Wulfric. You never have to worry about him. His bark is worse than his bite—"

"Allegedly," I say.

"You can't believe the rumors."

"It was more that I was scared I'd start laughing," I say.

"What could you have possibly found funny about that?"

"Well, you guys were…a bit intense," I say.

"And you thought that was funny?" he growls.

"Kind of."

He plants his hands on the arms of my chair. I have this sense that I'm a little bit in trouble from him. "Do. Not. Laugh at Wulfric."

"That's what makes it so hard! Because I know it would be terrible to do. I can't help it."

"You can help it."

"I try."

"Try harder."

I smile. He looks so handsome when he's being stern.

Not my boyfriend, I remind myself.

Notmyboyfriend notmyboyfriend notmyboyfriend, I chant—sense-lessly, for all the good it does me.

"And if you get any shit from Wulfric, you tell me. I mean it— one harsh word, he answers to me."

"Thank you, but it's not necessary. I can fight my own battles, remember?"

"Of course you can, but I need you to know…" His voice goes low. "If it ever comes to any kind of trouble…"

I can feel the smile fade from my face. There's something primal about the way he says that—a kind of feral darkness in his voice and in his eyes, like he's imagining terrible things.

I'm unsure what to make of Hugo's protective side. It's intense. And a bit…familiar. Like I've seen this version of him before.

And out of the blue it comes to me—that long-ago October night in Williston when Timmy Trask left drunken me on a park bench. I don't remember a lot, but I remember Hugo's expression as I told him how I'd come to be left there.

In my memory it had morphed into annoyance, because how could Hugo not have been annoyed? Annoyance was his default when it came to me, and here he had to drive twenty miles to Williston to rescue my drunken ass. Of course he was annoyed.

And later it got covered over with mortification that I had such awful judgement that I'd gotten myself into that situation.

But I'm back there with him driving me home, pressing me for details about what happened, expression hard and dark by the dashboard light.

Hugo's back to his boards. "I should've had a breakthrough by now, and Wulfric knows it."

I go up next to him. "You can do it."

He rubs off a stray mark next to a jumble of letters and squiggles. "The best thing for this process would be to give it a rest. To switch off to something unrelated and let it percolate, but this fucking deadline."

He's absorbed in the board, and I need to go, but I can't stop thinking about the look on Hugo's face. And Chewbacca.

"Halloween's coming," I say.

"Uh-huh."

"Are you going to dress up as Chewbacca again this year?"

"Chewbacca," he mumbles distractedly. "I haven't dressed as him in forever."

My heart pounds. Of course it was Hugo. Of course.

"Okay," I say.

He turns to me. "Why?"

"Why?" I say back.

"Why do you ask?"

"No reason," I say softly. "You should put on more cologne."

CHAPTER 41

HUGO

I take Stella's advice and get Brenda involved in examining a currency market inefficiency that I've had my eye on, and she produces a report that's surprisingly helpful.

We kick around trading strategies, and I send her away with a few potential research directions.

She's thrilled.

A few days later, she's in my office with questions, and I see her looking at my boards.

There's little chance she could help me with QuantumQuilt, but explaining my thoughts and the problems I've encountered with the approaches I've tried might help me get perspective.

"You got time to walk through this thing with me?"

She looks around, as if I must have meant something other than the boards.

I go up and wipe a stray mark off the corner. "It could take a bit."

"No problem!" she says. "Whatever you need." She's signed a

nondisclosure, so it's not as if she's going to tell anyone about it. Not only are the terms ironclad, but nobody crosses Wulfric.

I start at the beginning, explaining the parts that I know are right, moving to the other board to show underlying equations. Eventually we get to the problem.

Brenda stands there looking skeptical.

"What are you thinking?"

She points at an equation. "I just don't see how this one accounts for what you need it to account for. I don't see how anything can. Not that..." She pauses, realizing what she's saying.

"You don't think it's crackable."

"If anybody could crack this, you could," she says quickly, going on to rephrase this in several different ways, worried that she's annoyed me.

I'm barely listening. Have I gotten overconfident? Mathematicians who make big breakthroughs have been known to tackle problems that are beyond their abilities.

Brenda shows me her palms. "I wouldn't have thought AxiomPulse was possible. But you cracked that, so what do I know?"

"You know that lightning rarely strikes the same place twice, that's what you know."

"It'll strike if you make it strike," she says.

I nod. And the sun will be purple if you make it purple.

We stare at the board, and she asks me more questions. The questions are insightful. It's a long afternoon of staring at the board and going over the same ground from different angles.

"This was helpful," I say.

"We didn't get you down the road any," she says. "But I think it's brilliant—what you did in this section." She taps the solid section.

"Unless the goal is wrong," I say.

She shoots me a baffled look. "Excuse me?"

"What if I can't get down the road all the way because the vehicle itself is faulty?"

"Meaning the concept of the data model itself?"

"What if? What's the saying—you can't pick up a rug that you're standing on?"

Brenda seems to find that interesting. I like that she doesn't discount it; her instincts are excellent. "You can't solve a data model with a data model? But no, that's not it."

"But something like that," I say.

We regard each other silently. No way will I be able to present this month or even this year with a direction like that.

My quest with Stella is beginning to feel just as impossible as QuantumQuilt. The boundaries she puts up around our relationship are nothing short of maddening. We have a once-in-a-lifetime connection, yet she'll never sleep over. She won't dine out. She doesn't want to exchange details about our lives unless it's something she's burning with curiosity about.

And she still won't accept my gift.

I call Carruthers and purchase it. Felix promises to wrap it up for me and set it aside.

I'm not giving up. I can't.

CHAPTER 42

HUGO

"Maybe we should get pineapple on that pizza," I say one Saturday afternoon. It's breezy and warm for October. I'd have the windows open if not for the jackhammers outside. There's some underground pipe situation.

Stella's sitting up on my kitchen island, swinging her legs back and forth. "I know what you're doing."

I go to her. "What am I doing?"

"Trying to get me to ask about the pineapple. You think if I keep breaking my own rules and asking personal questions, you'll get to ask questions about me, and we'll just slide into dating, but you're wrong."

"I'll add pineapple on half," I say. I hit submit and put my phone aside.

"You're so evil," she says.

"Can't people in no-strings, no-life-details affairs order pineapple on their pizzas?" I ask innocently.

"Come on, fine, just tell me. Why does everybody at work think you're allergic to pineapple?"

"So you want to know my life details, but I can't know yours?" I skim my hands over her hips. "The gifts, the pineapple."

We just had a particularly vigorous round of kitchen-counter sex, and I still can't keep my hands off her.

"Tell me," she begs.

"You do realize you're being logically inconsistent."

"Logically inconsistent," she say in a robot voice. "Insufficient data. Alert! Alert!"

I give her a grumbly kiss.

"Please tell me."

"Why should I?"

"Because I'm begging." She pulls me to her. "I'm begging."

I groan. "So you know I wanted to work with Wulfric from the first time I was aware of him. Goblin that he is, Quantum Capital Partners had everything I needed to achieve my vision for that first data model."

"Your triumphant debut," she says.

"Not only did he have all the right pieces in terms of this company, but say what you will, he gives people the freedom they need to do bold work. The next best thing to starting my own firm, but I sure as hell wasn't going to do that, much as people thought I should. Bossing people is not how I want to spend my time."

"Being that you hate people."

"And people hate me right back."

"Fair point."

I grab plates and set them on the island. "So there was going to be this interview with him. It felt very high stakes to me, and I knew he was talking to other people. And of course I'd heard about his reputation for being mercurial and combative. And I was still in my early twenties, fresh out of a PhD program, not at all good with people. He invites me out to dinner at this steak place in the village—he's sending his jet to fly me up from MIT."

"That was the interview? A dinner out?"

"Yeah. I would've done anything for it to be on Zoom or maybe even text. I wanted to talk about my plans and ideas without worrying about ordering and eating and social niceties and all that."

"I bet." She glances in the direction of the street. The jackhammering is obnoxious, even with the windows closed.

"But my future was hanging in the balance, so obviously I said yes. I knew if he grasped my vision, I'd be in, so before I went, I ate a huge room service dinner. I figured I'd have a few bites of something when I was there with him, but I was there to talk. As it turned out, he was there to eat. This was apparently his favorite place and he ordered for us both."

"Nooooo!" She's laughing.

"I know. So Wulfric's watching me cut little pieces and move them around. He says, 'I told you to bring your appetite, did I not?' and 'I thought you said you liked steak.'"

"Wulfric's being all monster mash and you had to eat two dinners," she says.

"I think a normal person would've confessed that he'd eaten already in order to devote every bit of attention he could to the discussion, but it didn't come to me. These social interactions..."

"Not your forte."

"I got through it, though. I ate another dinner. I was stuffed. And then dessert comes. And I couldn't."

Stella's eyes widen. "Pineapple cake?"

"Pineapple tart and carrot cake, also with pineapple. Wulfric's a maniac about these desserts. I didn't know what to do, so I blurted out that I'm allergic to pineapple. *Deathly* allergic would be the terminology I used."

She's laughing. "You never lie."

"I panicked. I got the job, and I figured I'd better not eat pineapple in front of anybody. But he became obsessed with keeping pineapple away from me. I'm sure you've heard about all the things that he's done. The kitchens he's cleared like it's anthrax."

"What are you going to do? What if you told him? Is it possible he'd think it was a funny story?"

"Have you met the man?"

That's when the second jackhammer joins the first.

"You're seven stories up; how is that so loud?"

"Two doubles the noise," I say.

She goes to the window. "Fuck, there's another setting up. Is there not a law about this? Is that not possible?"

I go behind her.

"Screw the pizza. We're going out to eat."

"But—"

"You'd rather I go out by myself and drop you off at home?"

She gives me a hot glare.

"I could take you to your favorite restaurant that you don't know about yet."

Her glare heats.

I grab my phone. "Let's do it."

"It's not even five."

I smile. That objection tells me we're in. I check the hours. "They're open."

"And we can get in just like that?"

"Just made reservations."

"Must not be very popular," she says. "If you got instant ressies."

"It's not. A lot of people hate it and it's overpriced. I doubt it will be in business for much longer. It doesn't deserve to be."

"You've been there?"

I shake my head. I read a review of it in the paper when it opened. She hadn't moved here yet, but I saw the headline and imagined her liking it.

"But it would be my favorite?"

"Are you going to change? Or just go in my T-shirt?"

CHAPTER 43

HUGO

She can't resist, and that's how we're pulling up in front of a restaurant called The Melting Table on an early Saturday evening.

It's in the bottom of a decrepit office building on a busy street in Queens. We get out of the town car and suddenly she's clutching my arm, standing stock-still on the sidewalk.

"What's up?" I ask innocently.

She's staring at the sign—"The Melting Table." It has an image of a melting table done up like the famous melting clock by her favorite artist in the world, Dali.

"What is this place?" she whispers loudly.

"I bet you can guess."

She looks at me. "Is this a Dali restaurant? Is there Dali art all over the walls or something?"

"Baby, it's much worse than that."

She squeezes my arm. "How much worse?"

"So much worse."

We head in. The place is every bit the horror show the review I read suggested it would be. There is indeed Dali art all over the walls in addition to obnoxious lighting—think floor lamps with twisted poles and weirdly formed shades, like they were 3D-printed by a drunken clown.

The host—complete with a stringy black moustache glued partly to his cheek—leads us to a corner table with one normal chair and one chair that is so twisted and malformed, you couldn't sit on it if you tried.

"This is…amazing," she says.

"That's *one* word for it." I take the good chair, which is, in this case, the chivalrous thing to do, being that she's all in for the Dali experience.

She examines the bizarre chair and then turns to the host. "Awesome as this is, I might need another chair."

"What's wrong with this one?" he asks.

"Well, it's kind of…a melted chair stump thing?"

He acts like he doesn't understand. Other diners look on, amused. How many times does this scene get played out every day? I shudder to think. The host finally storms off to trade the stupid chair for a normal one, placing the stupid chair at an open table, ready for the next unsuspecting victim.

Stella couldn't be more delighted.

We order drinks and food. Stella's "surreal sangria" has exotic fruits and a plastic doll arm floating in it. My "galactic gin and tonic" contains colorful curls of ice, but luckily no arm.

Stella has a lot to say about the chair. She's telling me how Dali was fascinated with distorted imagery.

"Dali's work is the polar opposite of mine, in a way," I observe. "He's distorting reality and I'm trying to organize it."

"But you're both trying to get at something true," she says.

"What possible truth is in a chair you can't use?"

"The deeper truths of the subconscious. Impermanence."

The "cubist crostini" arrives just then; it's cut into abstract, geometric shapes, and there's half of a hard-boiled egg set randomly on the plate; it's made to look like an eyeball through the creative use of capers and other small foodstuff. Our "melted clock nachos" feature cheese and toppings that appear to be melting off the chips.

When Stella asks the waiter to exchange her weirdly twisted fork for a new one, she gets an even larger fork with more twists. This goes on for a while until she grabs one off of a neighboring table.

As if that's not enough, the waitstaff calls out the word "fish" at random times.

I stir my gin and tonic, which has turned a shade of brown due to the melting ice cubes. "You know this is taking five percent off my progress."

CHAPTER 44

STELLA

I tell him about a new client I got off of LinkedIn over our somewhat mediocre surrealist pasta.

"I'm going to pull together a freelance team for this project. A lot of the top creatives didn't go back inside after the pandemic. When you think about it, you can get better creative work outside of the creative agencies."

"That's interesting. Are you thinking about running that as a business?"

"No, just for this project. I could never actually run a company. Can you imagine the organizational demands? The detail orientation it would take?"

"So what? You have a strong vision for things. I think you'd be brilliant at it."

"Have you met my untied shoelaces? Would you like to meet my financial record-keeping and budgeting system? Oh, wait, I have none."

"You could learn it. You could hire some of it out."

I could not adore him more right now. Not just for tolerating this restaurant, but for thinking I can do these things. I'm so used to people thinking I'm inept. "It's just not in my wheelhouse. It's not me."

"And your evidence for that is…"

"Well…" I dunk the baby arm around in my glass, trying to come up with an answer. A time I tried to be an organized, together person and failed. Did I ever try? "Evidence, you say."

"You developed a successful career," he offers. "Before my letter."

"In a smallish city," I say.

"It was a successful career."

"Maybe so, but I didn't need any kind of organization skills for that. They would point me in a direction and say, make something entertaining that communicates this message. And I would generate ideas. I was like a wind-up monkey that generated and implemented ideas."

"So you have no evidence."

I'm about to laughingly say something about losing my keys, but I stop short. I've spent the better part of my life trying to prove to Charlie and my parents that I'm not that irresponsible, inept girl. It's almost like they're in my head. Maybe organization isn't my strong suit, but why am I trying so hard to convince Hugo?

"You're no wind-up monkey."

"Yeah, yeah, yeah."

We brainstorm different ways I could market my services. Hugo wants desperately to help—he really feels bad about what he did, but I'm starting to wonder if it wasn't a blessing in disguise—not just because it led to us being here, but what if I could run my own show?

Hugo comes up with some good ideas when the staff isn't bugging us by bringing random things, or a huge ceramic checkmark when Hugo asks for the check.

He rolls with it all, and I sit there working overtime to keep his violent rejection of the flawed orb in sight.

CHAPTER 45

STELLA

It's a week later, snowy November Sunday, and we're hibernating hard.

I adjust the couch pillows and flop my legs up on Hugo's lap, completing my perfect nest for our viewing of the next episode of our historical mystery on Hugo's giant TV.

"Comfy?"

"For now." I grin and shove more popcorn into my mouth. Hugo points to a stray kernel on the blanket.

I put on a surprised expression.

He raises his brows, because stray kernels of popcorn are always my fault, even when I'm pretty sure they're not.

"Fine." I grab the kernel and pop it in my mouth.

Playfully he narrows his eyes. "Gimme that." He takes the bowl and eats the popcorn and hits play.

We've discovered that we both like sleepy historical whodunnits, a genre of show adjacent to my love of the crime drama and Hugo's fascination with the strange and elaborate ways of historical folk. We've been introducing each other to our favorites; tonight we are watching one of Hugo's go-tos, a World War One-era affair where female codebreakers solve a murder.

And it's right then, lying there watching the opening sequence with cheeks full of popcorn, that I realize that Hugo and I now have shows.

Fuck.

We have great sex. We do kind things for each other. We talk about our lives. We cook. We've discussed birth control and STD tests and determined that we can have condom-less sex.

And we now have shows.

I would apparently suck as a mystery-solving codebreaker, being that this thing has migrated from a no-strings affair to relationship central, and I'm only noticing it now.

He hasn't been to my place yet—that is pretty much the only relationship thing we haven't done. What was I thinking? That if he didn't come over to see where I live, we wouldn't be dating?

How did this creep up on me?

And what should I do?

The devil on my shoulder says, "Can't you see that he's proving himself? Just go with it! You know this is what you want! You love being with him. Seal the deal. Also, don't forget that you saw some Trader Joe's peppermint bark in his cupboard."

The angel on my shoulder says, "Nooooo! Protect your heart! Be vigilant! Smell the cologne! Quickly, quickly! PS: you never saw peppermint bark."

I lean up, take the bowl from his hand, and suck in a nice big snout-full of Obsidian Valor.

He pauses the show and turns to me. "You just smelled my neck."

"Huh?"

"You smelled my neck. Are you checking for the cologne?"

"Checking for the cologne?" I snuggle back in. "I knew you were wearing it."

"So you wanted to smell it."

"Yeah."

"We're eating buttery popcorn, and suddenly you had to smell my cologne."

I hold out my hand for him to pass back the bowl.

He passes it over, but is in no way deterred from his line of questioning. "Those two smells aren't nice together at all. It's like putting toothpaste on an olive. It doesn't make sense."

"You mean, scents sense?"

His gaze sharpens. "In fact, every time we feel close, you smell my neck or you ask me to put on more cologne. What's up with that?"

"Why does something have to be up with that?"

"I'm a quant. Patterns are my business."

He's watching me, putting it all together because he's Hugo fucking Jones.

In my second feat of solving an obnoxiously obvious mystery, I see now that this cologne thing was a terrible idea. My heart is just pounding.

"It's something about my cologne. You smell it, and afterwards, you're more..." He furrows his brow, searching for the word. "Reserved."

I blink, slowly relegating the cologne from the *terrible* category to *top five worst ideas ever*, and there are some star-studded bad ideas in that category.

"Okay. Umm...this is going to sound...not good—"

He stands. "It reminds you of somebody," he says, appalled. "It's his."

My heart skips a beat. "Okay...uh."

"No, no, no. Wearing another man's cologne? Smelling like that jackass? No." He beelines across the place. "Fuck no."

"Hugo!" I follow him into the bathroom.

He turns on the shower. "I won't smell like your ex, Stella. I'm not him."

"I'm sorry, Hugo. It was messed up." My pulse pounds in my ears. What have I done? I love this man.

I love him. I always have.

He's about to peel off the clothes but then he seems to realize that they smell like cologne as much as he does, and he literally steps into the shower, fully clothed.

"Hugo! Your sweater."

"What do I care about a sweater?" He's fighting off his sweater under the pounding water, struggling with the sopping wet sleeves. I've never seen him irrational or impulsive like this. Hugo is orderly. Logical under fire.

I go in with him, Lululemon loungewear and all, and help him off with it. "Hugo."

"I'm not him."

"I know you aren't."

"Wearing another man's cologne. To hell with that."

I toss the wet sweater onto the shower bench. "I'm sorry."

He paws at his shirt buttons, popping one.

"Hugo." I grab his hands, stilling them.

"Why would you want that?"

"I thought it would help me remember how devastated I was. The damage of somebody deciding that your flaws are just too much for them—you don't know what that feels like."

"I'm not him, Stella." He looks me clear in the eyes, water streaming down the sides of his head. "This is me."

"I know! That's the problem, Hugo. It's you. It's always been you. The way I love you, it scares me—it's too huge, how much I love you. It's like it's been there forever. The idea of you deciding one day I'm this pathetic person..."

It would destroy me.

251

I shake my head. I can't even say it.

I start unbuttoning his linen shirt, afraid to look up. He called me courageous back when I came to town, but I don't feel courageous. "The fear made me stupid."

"Stella."

"Well, your nice clothes are ruined," I say, feeling confused and chaotic—even for me. I can't believe that I just blurted out that I love him.

"Stella." He squats to eye level and stops my unbuttoning activities. He presses my palms to his chest. He's beautiful under the pounding water, this man I've known and loved for so many years. "You love me."

"How could I not?" I smile. "I love you. I always have."

He looks so happy, and the feel of his beating heart under my palms, let's just say it's madness how much I love him.

"So let's do this," he says. "No more of this no-strings bullshit. I want all the strings with you. I want every string possible. I want to be together."

"I do, too, but—"

"No buts, no reservations, no fucking cologne. I'm not going anywhere, Stella. I understand that some facsimile of me couldn't see what you are really worth, and it hurt in a big way, but you need to know that I'm not gonna do that. I'm gonna prove it to you."

I suck in a breath. "You're a scientist. You know you can never say never."

There's this flicker in his gaze where logical-science Hugo realizes that I'm technically right and I regret saying it. "Screw it. I'm saying never. What do you think?"

I smile. "Screw it. Let's do it. It's too late, anyway."

Hugo's pulling off my tank top. "We're dating now. I'm calling it."

"We're dating."

Our clothes come off.

He's kissing me, and then he's kissing my breasts. I spare a glance at his poor linen shirt.

"Stop looking at it. There's nothing I wouldn't ruin for you."

"Nothing?" I ask as he pushes down my sopping wet sweats."

"Nothing." He kneels in front of me, clutching my ass, face to my pussy. "Also, don't think the tawdry and lurid sex is off the table."

We head out the door of his building later that day, on a mission to get falafel sandwiches from my favorite food truck, which is two blocks away, according to my app.

"How do you know about Jonathan?" I ask.

"Because Charlie keeps me updated," he says.

"So Charlie just blabs about my love life to you?"

He gives me a sly glance. "I get it out of him."

"You know Charlie would be very unhappy with this situation."

"Very," Hugo says. "But it's not up to him."

"He's just overly protective. The whole big brother thing."

"We're adults now. He needs to update his understanding of the situation. I always considered you off-limits, but you're an adult."

"You updated your code."

"More like I blew up my code," he says. "But you're worth it.

I link my arm in his. "Thank you."

"And you don't need his protection."

"I think he's protective of you, too. Mom said he was really intense about me not bugging you at work. He said I'm supposed to act like a normal employee and not approach you."

Hugo turns to me with a frown. "I never said you shouldn't approach me. He knows I'm in the weeds, but come on."

"And I should not bug you...Mom said I shouldn't act like I even know you."

"What the hell? Did Charlie tell your mom to tell you that?"

"I don't know. She seemed to think you pulled strings to get me the job?" I say. "And it could get you in trouble?"

"I could run through the halls naked and I wouldn't get in trouble," he says.

"I wouldn't object to that, you know."

I smooth a hand over the lapel of his thick wool coat. "So... you didn't say for me to stay away from you?"

"I was wondering why you didn't seem to recognize me. What the hell? Charlie knows about my problems with the data model, he knows how important it is for me to focus right now, but that was no reason for him to suggest I wouldn't want to say hello. It was just weird."

"It *was* weird!" I say. "And then I tried to give you the card and that was weird, but I needed to somehow thank you."

Hugo snorts. "I liked the card."

"I can't believe the communication ended up that I should treat you like a stranger. I guess the headline is that everyone thinks I'm so irresponsible, so unprofessional that I'll—I don't even know—burst into your office and ruin your concentration with Britney Spears-inspired dance routines each and every day?"

"I wouldn't object to that, you know."

"I get so sick of the way they look at me. And why should I care? But I do."

"Come here." He pulls me to him. "You're an intelligent, tenacious, stunningly impressive person."

"You know where that would've been amazing? In my letter of recommendation!" I tease.

"I'm so sorry," he says for about the tenth time. "I hate the effect it's had on you and your career. I feel like such an asshole."

"It's not all on you, being that it's Mom and Dad's fault you even wrote one."

I already told Hugo about the good letters I'd had lined up. I even let him read the one my old boss sent on my behalf. The letters are supposed to be confidential, but my boss sent me a copy of the one that he'd sent, and it had meant a ton to me, just seeing myself described as "a good leader with reliably excellent instincts."

"Your parents need to update their view of you, too, and so does Charlie. Yes, he's been a protective brother to you and a protective friend to me, but he's taking it too far. They call themselves scientists, but they never updated their data on you."

"Yes! Thank you! Thank you for saying that!"

We buy our sandwiches and take them to a sunny bench that's protected from the wind. They're so good, we practically inhale them while we admire the dogs being walked back and forth.

"When was the last time you spoke with him?" I ask, wiping my fingers.

"A while ago. Well before you started. With the time difference and being busy, it's been hard for Charlie and me to keep connected."

I think back to what my mom told me about Charlie being sensitive that Hugo stole the spotlight. Could that be part of it?

"But I'll definitely be having words with Charlie. Because insinuating I don't want to talk to you? Or that you should act like you don't recognize me? I did not appreciate that."

"No, don't. It's my thing to talk to him about."

Hugo growls the way he does when he doesn't agree.

"I got this," I say.

～

I'm pretty pissed off at Charlie—and my parents. But in a weird way, their behavior with this thing has been so outrageous, it's inspiring. Liberating, even, because they are so obviously wrong.

I join Kelsey and Willow for a walk down 11th Avenue to the park the next day and tell them about it. I tell them how I let Charlie and even my parents label me as this screwup, but I don't have to keep that label.

"That was me as a kid," I say. "And yeah, maybe there's a grain of truth in it now—I'm not the world's most organized person, and I don't always look before I leap, but I always come through on the things that matter."

"Rip up that script!" Willow says.

"If they want to give me that label, it's about them, not me."

"Fuck yeah!" Kelsey says.

Willow suggests an audiobook on mindset and getting new skills, which I listen to the next week while I'm doing my home workout with Kelsey's set of weights. It's as inspiring as Willow said it would be, all about how you can acquire any skill. It's not about how you were born.

Inspired by Hugo and the book and my friends, I volunteer to update the investor database, which entails organizing tons of data into a really neat and orderly form. Normally I would shun this task, and I would complain that it was the exact opposite of my abilities, but I'm on it.

When I run into trouble, I ask Viola for pointers. Not only is she excited to give them to me, but her pointers are actually helpful.

"I can learn this thing," I say, marveling at the wonder of it. "I can do database organization."

She looks at me, confused. "Why wouldn't you?"

I'm about to say because it's not in my nature, but I stop myself. I suppose in some ways I still believe it, but I'm chipping away at it. "Right," I say simply.

"The figure-it-out girl," she says proudly.

Hugo and I go to a movie one night and out for late-night dessert after. He really wants to know when I'm going to confront Charlie.

"I'll do it eventually," I say.

He grunts and takes another bite of marzipan cake.

The truth is, I'm hesitant. Charlie has always had the power to make me doubt myself, and I don't want him anywhere near my fragile new dreams where I grow beyond my old branding.

And I have this other fragile new dream: what if I do try to start my own tiny business?

I'm steaming through day two of the database update when Hesh pops his head over my cubicle wall.

"No chia project for you anymore?" he asks, adjusting his little glasses.

"Nope."

Jane rolls up. "Are you back to being free for lunch for once? You want to go to Ming's with us?"

"Into it," I say. "What time?"

"Twelve thirty?" Jane says. "Will that work? Is this thing deadlining?"

"No, I got it."

"Trouble in chia paradise?" Hesh asks.

"Okay…" I lean in and lower my voice. "I'm gonna tell you this but it's not for general broadcast."

"Wait…" Hesh does a comical double take. "Wait…no."

I smile enigmatically.

Jane leans in closer, red hair blazing. "You and Hugh-dini?"

"Ummm…yes!"

They look dumbstruck.

"I can't believe it!"

"Just to clarify—doing it," Hesh says.

"Hesh!" Jane says. "She doesn't have to go into details. Unless she wants to." She turns to me. "Like if there were some...sharable things. But she doesn't have to."

"*You* and Hugh-dini," Hesh says with disbelief.

"Well, is it *that* shocking?" Jane says.

"What? Hugh-dini goes after you know, leggy blonde finance bro-ettes who may or may not be ultra-high-functioning androids designed to look like supermodels. Not that Stella, you know—"

"Just stop talking," Jane says.

"I'm just saying Stella isn't a leggy blonde android," Hesh protests. "Stella is a hottie in her own way—"

"Oh my god! Zip it!" Jane says.

"It's fine. I don't want to be a leggy finance bro-ette."

"So...what happened? Did you guys bond over an annoying research project?" Jane asks.

"Here's the thing—we knew each other as kids. I wanted to tell you all month, but certain family members told me it was this big secret. Hugo was my brother's best friend when they were kids. He and I didn't really have much to do with each other, honestly, but then he helped me get this job—"

"He was your brother's best friend?" Jane asks. "Okay, we are gonna need a three-hour martini lunch to get through the gossip quotient here."

"Hugh-dini was a kid?" Hesh jokes.

Jane chucks a paperclip at his face.

"A very serious kid," I say. "And don't worry—I didn't breathe a word of Hugh-dini, a name that is completely hilarious, for the record."

Tinley wanders up. Hesh points at me and mouths the word *lunch*.

Needless to say, the three of them pump me for details over lunch. I'm not one to kiss and tell, but there's a lot to tell outside of kissing. I also omit the Chewbacca attack, and the truth about pineapple. Hugo's right—Wulfric can never find out.

Tinley fills us in on the Lola gossip—apparently Lola's stalker ex-boyfriend, Roger, got her kicked out of where she's living— the man broke into her apartment. She and her roommate weren't there at the time, luckily.

"The man's dangerous," Jane tells me. "He's a bouncer at this horrible club in Soho. A big guy. I feel like there's a bad story there."

"Poor Lola," I say. "Doesn't she have a restraining order against him or anything?"

"Like those do any good," Jane says. "This Roger guy left a rabbit's foot on her bed because he used to call her 'Bunny,' and he stole a few things, and the roommate just wants her out. It's a sublet, and the roommate's like, you have to be out of here."

"Lola needs something secure," Tinley says.

"Like doorman-secure," Jane says, "but that can be expensive. And she feels like she needs to disclose it to potential sublets, so not a lot of interest."

"You'd think Wulfric could help her," Hesh says. "If nothing else, he's gotta know he'll never find another Lola."

"She doesn't want Wulfric to know," Jane says. "She's very private about all this. This stuff is cone of silence, obviously."

Everybody looks at me here.

"Don't worry, cone of silence," I say. "Though I think there's someone looking for a subletter in my building. I don't know if it's immediate, but I could ask. And we have a doorman and cameras and the whole thing, so the boyfriend might not be such an issue."

"You have a doorman?" Hesh is surprised. "A human one?"

"Yeah. He's awesome." I grab my phone and shoot Kelsey a message.

"Posh," Hesh says. "That is some posh shit right there."

"I know! And rent's not even that bad. Somebody's billionaire boyfriend bought it and did upgrades. You should see the lobby and the rooftop deck."

"Sweet," Hesh says. "We have a cyber doorman that does facial recognition. So apparently, I can never grow a beard."

CHAPTER 46

HUGO

I'm lying on Stella's bed in her little bedroom in her West 49th Street sublet share, looking at the collection of photographs on the walls—a still from *Blade Runner*, a shot of mountains. A Dali print. A pair of photos of farm workers in the 1930s. "So I'm guessing your décor theme might be called, 'I hate décor themes —I'll put up whatever I want.'"

"Oh, is that what you think?" She tugs playfully at my T-shirt. "So little faith."

"Yes, it is what I think."

She snorts. "Sorry, Mr. Quant and boss seer of patterns. There's a theme, and it's awesome."

"Oh yeah?" I shift to get a better look. It's a Saturday, not that it matters. I spent the day at the whiteboards, pondering until I couldn't see straight, and now I'm here. I shouldn't be here, but there it is.

"It's all about the lighting. There's a story in the lighting of all of these. I love looking at them and being inspired." She goes on to explain the lighting story in every piece of art.

"I love that," I say. "You look at it like a serious artist."

She gets on top of me and kisses me. "I'm not a serious artist, Hugo. I'm a marketing filmmaker."

"You have an artist's eye for light." I slide my hands over her hips. "And a passion for it."

Another kiss. "Fine."

"You entertain people. That is an art. You have this intuitive sense of what will engage people."

"I have an intuitive sense about what will engage you right now."

"Don't act like it's not true, Stella. You have a sense of people. With your family? You alone could get them out of their books and whiteboards. You said the other day that you were the black sheep, but you know that's not true, right? You were the North Star. You were the one fun person in a very unfun family."

"Uhh, not so sure the Woodwards would agree with you there." She says it lightly, but there's nothing light about this bullshit she absorbed from her family.

I tuck a chunk of hair behind her ear. "I was so obsessed with pretending I didn't see you that I missed some really important things about what was going on in that house, like with Charlie being pretty unfair to you. But I didn't miss everything. I know they didn't know what to do without you."

"Excuse me? What they would do without me was follow their passion, unbothered by my antics."

"No, Stella, you were the star in that family," I say. "You had the spotlight in that family. You livened things up."

"Are you sure you didn't have the spotlight? Because I think it was you."

"Are you kidding? When you weren't around, do you know what the dinner table conversation was?"

"The circumference of tetra-rhomboids?"

That's not a thing, but I don't say that. "We barely talked at all."

"Like, at all?"

"There'd be a bit of it, but mostly we had our phones out, and we'd eat fast, and it would be over. It wasn't dinnertime the way it was when you were around."

"You wouldn't even talk about math?"

"If you haven't noticed, math is a pretty solitary endeavor."

"What about Dad's math jokes I never understood? I'm sure he at least told those."

"Your father's math jokes were only funny when you were there. Remember that chair dance you'd do when he'd tell those jokes? You'd flail around. Or you'd blurt out the weirdest answer you could come up with and then you'd flail around."

"I can't believe you remember that. You know that was my strategy when I didn't know an answer or hated the conversation —I'd do that weird Muppet chair dance."

"Well, it was hilarious. You created fun. Remember game night?"

"Yeah. They only did it because I badgered them so much. But nobody wanted to—including you."

"What? We all wanted to. We all did."

"Then why did they stop doing games as soon as I started going out with my friends?"

"Because it wasn't fun when you weren't there. You'd over-react to everything and get people laughing. We played without you a few times, but it seemed pointless. Sometimes we'd bring you into it, anyway. Your mom or dad would say things like, 'if Stella were here, she'd be so pissed that you played that,' or, 'remember when Stella got three of those in a row?'"

It takes her a while to comprehend this. "I thought everyone was relieved when I lost interest in game night."

"How could you think that?"

She frowns. "Charlie acted like it was this huge millstone off the neck of the family."

I straighten. "That is completely false and outrageous. Your parents outright wished you were there. Your mom seemed devastated."

"My parents wished I was there?"

"I can't believe you don't know that. Or that Charlie would let you think the opposite. It's not cool. Or this shit where I supposedly didn't want to talk to you at work?" I nudge her off of me and sit up, angry on Stella's behalf.

"People *liked* game night?" She's still on that.

"I say we call him. We can tell him we're dating now, and we can ask him to explain this bullshit. What time is it in Japan?" I grab my phone.

"Hugo, no!"

"I'm calling him."

"This is my fight."

"Then you call."

"I'm not going to call him up out of the blue to tell him we're a couple and yell at him about being a mean yet weirdly overprotective brother."

"Why not?" I ask.

"What good would it do?"

"It would make me happy."

"I'll say my thing to Charlie, but I don't want to be forced into it."

"I get it." I trace a gentle line over her shoulder and down her arm. "It's your thing."

"I know it probably sounds like I'm wimping out, but in a way, I'm still really digesting it all and sometimes I feel like he's in my head. This voice. 'God, Stella, can't you do anything right?'

I'm a lot more interested in ejecting that voice than having some showdown."

I nod, impressed at how thoughtful she's being. I want to fix things for her—the damaging letter I sent, this issue with Charlie —but Stella's determined to manage things her way, and I respect that.

"I'll say something when I get the urge to. Also, I hate that this is causing problems with you two."

"There are problems with Charlie and me right now, and those problems are a hundred percent caused by Charlie."

She gets this mischievous glint in her eye. "Who do you think would be angrier: Charlie seeing us in bed together? Or Wulfric discovering you're not allergic to pineapple?"

We debate that for a while. We're definitely leaning toward Wulfric when Kelsey texts, asking us if we are in for pizza with Willow and Lizzie.

"What do you think?" she asks. "It's okay if you don't want to deal with my friends. I can tell them that you're working on the most important and difficult product of your life with an impossible deadline."

"No, I'm going to hang out with my woman's people."

An hour later, I'm eating pizza with Stella's new girlfriends. I've met her roommate, Kelsey, of course, but never really spent time with her. And then there's Willow, who knows her way around an algorithm, as it turns out. I meet Lizzie, the woman behind all of those cookie stores that have been popping up like mushrooms, as well as Mia, who is starring in the musical with Kelsey.

A few other women drift in; I'm starting to feel a little like a zoo animal that everyone in the building wants to come and see. I greet people and do jokey small talk about the construction. I've had to gain some ability to be in social situations, but I still don't like them. They're still an exercise in focus and remembering how to do it.

"You okay with this?" Stella asks.

"Ripping off the Band-Aid," I grumble.

Later still, the door opens and none other than Lola walks in. "Oh!" She looks between Stella and me.

"Lola!" Stella says. "Um..."

A tall woman with a cake crowds in and around her and puts it on the counter. "Lola and I made carrot cake!"

Lola comes near. "So..." She toggles her pointer finger back and forth between us.

"Busted." Stella shoots me a nervous glance. "Don't tell Wulfric."

"Hey, I don't care if you tell Wulfric," I say.

"Don't worry," Lola says. "Wulfric and I don't discuss things like that. It's more commands and demands, so I don't see where it would come up." She goes and hangs her coat on the crowded coatrack.

"Heads up now that everyone's here!" Kelsey waves a sheaf of papers, long silver nails flashing in the light. "I'm passing these around. I want you to put them on your refrigerators, in the hallways, on the elevators, and burn the image to your eyeballs, too. All doorman staff will have a stack at all times."

Stella takes a couple of them and hands one to me. The flyers show a man with puffy cheeks, thick brows, and about twenty arrows pointed at his face. Kelsey has really taken up the battle of Lola, apparently.

"This is Roger, Lola's ex," Kelsey says.

Lola sheepishly raises her hand. "And greatest lapse in judgment."

"Fuck that. Your lapse in judgment didn't make him go feral," Kelsey says. "His name is Roger Bancroft Junior, and we are protecting Lola from him. Roger is dangerous, probably armed, and a jackass."

"This is a pretty high-security building," Lola says. "I'm not expecting him to make trouble, I mean, he's generally very cowardly, but I'm sorry you have to even think about it."

"Don't be sorry," Kelsey says. "We are going to make *this* motherfucker sorry if he breaks that restraining order. If you see this face anywhere on the premises, you need to call 911. Take a picture of him too. He needs to know he's not messing with our girl." She points at me with one of her extra-long bejeweled fingernails. "He shouldn't be anywhere around your place of employment, either."

"On it," I say.

"Lola, tell them what a psycho this guy is," Sienna urges. Sienna seems to be Lola's new roommate.

Lola's clearly reluctant to go into the full story. Stella already told me about how Lola got kicked out of her last home because of this Roger. The way Kelsey and the rest of this group have embraced her, that won't happen here. I'm happy to see that Stella's found her way into this fierce group.

After Lola tells ex-boyfriend horror stories, the group falls to discussing imaginative and somewhat frightening ideas for booby traps that I definitely wouldn't want to be on the wrong end of.

Lola wanders over. "This kind of thing probably wouldn't come up with you and Wulfric, but I'd rather he not be involved. Not that he'd ever care or want to be involved, but you just never know with Wulfric. In certain moods he's unpredictable."

"If not volatile," I say.

"Right! Involving him feels extreme," she says.

I nod. Everything with Wulfric is extreme.

"And I am handling it," she adds. "I have a solid strategy

beyond this." She gets this mysterious expression. "I'm in a secure building and I have a golden strategy."

"Good," I say, resisting the urge to ask about this strategy of hers.

The talk spins to *The Bachelor*. Lola also has a lot of feelings about the new season.

Stella climbs into my lap. "No opinions? Not even on *Bachelor* versus *Bachelorette*?"

I pull her close. "None whatsoever."

She grins. "You sure?"

"So sure."

"I just took the cutest picture of you two," Lizzie says. "Sorry, but you were looking so cozy. I'm forwarding it to you."

Stella's phone pings. She grabs it. "Love!" She shows me the picture. The way we're looking at each other, we're in our own world.

"Is that what we look like all the time?" she mumbles at the phone. "Like a bomb could go off and we wouldn't notice?"

"Well, I'd notice a bomb."

"So romantic," Stella says, and then she gets this mischievous look on her face.

"What?"

"Wait." She's texting furiously. Then she shows me her phone with an as-yet-unsent text to Charlie. It's the image of us looking like we're in love along with a message:

> Me: Hugo - best boyfriend ever!!!!!

"I'm sending it," she says.

"Wait, don't," I say.

"No?" she says. "I really, really, really want to."

"Not until I fix it." I take the phone and add a line at the end: "Stella Woodward - best girlfriend ever, signed Hugo."

"Love!" She hits send and turns to me. "Am I having a bad influence on you?"

"Yes," I say, "you're taking me down at least five percent a day and I am loving every minute."

CHAPTER 47

STELLA

I spoon a bunch of turmeric into the bubbling pot. It's a Sunday afternoon and we've decided to make a curry dish. We're acting more like a couple every day. This weekend we're actually going to some industry event together.

"What did you just do?" Hugo asks.

"It calls for two tablespoons of turmeric," I say.

"The tablespoon measure is over here."

"Normal spoons are like a tablespoon if you get it heaping."

"You have to measure things properly," he says.

"Measurements are just estimations."

"Not at all. Cooking is chemistry. This is a chemical formula."

"It's gonna be amazing," I say.

"Don't you want to do it correctly?"

"Correct is in the eye of the beholder."

Hugo gives me a growly kiss and sets me up on the counter. "I'm giving you a time-out." He measures a teaspoon of cumin exactly, leveling off the top so that it's a perfect teaspoon.

"I'm gonna sneak some extra in when you're not looking," I tease.

He comes to me. "I'm gonna tie you up so you can't."

"Are you gonna tie me up and force me to watch you make soup with the precision of a Swiss watchmaker? Because I suppose I would be down for that."

He passes the bowl of potatoes. "Dice."

"Do they have to be the size of an actual dice?"

"Die, you mean? Yes."

"Fuzzy dice?" We fight over the potato. Fuzzy dice.

At some point the stovetop is turned off and we're over on the couch for some very amazing pussy licking that blows off the top of my skull, and later we're in the shower where I try to bring him down another percent with a mind-melting blow job.

We towel off and dress in his clothes—both in matching button-down shirts and sweats—and then make the very not-difficult decision to put the curry parts in a Tupperware to make tomorrow and order to-go food.

A few minutes later, there's pounding on the door.

"That was fast," Hugo says.

"That's no Vietnamese food," I say, pulse racing. "I'd recognize that pounding anywhere."

Hugo scowls. "Charlie."

"How he got past the doorman…"

"He's on my list." Hugo heaves himself up and strolls across the place. With a quick glance of solidarity at me, he flings open the door.

"What the hell?" Charlie's holding up his phone. "Are you fucking kidding me?"

"Hi, Charlie," I call.

Charlie storms in. His clothes are wrinkled, and his hair is impossibly mussed. Did he just come from the plane?

Hugo shuts the door calmly and follows him in, coming

around to where I'm standing. He wraps his arms around me and sets his chin on the top of my head. "What?"

Charlie's fingers look white. Even from where we're standing, I can see it's the text with the picture I sent.

"What the hell is this? She lands in this city, vulnerable, completely without resources, and you move in on her?"

"Hello, I'm right here!" I say.

"You just swoop in on her?" Charlie adds.

I break away from Hugo and walk right up to Charlie. "This is none of your business, is it?"

"It's very much my business when you send me this." Again with the phone. "You don't know what you're doing. Neither of you are seeing clearly the train wreck that is happening here."

"It's not a train wreck, and your sister is neither vulnerable nor without resources," Hugo says with icy calm.

"Yeah," I add, loving his icy calm. "So you can take yourself and the bullshit that you've been peddling right out of here."

"Me peddling bullshit," Charlie says. "You think *I'm* the one peddling bullshit?"

"Yeah," I say. "Like this thing where you told Mom to tell me Hugo didn't want me anywhere near him at work? Because I might accost him or whatever?"

"And I'm guessing that's exactly what you did, isn't it? Because whatever this is—"

"Oh my god!" I get in his face. "I'm so tired of you thinking I'm this ridiculous child. I'm done with it."

A hand on my shoulder.

Hugo.

"I don't think you've seen your sister clearly for a very long time," he says, standing with me, shoulder to shoulder. Something new washes over me. Like I'm not alone here. We're in it together. We're a team. And unlike Charlie, Hugo respects my judgement.

Charlie gives Hugo a hard look. "So much for your famous fucking code of honor."

My chest tightens. Charlie knows exactly where to hit. Happy as we are together, Hugo's not proud to have broken one of his own self-imposed codes.

"Please with the codes," I say. "I'm an adult, and it's not 1872, with codes around womenfolk and all that."

"You don't go after your best friend's little sister," Charlie says. "That's always a thing."

"It's not always a thing," Hugo says, "and even if it were, the love that I feel for your sister transcends codes."

Warmth rushes through me for how he says this. Transcends codes.

Charlie isn't feeling it. "I get that you may believe you love her, Hugo, but we both know how this goes." Charlie turns to me now. "Look, I'm sure Hugo believes what he's saying, but he'll never be in this thing like you are. Food, water, shelter, sex, it's all there to serve his work, his quest for the next breakthrough. No woman will ever fit his ideal, no equation will ever be good enough. The distraction you create may be helping him in some way but it's not what you think it is."

"You're pushing it," Hugo says, voice filled with menace.

"Yeah," I say.

"Hugo loves math and logic and data and perfect accuracy. That is his true love. In fact..." Charlie turns a cold smile on us. "Ask him what he's working on."

"I know what he's working on," I say. "A data model to predict the markets."

"Ah. So you know what the goal is."

I look up at Hugo. "Being that he works in a hedge fund, I do believe the goal is investor profits."

"Have you explained it to her? Like really explained it?" He turns to me. "Hugo makes lopsided circles into squares, Stella. He tames chaos. He looks for rough edges and smooths them right out, buffing out all of the deviation. He makes the imperfect perfect. He makes nonsense make sense."

Hugo's shaking his head. "That's a ridiculous explanation, Charlie."

My heart is pounding. I'm thinking about the torus orb. His hatred of the imperfection.

"Look at her," Charlie says. "She knows I'm right. You think he loves you the way you love him, Stella?"

"Dude," I say to Charlie. "If you didn't like the picture of us that I texted to you, you should've just thumbs-downed it. You didn't have to come all this way. Because we're not buying what you're selling."

"He's gonna break your heart. You thought the thing with Jonathan was bad? And you." He turns to Hugo. "She's my sister, for fuck's sake."

"If you can't be happy for us, you can leave," I say.

"This isn't your home."

"You heard her," Hugo says.

"I'm trying to save you both a lot of misery."

"If this is saving us misery?" I say. "I'll take the misery, please. Double heaping helping, please."

Charlie buttons his coat. "Consider this an advance '*I told you so.*'"

With that he storms out.

CHAPTER 48

STELLA

I'm sitting at the kitchen island watching Hugo set the table in preparation for the coming takeout. He lines up the forks just so. Napkins are squared off with the edges.

I've been acting breezy since Charlie left, like his words didn't bother me, and Hugo says Charlie will get over it and apologize, but the whole thing bothered me. A lot. And Hugo's weirdly exact place settings make me think he feels as unhappy as I do. Like lining things up perfectly will bring some order to things.

The air feels tense and awkward, like neither of us knows what to say to make things okay.

Hugo grabs a bottle of wine and holds it up. I give him the thumbs up, and he opens it.

I shouldn't drink on an empty stomach, but I do.

"I don't want it to be like this. With the three of us," I confess, because it's easier to talk about the Charlie part of my bad feelings than the Hugo part. "I feel shitty now."

"What's shitty is that he didn't apologize to you. He owes you an apology, and I didn't hear one."

"I could've handled it better, though. Maybe not sending that text out of the blue?"

Hugo fills waters. Two matched glasses three-quarters of the way full. "Both of us were involved in sending that text, as I recall."

I down my wine in record time and put out my glass for more.

Hugo pours and takes the seat next to me. "You know Charlie. He can be moody and controlling, but he'll think about it later. He'll see he was acting like a jackass."

"I don't want your friendship to be messed up, either."

"Let me worry about that," Hugo says.

"I didn't tell him I loved you," I say.

"What?" Hugo says.

"I never said I loved you to him. But he knew I did. Did he know all along? But of course he did," I say.

"He cares about you. He's not seeing us right."

"Yeah," I say. "Also? Not a fan of the advance I-told-you-so. Is that even a thing?"

"We pushed his buttons with that photo, and he came out blazing."

I slide my finger around the rim of my glass in the silence that follows. "As if you're making lopsided circles into squares. I mean, right?" I say. "That's not right…"

Hugo recognizes this as the question that it is. "Baby, Charlie put it that way because he knew it would bug you. He went out of his way to paint things like that. As if I'm enforcing some sort of uniformity."

The next knock on the door is the food. Hugo goes to grab it.

"He was right about one thing," Hugo says, dishing sweet-and-sour shrimp onto our plates while I take out the egg rolls. "The girls I hooked up with in high school—I was going through the motions. That's what he's basing his ideas on."

"He once said you didn't give them anything. He was like, 'Hugo doesn't give them anything.' I always wondered what it meant. Like, I wondered a lot."

Hugo grabs the rice. "I had very little to give them," he says. "Between the energy I spent on my studies and the energy I spent burying my infatuation with you—" He looks up. "Under ten tons of granite."

"The way you wouldn't even look at me. I thought you hated me."

"I definitely worked overtime to keep it hidden—even from myself. Hiding things even from yourself takes a lot of energy. Rigid compartmentalization."

"You were very successful at it," I say.

He shrugs.

I grin. "Mom says you're a rigid and hard-driving boy."

"I'd like to banish that idea from my head please."

"You know, she used to worry about you. Oblivious as she could be, it was really important to her that you felt welcome in our home."

"It meant a lot. You have no idea."

We talk about the mathematical precision Mom would bring to balancing the food groups according to the food pyramid. Talking about the old times makes me soften on Charlie...a little bit.

"Are you going back for Thanksgiving?"

He leans back, stares at the ceiling. "Holidays are not my favorite with my parents. It's better to go on an ordinary week. Less baggage."

I ask about how they're doing. He's been paying their bills and giving them an allowance, and his parents don't seem to thank him.

"They spent their allowance on booze this month and tried to go over my accountant's head to ask me for more, but they know the rules. When they spend their allowance, my accountant has the power to arrange funds for rehab or a ride to a food shelf. Those are their only options."

I imagine the boy he was, craving rules and some kind of order. Now he's imposing it on them. "Do you think they'll ever say anything like we're sorry for...you know..."

"For being drunk and out of control most of the time?" Hugo supplies. "They have a disease, and a part of that disease is not taking responsibility for their actions. So, no."

"I'm so sorry," I say.

"I don't think about it a lot, to be honest. My accountant manages their bills and their finances on a day-to-day basis just like she manages mine, and I don't deal with it. I don't have time."

"Is this part of your one-percent-a-day improvement plan?"

"Yes, and money is boring."

I snort, loving that he said that. "Thanksgiving's next week. I'm sure Charlie will stick around for it. Come to Illinois and celebrate with us—Mom and Dad would love to have you. And we can talk to Charlie."

"The man owes you an apology first," he says again.

"I just feel like, let's get in a room and talk. More communication is always better than less communication."

"Sometimes," Hugo says, and I think he's probably thinking about his parents and their useless drunken communication.

"Yeah, sometimes." I swirl an egg roll in rich, brown sauce. "Do you think you like data models because it's a way to create order out of chaos?"

"You need to get Charlie's bullshit out of your head."

"You don't think it has anything to do with it?"

"I'm not creating order out of chaos. More like predicting how chaos will move."

"But how is that even possible? Hello, it's chaos!"

"There's always a pattern to find. My old data model predicted the velocity of chaos. My new one will predict its shape even before the chaos occurs."

"Are you getting into the psychic business, Hugo?"

"I'm in the observation business, baby. The observation business always looks like the psychic business."

"Dude, you're trying to predict the unpredictable." I'm trying to act light about it, but my pulse is racing. I don't know why this is bothering me so much.

"It's not unpredictable if I can predict it and put numbers to it."

I spoon rice onto my plate. "But the world is full of weirdness and mystery, and people who do things for different reasons. You can't go, here's a math equation for that."

"Actually, that's my entire job description."

"But isn't that the wonder of life? That nobody's perfect and nothing's predictable?"

"Give me a little time and I can create an equation for the wonder of life."

"You'd better not!" I say.

He chuckles.

"Well, is there a place where I can opt out of the data model," I ask playfully. "I don't want an equation to predict me. I want to be grossly irrational and unpredictably imperfect."

Hugo snorts. "Too late."

I go around the table and stand behind where he's sitting. I wrap my arms around him. "Take me out of the data model," I whisper into his ear.

"No can do."

"Maybe I'll act extra messed up in there."

Hugo gets out of his chair. "Please do." In one swift movement, he's carrying me across the room. He plops me down on the couch.

"I mean it," I say, gazing up into his gray eyes. "Take me out of your data model or else."

"I can't."

I start tickling him. He pins me down.

"Take me out," I say. "And you, too. I want us to live outside of the data model."

He kisses my neck in the way that I like, the way I sometimes can't resist.

"I'm telling you, Hugo, I'm going to wreck your data model if you leave me in there. I'm gonna flip the tables."

"Do it," he says, kissing me. "Flip all the tables. My data model can handle it."

"And then I'm gonna bust a hole in the side and leave."

We're laughing, and I wrestle out of his hold and clutch him to me and hold him close, warm and luscious against me.

His body against mine is everything nourishing and good, and I never want to let him go. And I don't want Charlie to be right.

CHAPTER 49

STELLA

Kelsey's friend Vicky has a dinner party at this amazingly fancy boutique hotel that she and her husband, Henry, own.

I know most of the women from the apartment building; it seems like everyone's lived there at some point, and a lot of them are with billionaires. Willow is laughing and trying to do the math on that. I tell them Hugo's not really like a billionaire. "He thinks money's boring," I explain.

"Hah! Don't tell Wall Street," Tabitha jokes.

"Right? He only wants to think about math. But...a billionaire. He doesn't act like one."

Kelsey snorts. "His limo says otherwise."

"That's a town car, and Wulfric supplies it," I say. "Wulfric's weirdly protective of Hugo because of this big project he's working on."

"The new data model?" Tabitha asks.

"Yeah," I say, surprised. "How do you know?"

"Because my man, Rex, is very curious about that data model.

Very curious," Tabitha says. "You know everybody's holding their breath, waiting to see what he comes up with. Rex joked that if you got drunk and started talking about Hugo's ideas, I was supposed to record it. Which, no."

"Guys," I say.

Hugo's working from home tonight. I brought him donuts this morning and discovered he'd been up a full twenty-four hours. He told me that he made what he termed a minor breakthrough that's "more of an iteration." He was very glum about it. I pointed out that it's at least progress, but an iteration is apparently not progress to Hugo. Nothing short of a brilliant game changer will be progress to Hugo.

"And Wulfric Pierce?" Tabitha says, breaking me out of my reverie. "Rex has lots of feelings about that guy."

"What kinds of feelings?" I ask.

"Intensely negative man feelings," Tabitha says as we watch Mia set out two blue and orange boxes. "Poor Lola and I did the full download on it the other day. She's like, he's not so bad. I mean, really? Because it's eight on a Friday night, and Lola really wanted to come to this dinner. Why isn't she here? Wulfric is making her work. I don't know how she tolerates that man."

Kelsey claps. "Mia bringing the Peanut Butter Kandy Kakes!"

"Nice and fresh. All the way from South Jersey," Mia says. "Double-filling ones!"

People go for them like locusts. The conversation fizzles out as everybody eats the strange little desserts, which turn out to be these vanilla cake bites with peanut butter filling, all covered in chocolate.

Even Vicky's man, Henry, stops by with their two dogs, Smuckers and Spencer, and grabs a Kandy Kake.

Vicky narrows her eyes at him. "Did you time this?"

"Plead the Fifth," Henry says.

"Of course he timed it," Mia says. "Who can resist?" She grabs another. "Just don't fall for the fake ones. Fake Kandy Kakes flip my bitch switch."

The two dogs grab center stage, getting lots of petting while angling for table scraps. Francine, a dancer who seems to have been all over the world, sneaks the little white dog a corner of one.

"I saw that!" Jada says. Jada's fun—and she loves filming things as much as I do.

Tabitha comes over and asks me whether I'm going to the Fernhauser Gala on Saturday.

"Is that the thing at the Regis Ritz? Hugo said something about it. Finance people are going?"

"Yeah. What are you wearing?"

"I don't know," I say. "Maybe a cute skirt and..."

"Were you about to say cowboy boots?" Tabitha demands.

"Maybe?"

"Stella, no! This is the Fernhauser Gala."

"Umm...high heels?"

"You understand it's a black-tie gala, do you not?"

"Wait—black tie? It's a formal ball?"

"It's a hugely formal ball for Wall Street people. It's supposedly for charity but it's really just a schmooze fest. And an excuse to wear movie star shit. How could he not tell you this?"

"He's pretty much consumed with work. But if it's a dress up thing...shit, it's tomorrow." I turn to Kelsey.

Kelsey holds up her hands. "My most formal dress has a metallic lightning bolt on the front and peekaboo holes on the sides. I guess it's better than your cowboy boots and blazers."

Tabitha perks up. "Style makeover time!"

"Excuse me?"

Everybody's excited.

Lizzie's dragging me out of my chair. "We're going shopping."

"At nine at night?" I ask.

Mia claps. "I call DJ!"

An hour later, Tabitha's unlocking one of her style storefronts and the group of seven of us bound in. "Is this a shop?"

"Kind of. It's this whole business concept that involves personal stylists. Tabitha runs it," Kelsey says, breezing by us. "Did we not tell you what a style maven our Tabitha is?" She points. "Is the formal section in back?"

"You know it." Tabitha's pulling little bottles of champagne out of a refrigerator behind the counter. Francine passes them out.

Jada grabs glasses. "So ready for a fashion show."

"Wait...am I the model here?"

"Fuck yeah," Mia says.

Shy Noelle raises her hand. "Calling it! You're an autumn like me. Your skin has gold tones, and your brown hair is in the warm end of the wheel. She's an autumn, right, Tabitha?"

"Hundred percent." Tabitha grabs my arm. "Come on."

We head into the dressing rooms. Dresses are brought to me.

The group drinks little bottles of champagne. Mia DJs it up, coming back for sneak peeks and changing the music based on the dress.

It comes to me around my tenth trip down the makeshift runway that this whole thing is as much for everybody's entertainment as it is for helping me get something to wear. Once I realize that, I start playing it. Now and then I strut out in a way-too-va-va-voom one and do a little wiggle as I spin.

People scream.

Basically, I'm forced to try on pretty much every gown in the store that's my size, including a few that are too tight and a few that are "all wrong for an autumn," according to Tabitha, but she sends me out anyway.

It's the most fun I've had in ages, and at the end of the night, I have a loaner dress and shoes in a pretty blue bag, and this thought that I must have sacrificed myself on a burning pyre to save a horde of sad-eyed orphans in a past life.

What else could explain my extreme luck in hooking up with these women?

Kelsey and I share an Uber home, and I look out at the nighttime bustle of Manhattan, so thrilling and glamorous, like an endlessly churning tide of big, bold life, and Charlie's warnings don't seem so dire.

CHAPTER 50

HUGO

Stella comes out her door in such an outrageously sexy golden gown, I forget how to breathe. The way it hugs her curves, and her skin looks smooth and golden, and her breasts…

I'm a mathematician with zero belief in witchcraft, but the compulsion I feel to kiss her everywhere, to touch her every-where, to press my face to her breasts that are plumped above the dress, it's like I'm under a spell.

"Hugo?" I realize that she's talking. "Are you okay?"

"You…"

"Hugo?"

I force my gaze to her eyes. "You look beautiful."

Her face lights up. "You're not so bad yourself, handsome." She tugs at the corner of my bowtie. "Very double-oh-seven." She informed me last night about this dress code, and in the morning, Lola had Wulfric's tailor send over a tuxedo.

"Have fun, kids!" Kelsey calls from somewhere inside the place.

I cannot take my eyes off Stella. Not in the elevator down to their lobby, not on the sidewalk outside her building, and definitely not in the limo.

"Maybe we should stop off at Hotel Luxe," I suggest.

"If you think that I'm going to skip my first Cinderella-type gala—"

"We'd have so much more fun. And there'd be no people except us. That's always better."

She presses her hand to my cheek.

I grasp her wrist and kiss her palm. Her hair is piled up on top of her head except for two long curls. The gold of her dress gives her hair a richness—it really is some kind of magic.

"Or we could just stay in here," I try.

"I have a data model to predict that," she jokes. "It's a giant zero."

"That's your model?" I chuckle. "A zero? The numeral zero? How would you present it?"

"It would be a three-dimensional zero that I sculpt out of wire and little bits of debris to show my disdain for the idea of missing this gala."

"Maybe I'll bring your data model to the presentation," I tell her. "It sounds better than the pathetic iteration I've managed to develop."

"Oh poor baby." She does a fake frown. "Are you saying it's not the most perfect thing in the world? Are you having to settle for mere excellence?"

I slide a finger under a curl. "My first one was bold and disruptive, but this one is weak." I can't get my mind off of that fact.

"What does Brenda think of it?"

"She thinks it's brilliant."

"Oh my god, you suck!" She hits my shoulder with her clutch. "It's not brilliant."

She's shaking her head. "But hey, if you hate the idea of a perfectly decent data model, you could aways borrow my sculptural zero to present to the people. What do you think Wulfric would say to that? That would be bold and disruptive. Can you imagine his face?"

I snort. "Wulfric would not be amused."

"You could bring it out in a box and unveil it with a flourish," she says. "I present to you, Wulfric"—she raises her hands in a theatrical gesture—"the boldest and most brilliant data model you've ever seen. I give you...a zero—made entirely from garbage."

"Very funny."

"If you really wanted to be disruptive," she continues, "I'd go with something that has a performance aspect. Imagine this—you unveil a cutting board, a knife, and a pineapple."

"Jesus."

She grins. "You wanted bold and disruptive."

I sigh and lean back in the seat.

"Poor grumpy-stuff," she says. "Maybe you'll actually have fun. Parties *can* be fun."

"So I've heard."

"Sometimes they are," she says. "Even a stopped clock is right twice a day."

"Not necessarily. Considering leap seconds."

"Leap seconds?" She pulls back. "Did you make that up? You made that up."

"I didn't make it up. Earth's days aren't all exactly the same length. Leap seconds get inserted now and then to compensate for the earth's uneven rotation."

"What? Days aren't all the same length?"

"They're not," I say. "They add and subtract seconds here and there to even things out."

"Somebody's been adding and subtracting random seconds to time? Does this person live in a giant cuckoo clock?"

"Hardly." I grab a water. "This person works at the International Earth Rotation and Reference Systems Service."

She furrows her brows. "I don't know what I'm more amazed by: that there's an actual place with that name, or the fact that somebody's been inserting seconds without people knowing it."

"So as you see, stopped clocks can be right only once a day."

"I'm still going to say it the old way," she announces. "It's the spirit of the saying that's important."

"But wouldn't you want to get it right? Now that you know the correct way to say it?"

"No, because saying, 'a stopped clock is right twice a day' is way better than, 'a stopped clock is right twice a day if you ignore the presence of leap seconds, which are used to compensate for the earth's uneven rotation.' Do you want to know why?"

I smooth my thumb over her cheek. "I think you're being a smartass."

She grins. "I'll tell you why: because I'm not a fucking nerd."

"The second way is better. It's objectively better."

"But it's *not* better," she says.

"It is better, because you should want to be accurate," I say. "You'd have to change it to, 'a stopped clock is sometimes right twice a day.'"

"I would hate that," she says with an intensity that surprises me. "I would never say that."

Is she upset that I corrected her?

"What's wrong?" I ask.

"Nothing. Just...sometimes it's the spirit of the thing that's valuable. Maybe you want to preserve the heart of it, you know?" She opens her little clutch and extracts lip balm. "Just never mind."

"No, I want to know. What's going on?"

She smooths the balm over her lips a few times, then pauses, then smooths on some more. Finally she puts it back. "I don't want to be having a fight about leap seconds."

"How about this—your way of saying it is more evocative."

She does a subdued version of the Muppet flail she used to do at dinner.

"Okay, wait," I say. "That means you hate the conversation, or you don't want to give an answer."

"Right now it means we are pulling up to one of the grandest hotels in the city and you look like a dashing secret agent and we're in love and I'm so off of leap seconds."

"No more leap seconds," I say, making a mental note to come back to this later. Stella's upset, and I don't want to just leave it.

"Holy crap," she breathes as we reach the balcony overlooking the ballroom floor, which is dripping with chandeliers and ornate Victorian-era flourishes.

It's the lighting she's looking at—of that I have no doubt. I follow her gaze, wondering if it's the warm glow coming off hundreds of flickering candles she's marveling at. Or the way the light makes the chandelier crystals seem to flash. Or is it the interesting shadows around the fussy medallions and moldings that frame the bone-white walls?

I grab champagne off of the tray of a passing waiter and hand her a glass.

"Amazing," she says.

"Now can we go to the hotel?" I joke.

"Hell no!"

I take her hand and we descend the marble stairs and join the throng. I guide us to a sparse corner as she tells me about her night with her new friends from the apartment. Waiters circulate with finger foods, and Stella insists on trying it all.

"Oh my god. Hey—" She points at the upper level. "Look! It's Lola and Wulfric! See? In front of that marble statue thing! God, why would Wulfric make her go to something like this?"

I look up there. I recently informed him that Stella and I were dating. His answer was exactly what I knew it would be: he cares only about the data model.

I used to care only about the data model, too.

CHAPTER 51

STELLA

I take Hugo's hand and pull him over and say hi to Wulfric and Lola. People try to catch Hugo's eye—they really do seem to want to talk to him, but every time I look back, Hugo's watching me. He's oblivious to people as a rule, and this glam golden dress is not helping.

Score!

I hug Lola, who is wearing a very chic red gown. Wulfric is immediately grilling Hugo on the data model. Hugo mumbles something about testing methods. Even I can tell he's being evasive. Wulfric will probably love whatever data model he comes up with, but Hugo sees the flaws, just like with that orb.

Hugo loves math and logic and data and perfect accuracy. I try to shake Charlie's words out of my head. He was being an asshole, that's all. He knows the soft spots. Of course Hugo cares about math and data and perfection—but caring isn't the same as worshipping!

"I'm stealing Stella!" Lola drags me to the auction table. "Help me pick something in the mid-six-figure range for Wulfric to bid on."

"What does Wulfric like?"

"Wulfric hates everything. He'll probably be giving it away as some kind of bonus." She turns to me. "Maybe even to Hugo if he kills it with the model, which he will."

"He's been at that thing nonstop," I say. "I think they should move the presentation."

"They can't. Or won't. Math dudes flying in. High stakes and heads rolling. Finance bro come-to-Jesus moment and all that." Lola inspects the card for a spa package and pronounces it a bore.

I tell her about Vicky's dinner and my style shop adventure. "I wish you could have come. We missed you."

She examines a crystal box that contains a Fabergé egg. "I was pissed AF that I couldn't go."

I look over at Hugo and Wulfric. "Does he always bring you to these fancy things?"

"Yeah. But I'd be working either way, what with him texting me for research on people he sees. Trying to figure out whose company is in trouble and all of that. This way I can do it on the spot. Plus I get a new dress and an amazing meal. Wait till dinner, Stella. Don't worry, though. Wulfric nearly came to blows with a few people over a pineapple item on the menu."

"Wow. Okay."

Lola picks up a card for an archery tour to Scotland. "If I was bidding, I would get this in a heartbeat."

I look over the auction items, but the thing I want most is whatever mysterious gift Hugo had for me. And for the presentation to go well. And for Wulfric to never find out about the pineapple.

"Look!" Lola shows me an auction item where tiny fish give you a pedicure. "Not for all the tea in China!"

I select a tiny gold rocket, which is a stand-in for a rocket ride to the space station. "You couldn't pay me enough."

"Hell no. Gimme the biting fish over the bro rocket."

The auction is a lot more fun once we start competing on who can find a worse present than the rocket ride.

Lola finds a gift certificate for cryogenically freezing your body at death.

"Rich people are out of their minds," I say. Then I add, "I want little fish to eat my body after death. Or else piranhas. I'd bid on that. And I want to be in a rocket while it happens."

"What? Noooooo!" Tabitha butts in and slings an arm around my shoulder. "Stella, do we need to buy you a happy light?"

We make Tabitha choose her worst gift. She takes it really seriously and discovers you can bid on a piece of cake from Prince William and Kate's wedding.

We move on to picking the worst possible gifts for each other. Drinks are had. Finger foods are eaten.

At some point I notice that Hugo is in a large circle of people. I can feel him hating the attention from across the room. "I'm going to do a rescue," I say. "You two—keep your guys away from each other. I don't want to see Wulfric and Rex in a rumble."

Lola and Tabitha grin.

I go up and link arms with Hugo, who introduces me to Meredith, a statuesque redhead who looks like one of those models where they put glasses on her and pretend she's a librarian. But Meredith went to MIT with Hugo, and I have no doubt the glasses aren't a smartness prop. And then there's Maria and Sergei and Ethan, who also went to MIT with Hugo, and some industry people with names I didn't catch.

Hugo puts his arm around me.

"I hear you two met at math camp," Meredith says. "What's your area of specialization?"

"Ummm…" I grin. "Videos about sports drinks?"

Meredith snorts. "Really?"

"Stella's a marketing wiz," Hugo says proudly. "Her videos win awards."

"Ohhhhh! That's amazing," Meredith says in the way that you say it when you don't think it's amazing at all, and maybe you're even embarrassed on the person's behalf.

Everybody agrees that it's "amazing" that I'm in marketing with amazing definitely being in quotes.

Sergei frowns at me. "Though you're aware, I'm sure, that Hugo is literally the world's top expert in blending microstructure with systemic macrostrategies."

"You don't know how lucky you are," Maria says, and the emphasis is a lot more on the "you don't know" part than the "lucky" part.

I squeeze his hand. "Of course I know."

Hugo gives me a dark *can-we-go-now?* look that makes me just love him.

"People look to him. They follow him," Meredith says.

Hugo's bristling so hard at the praise, it's a wonder quills of annoyance aren't shooting from his skin.

Meanwhile, I'm rethinking the wisdom of that Hotel Luxe offer.

"Hey, did you all see that we can bid on a rocket ride to the space station?" I try, hoping to change the subject, and definitely also hoping that it doesn't seem like I'm directing the comment entirely at Meredith, Sergei, and Maria, though I really would send the three of them off in a rocket if I could.

They ignore my conversational gambit; they're talking about things that involve divergences and dynamics and other words I don't know. The rest of the group joins in, and it's off to the races. People keep asking Hugo questions and trying to get his commentary on things. Sergei even shows him his phone with a photo of a whiteboard on it, and Hugo has annoyed things to say about what went wrong.

Do Hugo's peers seem to see this gala as a special window of opportunity to get Hugo's insights? I'm thinking yes.

So rude.

We get herded to a table with the group of them, but I'm determined to make the best of it. I ask Sergei and Maria, who are obviously a couple, how they met. It turns out that they met in Singapore. I ask a lot of questions about that.

Hugo gives me a sly sideways glance. I grin. Yeah, I'm changing the subject like a boss!

"Our first kiss was in Cloud Forest," Maria says, looking at Sergei. "It's this gorgeous botanical conservatory. Huge."

Another couple at the table, Joe and Verna, say their first kiss was in the MIT robotics lab.

People turn to Hugo and me.

"Our first kiss was in my office," Hugo says.

"Well, but really the music room at my family's house," I say. "Remember?"

"But that wasn't officially our first kiss," Hugo says.

"It was our first kiss."

"But not really," he says.

"It was a kiss. It was between us. And it was first."

Hugo is wearing his expression of consternation. He is really not agreeing.

"What?" I say to him. Does Hugo reject our wonderful, precious first kiss?

"First kiss is in the lips of the beholder," Maria jokes.

Somebody points out that there are different kinds of kisses.

Others chime in, because it's getting weird.

"Sure," I say. "Different kinds of kisses." But I loved that kiss. It felt passionate and wild and forbidden. I lived on it for years. It was everything to me, and it's a part of our journey together, which makes it doubly precious.

And he'd disown it?

I tell myself it's not a big deal, but it kind of is.

Also, I feel like everybody is thinking that we don't belong together, and I'm hating that, too.

Lola and Wulfric are there, suddenly. Wulfric pulls up a chair so that Lola can sit by him, forcing people to squeeze together to make room.

They're just starting to serve, and a young manbun waiter comes over, clearly intending to ask Wulfric to move, being that the tables are designed for eight people, but then he seems to sense something foreboding about Wulfric, like a small animal sensing the presence of a malevolent force. He hesitates, then he pulls a place setting off a nearby table and sets it on ours.

"Thank you," Wulfric says. "And I cannot stress this enough: I don't want to see one speck of pineapple anywhere on this table. In fact, if I hear that even the tiniest molecule of pineapple is present anywhere on this floor or back in the kitchen, people will answer for it."

"Yes, we've been made aware, sir."

"Is somebody allergic to pineapple?" Sergei asks.

"Hugo is. He's deathly allergic," Wulfric barks. "I thought you went to school together."

Meredith turns to Hugo. "You're allergic to pineapple?"

Sergei says, "How did I not know this? We were roommates!"

"For crissake, what's wrong with you people?!" Wulfric says in the most terrifying tone possible. "Pay attention! You could've killed him!"

Sergei looks pale. Meredith mumbles something about not knowing.

Hugo has his usual stormy poker face, but I, for one, am panicking. I reach for my water and deliberately knock it over into the breadbasket and condiment area. People jump up from their seats.

Waiters descend onto our table to clean it up and replace things.

The conversation never quite goes back to Hugo's supposedly deathly allergies.

Even so, I'm quaking in my heels, hoping none of them will remember a specific instance where Hugo ate pineapple, or God forbid, produces photographic evidence.

Lola sits like a beautiful and mysterious sphinx, and when the fish is served, she points to it with a significant look at me and makes minnow biting motions with her fingertips.

CHAPTER 52

HUGO

The road in front of the Regis Ritz is jammed with limos and taxis, and nobody seems willing to let anybody in or out. In other words, gridlocked.

Stella stares dolefully out the window at the throngs of people on the sidewalk.

"Quite the diversion back there," I say. "Thank you."

"Sure," she says, clutching her golden purse, hopelessness radiating out from her.

"What's wrong?" I ask. "Is it the pineapple?"

"No, it's not the pineapple."

"What, then?"

She turns to me, eyes shining, and not in a happy way. "How can you say that wasn't our first kiss?"

"What are you talking about?"

"Our first kiss wasn't in your office. It was in the music room of my parents' house."

"But that wasn't a real first kiss," I say.

"Of course it was real," she says.

"You didn't know it was me. It was a kiss for another guy. I was sleeping at the time."

"But then at some point you knew it was me. And I knew it was you. And that's why it was special, because we'd found our way to each other."

"And you were grossly underage," I remind her.

"*You* were underage, too!" she says. "It doesn't count if both people are underage."

"In some states it does. Anyway, you were also drinking at the time. Possibly drunk."

"Hardly," she bites out.

"Everything about that kiss was wrong," I say.

"But I loved that kiss. It was precious to me. You realized it was me at some point, and I realized it was you, and remember how awesome it was? It was this sense that we'd found each other across the desert for one stolen moment in time. And the way you held me, like you couldn't bear to ever let me go."

"But it wasn't the two of us deciding to kiss each other out of a feeling of mutual attraction."

"So?" she says. "I suppose you're going to say the elevator wasn't our first time making love."

"It depends on how you define the phrase 'making love.'"

"Oh my god. Seriously?"

"The elevator—it wasn't deliberate so much as a failure of control. We could've been a couple of ferrets."

The moment it's out of my mouth, I can see it was a mistake.

"Ferrets?" she says.

"Maybe not ferrets—"

"Us in the elevator was the best ever. It was one of the peak moments of my existence."

"This is an argument of semantics," I say.

"No it's not! We had that mistaken-identity kiss, we fucked in an elevator. That was our journey as a couple, and it's not good enough for you?"

"It's not about *good enough*," I say.

"What if we had a kid and their first step was in a pile of shit —would you reject that too?"

"Of course not. I would love anything a kid of ours does," I say, stunned we're talking about kids, but I'd go there with her. "I'm defining terms, that's all."

"How long until you're wishing I was different, just like your torus orb? You thought your data model was okay, and Brenda says it's brilliant, but now you think it's a piece of shit? Why, Hugo? Because it doesn't reach your perfect ideal? And what about me? How long until you start seeing flaws you can't unsee? You'll start tearing me down—you won't be able to help it."

"Don't make me pay for the sins of another man, Stella. I would never want you to change, or to change you."

"But it's already happening! What we have built together already isn't measuring up. This is the messy, imperfect history that we've created together, and you're editing it to fit some perfect ideal. And someday you'll look at me that way, too."

"No—I love our history," I say. "I love you."

"But you're already changing things, don't you see?" She wraps her arms around herself, looking so hopeless. "It scares me. I can't help it. It's so déjà vu."

My blood goes cold. Is she leaving me? "Stella, no—I love us, and I love you," I say simply. "I love you exactly the way you are. I know I can have exacting standards, and it's something I probably need to work on."

"I'm not going to leap into a relationship with you only on the condition that you work on something. That's not fair to you or to me, and it's just a rule."

"So where does that leave us?"

"I don't know. I want to take the time to look before I leap.

The way I've been feeling, I think this relationship is worth the leap no matter what. The love I feel outweighs the rest. But I want to take the time to overtly decide to leap instead of just falling into it. I want to stand up and get right in your face and tell you it's worth the leap no matter what."

"I don't want to not see you."

"Work on your presentation, and I'll...well...I don't know. I just need to think. Or something."

CHAPTER 53

STELLA

I'm in bed in my pajamas, half-reading a book, when I hear Kelsey come in the front door, back from her Tuesday evening rehearsal.

"Don't worry about being quiet!" I call out. "I'm up."

"You got a package!"

"Okay!"

I've been miserable without Hugo. Miserable at work without seeing him. Just miserable. It's been three days, and I haven't figured out what to do. I feel like I can't live without him.

"Not from Amazon!" she calls. "It's a Brooklyn address."

"No name?"

"Would I not say the name if there was a name?"

I pull on my robe and plod out there. "I was gonna make avocado toast anyway."

"There's only half an avocado left."

"Sigh." I spot the package. It's the size of a microwave, all wrapped in brown paper.

"You know anyone in Brooklyn?" she asks.

"Nope." I tear it open. The box is filled with several varieties of packing materials, and whatever is in there is wrapped in tissue paper inside a layer of bubble wrap like it's the most precious thing ever.

"What is it?"

"I don't know. Some kind of silver dish?"

As I unroll the layers of packing, my heart begins to pound.

It's a cheese ball tray, but not a conventional one where you smush it onto a plate and surround it with crackers. No, this is a cheeseball tray just for a cheeseball. There's a small cup with a spike where you put the cheeseball itself, and little arms on hinges can be bent in to hold the sides in place to help it keep its spherical form, but you can bend them back out if you want to get at a yummy part.

"What the hell," I breathe. "How is this even possible?"

"I'm looking at it, and I still don't get what it is."

"Magic is what it is. From Hugo." I unwrap a little silver spoon. There's an owl on the end of it. It doesn't officially go with the tray part, but it's close enough. And it has an owl.

"Cute," Kelsey says.

I set it out on the coffee table. "It's the perfect cheeseball tray for spoon-eating a cheeseball."

"There are more of you out there?"

"I guess!" I turn it, marveling at it. "And you know what isn't here? A place for crackers."

"You could stick it on a plate and add crackers if you wanted," Kelsey jokes. "But why would you?"

"This is so…everything."

"It actually is kind of amazing that he thought of this for you."

"Really amazing. He thinks he doesn't know people's hearts, but he does."

Kelsey sits down and toys with one of the little arms. "Are you gonna give him another chance?"

"I don't know. I love him. But I also know that he eventually rejects everything that's not perfect. I'm not perfect." I sigh. "But I also love him."

"Totally get it." Kelsey grabs a microfiber cloth and starts polishing the spoon.

"And he wants to change," I say, "but you can't go into a relationship expecting a man to change. That's a recipe for heartbreak."

"Don't you bake that recipe," Kelsey says.

"Yeah, no, I know...I just, I don't know..." And I really don't know what I'm saying, what I'm feeling.

"Aww, sweetie," Kelsey says as she comes over and puts an arm around me. I glance again at the cheese ball tray. My eyes feel hot and misty.

CHAPTER 54

HUGO

I'm sitting at the poker table, studying my hand, at a loss, for once.

I'm not confused about how to win. I'm reasonably sure Cooper's got three eights and Leon has a low straight. Fergus could have two pair. Odds are high that what I need is still in the deck, and it's nearly my turn.

But I'm trying something new. Maybe.

"What's going on?" Fergus asks.

"Thinking." I rearrange the cards in my hand.

Five pairs of eyes turn to me.

I never take this long to make a decision on cards, but I spent the entire night walking around the city, turning over what Stella said to me.

She's not wrong. I'm critical of anything falling short of perfect—in other people, in objects, in myself.

But I'd never be that way to this woman I've loved for so many years. I'd never make her feel less than.

But why should she believe that? I do it with everything else.

Do I have a problem?

And even if I proved that I'd never do it to her, even if she believed me, why would she want to spend her life with somebody who does that, even to himself?

"Do I need to go make a sandwich?" Leon barks.

"Like you haven't ever taken a few minutes to make up your mind," Cooper chides.

"Patience," I growl.

At some point during my walk, right about when I was passing the Guggenheim with its shapes and spirals, I realized... I'm exhausted.

Just fucking exhausted.

I ended up home just as the birds started singing, and I did what I always do when faced with a lack of knowledge: went into research mode. I found techniques. I found a therapist. I found books on stopping with the inner critic. On not being a perfectionist. On embracing imperfection.

The idea of embracing imperfection is annoying, ludicrous, and probably the exact thing I have to do. One of the books I dug into suggested perfectionists should learn to enjoy the journey rather than focus on the outcome.

God knows how you do that. The journey? This is a thing?

But I want to do better. Could I just try it?

I look at my hand, which is decent enough to win with, depending on what I get if I ask for more cards, which I really should, but I'm thinking about the journey thing. It comes to me that if I rearrange it, there's an interesting pattern to it involving prime numbers. Well, why not?

"Stay," I say with a queasy feeling.

"With what you've got facing up?"

"That's right," I say, feeling like I'm on a high wire.

Everybody's staring at me now.

"What the hell do you have?" Ronan asks.

"It'll cost you," I say.

"Not on this hand." Ronan folds. Fergus, Cooper, and Leon fold, too.

Only Luther is reckless enough to call. He lays down a mediocre hand involving two pair.

I show my cards.

"What the hell is that?" Leon demands.

"It's a prime number pattern," I say.

Fergus laughs. "Good god, the data model's finally sent him round the bend."

"Works for me." Luther takes the chips.

"What have you done?" Ronan demands. "Why not take cards?"

"I'm enjoying the journey," I say.

The guys all scowl. All except Luther, anyway.

"I've realized I have a problem with perfectionism, and one of the strategies I've decided on is to focus on the journey rather than the result."

"The journey of poker? Instead of the result?" Leon barks. "Hugo. That is some bullshit right there."

"I don't know whether to kick you out of here or try to get in a few more hands before you come to your fucking senses," Cooper says.

"Is this about a woman?" Fergus asks. "No, wait. Don't answer. It's a woman."

"Well…" I pick up my drink and swirl the ice.

Everybody groans.

"Out with it," Cooper says.

"We're here to play poker," I say.

"You're not," Luther says. "You've got an art project going on. Much as I enjoy taking your money, you can't be playing by weird-ass rules."

"So she thinks you're too perfectionistic?" Cooper asks.

"Yes. And I bring impossible standards to everything."

Fergus nods slowly. "She's not wrong. You almost never make a mistake, but when you do, you're very unhappy."

"I'm probably going to want to kill myself for telling you this," Ronan says, "but your quest for perfect play limits you. You don't bluff. You play purely on probabilities, and yes, you win most of the time, but you don't utilize all of the possibilities of the game."

Cooper groans and tosses a peanut at Ronan. "Maybe you don't regret telling him that, Ronan, but I know I regret it. If Hugo starts bluffing?"

"So we double his ante again," Ronan says.

Luther gives me a hard look. "Ronan's right. Your purely mathematical game means you can never level up."

"But how can I ignore what I know?" I ask.

"You need to take risks, man," Luther says. "You need to break a few things—that's how you level up. You know how to bluff. Commit to a losing hand once in a while."

My heart races. It's not me.

"So, there's trouble?" Fergus asks. "With the woman?"

"Yeah."

"Out with it," Cooper says.

I balk—we're not that kind of group. We do cards; we don't do feelings.

Ronan demands the story. Even cold-hearted Leon chimes in. The prospect of them doing some kind of group analysis of my problems is too much attention. What's more, I've never helped them with their problems. It would be uneven.

But maybe this is part of breaking things. My mind flashes on Stella's brilliant recklessness, her genius for risk and abandon. It inspires me.

So I go for it. I tell my friends what Stella said. Before I know it, I'm telling them about our first-kiss argument, and the leap seconds, and my piece-of-shit data model. How I screwed up her career. I tell them about her love of Dali and of light and shadow, and how determined she's been to be more organized and how we never run out of things to talk about. To laugh about.

"It sounds like she's still yours to lose," Ronan offers, managing to look impossibly regal, even in an old sweater.

"Agree," Cooper says. "She's thinking about it—that's a good sign."

"But you can't wait around for her to decide," Fergus warns. "You need to take action. Get in front of this."

"She wants to think about it. She sees being with me as a gamble, I think."

Fergus suggests I show her the books I plan to read.

"No, think big—bigger than books, bigger than words," Ronan says. "You need to show her you're invested in changing. And whatever you come up with, go even bigger."

"Easy for you to say," Cooper says. "Mr. The-planet-is-my-oyster."

Ronan shrugs. He probably has stories to tell—he really seems to be from a different world, but he's the most intensely private man I've ever met, so he stays with the shrug.

They argue about whether change can actually happen that fast.

"I agree, it has to be big," Cooper says, ripping open another bag of chips. "Embrace that imperfection where it counts. Go for a home run."

"But embracing imperfection doesn't mean you don't get to do your best," Luther says. "Some shit like you've decided to button your shirt wrong or play poker by rules that are just fucked? No."

"Yeah, no more throwing the game," Leon warns. "We get you don't give a shit about money, but come on."

"No more playing like an asshole," I say. "But maybe I'll bluff."

Cooper shoots Ronan a dirty look. "You see what you've done? You've created a monster."

I lean back and cross my legs. "Are we dealing or what? Things are about to get wild. Maybe."

Cooper throws another peanut at Ronan.

"Fuck off," Ronan says.

Leon deals.

The game is suddenly...interesting. Nobody's sure how I'm going to play.

It's my turn. I should take a card, but I pause, just to mess with them.

Everybody's laughing.

I make the logical choice, but I won't always do that.

And right there, it hits me: ridiculous as that last hand was, embracing an obnoxious new goal led to one of the best poker experiences of my life. My guys and I had an interesting conversation where I got to know them on a deeper level. They helped me process this situation with Stella, they gave me some damn fine advice, and I saw a way to improve my strategy.

Luther was right—you need to break things to level up. To disrupt things.

I was trapped in the math of the game. I was trapped in a two-dimensional world. I was trapped in a whiteboard.

I'm trapped in the whiteboard.

I stand up.

"What now?" Cooper complains.

"I'm folding. I have to go. I just realized something about my data model."

"Don't you want to see who won?"

"I already know." From what I've seen, there's a 90 percent chance Ronan will win, but I don't say that. Again, not an asshole.

I head out. Everything's different. Everything's new.

311

CHAPTER 55

STELLA

There are so many places in Manhattan that I've never seen, and Kelsey's been introducing me to her faves.

We just had the most decadent build-your-own donut-ice-cream sandwiches at Holey Icewitch. I nearly keeled over from the yumminess of mine: cookie dough ice cream sandwiched in a warm french-glazed donut, all topped with hot caramel and toffee bits.

Now we're strolling down Fifth Avenue.

"I love this area," Kelsey says. "I love looking at the glam shit."

I'm gaping at the strangely dressed mannequins when she clutches my arm. "Is that Lola? In a giant fur coat?"

I scan the crowd and spot her. "Wow, she's really dressed up. Who's the Neanderthal? It's not her evil ex, right?"

"No way. I memorized that guy's face. It's not Roger."

"Wait." I squint. "I think that's Pico, one of Wulfric's bodyguards."

Kelsey waves and shouts across the place. Lola doesn't seem to notice, so we just beeline over.

Lola gets this weird look when she sees us coming, like she's been caught at something.

"Nice coat!" Kelsey says. "This is like…" She touches it with a look of wonder. "You're wearing sixty thousand bucks right here."

"This old thing?" Lola says.

"Are you being funny?" Kelsey says. "I know what a real fur coat feels like. Back in my youth I used to pretend I was rich and go to nice stores and try them on."

I introduce Pico to Kelsey, since Lola is really off her game. "We were just going to…" I say.

Lola and Pico exchange glances. Something secret is definitely going on.

"Wait! Hold the phone." Kelsey grabs Lola's hand. "What. The. Fuck."

I look down at the massive rock on Lola's hand.

"It's not what you think!" Lola says.

"I don't know what to think," I say.

"I'm going with secret engagement," Kelsey says. She looks at Pico, but I happen to know Pico's happily married. Lola has talked about how much he loves his wife.

"I know my bling. This is Saudi-prince-level shit," Kelsey says. "Tell all."

"Fuck!" Lola says, exchanging glances with Pico.

"You have to tell them," Pico says.

"We're tricking Roger," Lola confesses. "He thinks I'm engaged to Wulfric and that Wulfric wants to kill him."

"What?" I say. "Is Wulfric in it, too?"

"No! Don't tell him!"

"Don't worry," I say.

"It's so stupid, but Wulfric gave me this heirloom family

diamond to put in his safety-deposit box one time, and I put it on. It was just so beautiful, and so I wore it while I did errands before hitting the bank, and I ran into Roger, and he went ballistic when he saw it. So I told him it's Wulfric's family's ring, which it is, and that Wulfric and I have a secret engagement. The way it backed him off, it was like magic."

Pico grins. "The man is a piece of shit, but he's heard the rumors about Wulfric."

"And Pico has been so cool. He got the idea to get a fake copy made so I can wear it around."

"It's a famous ring," Pico says. "I guarantee you, Roger looked it up online."

Lola looks at Pico. "Sometimes we pull this coat out of Wulfric's storage and I wear it when I think Roger might be shadowing me."

"Another heirloom?" Kelsey asks.

Lola nods.

"You think Roger's out there?" I ask.

"He's watching us right now," Pico says. "Don't look around. Don't show we know."

"I want to see him! I want to punch him," Kelsey says.

"Don't. We're good. Wulfric is an amazing deterrent," Lola says.

Pico says, "I've let Roger know in so many words that Wulfric is looking for an excuse to kill him—painfully." He crosses his arms. "Delivering threatening messages to Roger is one of my favorite pastimes. I've told him what Wulfric plans to do if he comes within a hundred feet of Lola or shows up anywhere near her new place. My wife had a stalker. We're both very sympathetic."

"I think it's working," Lola says. "Roger's out there, but he's really backed off."

Pico grins. "The man is scared shitless of Wulfric."

"So it's a secret engagement that's so secret, even Wulfric doesn't know," Kelsey observes.

Lola grins. "Exactly."

I nod, thinking about Hugo's pineapple secret. "You gotta do what you gotta do."

CHAPTER 56

Stella

I meet Charlie under the bright red awning that stretches out in front of our building.

He's clearly nervous, and I wasn't really in the frame of mind to talk to him, but he texted, asking to see me. Kelsey and I were still in our pajamas, rearranging our living room for the tenth time, and I wasn't ready to go for an eleventh.

And of course, I can be a bit of a softie.

"Come on," I say, leading him around the mob of people at the bus stop. "We can walk down to the park, and if we're really ambitious, loop over to the High Line."

"You sound like a real New Yorker already," he observes.

"Hardly," I say. We walk past Gourmet Goose and he's outraged when I tell him about Greta refusing to sell me a cheeseball. He really wants to go in there and yell at her and maybe even sue her. It makes me remember how much I love him.

"Stella," he says, sounding really serious.

My heart pounds. I don't know what to say. I don't know how to navigate through my ugly mixture of emotions, and also my general avoidance of difficult conversations where I might cry.

"It's fine," I say.

"Definitely nothing is fine," Charlie says. "I have no excuses—I was an asshole, Stella. I was a runaway train of assholeyness—not just last week, but growing up—"

I stiffen. "You don't have to say that. You weren't an asshole."

"Let me say my thing, Stella. I wasn't always a good brother to you."

"Charlie—"

"Hear me out. I should have been helping you and cheering you on. Instead, what did I do? I was so fucking insecure, I would tear you down."

We come up on a DON'T WALK sign and I turn to him, blown away. "You were insecure? You were the brilliant one who took after them."

"No, Hugo was the brilliant one. I was never good enough. Don't you remember how they were constantly praising Hugo? Constantly comparing us?"

"But they were proud of you," I say. "You know they love you, Charlie."

The light turns green and we walk.

"Maybe it was their way of inspiring me to reach higher, who knows, withholding their praise and lavishing it on Hugo, but it sucked," he says.

"They did praise him a lot. No, I get it, Charlie. It never crossed my mind that you'd feel bad."

"Well, I did, but that's no excuse to turn around and make you feel excluded. You brought the family feeling to the house," he continues. "Every time you came home from cheerleading, every time you clomped down the stairs yelling things or had a fit about homework, that's when Mom and Dad came alive. I felt like the three of us were waiting around for the next thing you'd do."

"I always felt like I was too extra."

"Not at all."

We've hit the river park. My mind is spinning. I'm thinking about what Hugo said about game night.

"If our family was a math class," Charlie continues, "you were the adorable one, Hugo was the star, and I was the nobody. And I have a lot of anger towards them that I need to address with them, but what I need to address with you is what a shitty brother I was, always acting like you were this worthless screwup. You were a happy, well-adjusted girl. You were great at making friends and sports and dancing, and they never gave you any props for that, and I piled on, and I wanted to apologize."

"You don't owe me an apology. Kids do what they have to do to get love."

He gives me a look. "How did you get so smart?"

My heart skips a beat. Charlie's called me a lot of things in my life, but never smart. "Stop..."

"It's true," he says. "You're smart about a ton of things, and I felt like an outsider. Not quite making the grade."

My pulse races. The sky seems too bright. "Is that why you moved to Japan?"

"Partly."

"I didn't know," I say.

"And when you two sent me that picture of you together, I was blindsided. I went ballistic. I suppose deep down I sensed he was in love with you, and I was jealous. And I kept you apart, acting like I was being protective, but it wasn't entirely about protection. It was about not wanting to lose my friend. And then this image of you and Hugo and Mom and Dad. The perfect family."

"No!"

"It's how it felt. It's not rational, I know."

"I shouldn't have told you that way," I say.

"A normal brother would be happy. His best friend and his kid sister? Two people he supposedly loves? Together? But I couldn't see straight." He turns to me here, serious. "Growing up, I couldn't see my own worth, and I turned on you, made you not see your own worth, but you know who does see your worth? Hugo. He always has."

"Charlie." I wrap my arms around him right there on the seawall with people streaming by. "You are my family. Always, always, always." I hold on to him tight. All this time, feeling like not enough. I never thought Charlie felt that way, too.

"We're good," I say as I let him go.

"I owe an apology to Hugo as well. I'm not going to stand in the way of you two."

"Come on." I buy him a pretzel at a streetside stand and we settle on a bench overlooking the water. A giant barge moves lazily down the river.

He says, "You two being together, it's so obvious. So perfect."

"Maybe." I dip my pretzel in the little cup of mustard sauce.

"Whadya mean, *maybe?*"

"I mean I don't know that it's going to work out. You weren't wrong in what you said about his impossible standards. His love being math and data and perfection and all of that."

"I said it because I knew it would do damage."

"It only hurts if there's truth in it. You know how Hugo is. He has these standards of perfection, this drive to measure up to some ideal in his mind. I'm gonna tell you right now, I love him— I really do—but I don't know if I'm willing to submit myself to the Hugo Jones mania for perfection."

"Stella—"

"I'm not a perfect person with every hair in place and all of that. I don't know where my keys are half the time. I'm challenged in four out of five adulting areas, some of which I'm working on, but I'll never measure up to pie-in-the-sky ideals, and that is not gonna work for him on a long-term basis."

He wipes his fingers and folds up his checkerboard carton, seeming lost in thought.

"I'm a barrel of flaws. I need to be with somebody who can roll with that."

"You want Hugo to roll with your quirks and flaws. Can't you roll with his?"

"He has none. He's hammered every flaw out of his life, and he gets 37% better every year. No, excuse me—37.78%. Sometimes we joke that I'm making him lose a percentage here and there, but I think I kind of am, and I think he knows it."

"Don't you see, Stella? That is his flaw. Brutal, isolating, relentless perfectionism."

"Hold on..." I narrow my eyes at the barge, turning this over in my mind. "The quest to be perfect *is* his imperfection? Charlie, is that one of those questions designed to short-circuit a robot? And then smoke billows out its ears and it falls over?"

"I mean it. You think Hugo wants to be that way?"

"You think he doesn't?"

"Of course not, Stella; it's a compulsion. And look what it's costing him—he clearly loves you, and this thing you two have going is jeopardized now."

"But is it enough that he doesn't want to be like that? I don't know if it's enough." I tell him about the first-kiss fight and give a G-rated version of the elevator-sex fight. I tell him about the Salvador Dali restaurant, which he finds hilarious, but it's not funny to me. "Hugo was a champ to go, but he was barely tolerating it. I've been on the receiving end of being barely tolerated. It feels like poison in your veins. I've been there."

"That would be awful."

"It is," I whisper.

"Don't forget, I met that Jonathan a few times. He never looked at you the way Hugo does. He turned out hyper-critical, but this is Hugo. Can't you give him a chance to do better?"

"But what about the thing where everyone says you're not supposed to go into a relationship wanting to change the person?"

This seems to stump Charlie, and he folds his carton some more.

"Even reality can't live up to his high standards," I add.

"I get it, Stella. But when I burst in on you two at his apartment, you know what I saw? A man who had your back."

I smush my stub of pretzel around, sopping up the last bits of salt and mustard, remembering how nice that was. We felt like a team. Hugo and me against the world.

Kelsey's been crying when I get home. Not actively, but there are mascara tracks.

I sit down with her and make her spill all. The man she's been dating broke up with her, and it wasn't enough to tell her he didn't want to date anymore; he had to inform her that the reason was that she looked and acted like a hooker, and it was too much for him.

"Oh my god! Fuck him! I love your style!" I tell her. "Everybody loves your style!"

"Not him," she says. "He thinks I'm trashy!"

"To hell with him!" I say.

"I think your mom thought so, too."

"My mom likes prairie dresses with lace collars. She's practically Amish." I make her show me his Instagram. I want to punch him through my phone so bad. I point out what an unbelievably boring loser he looks like.

We find a picture where he's got a fish on the end of a fishing pole.

"Are you even kidding me?" I say. "A fishing pole pic. This is what he put on his profile."

"Oh my god," Kelsey says. "How did I not see this?"

We make pink barbie cocktails and popcorn and laugh about the fishing pic.

After the third drink, we make each other Taylor Swift eras bracelets. I think she's feeling a little bit better, but some insults cut clear to the bone.

I so want to punch the guy.

CHAPTER 57

STELLA

"Hey." Lola's at my desk. "I'm supposed to grab you for note-taking. Wulfric's instructions. Right now up on ten."

"Is this Hugo's data model presentation?"

"Yeah."

I wince. "I'd really rather not." I lower my voice. "Things are weird with Hugo and me. Can't you get someone else?"

"Are you asking me to go to Wulfric and tell him that'll be a big N-O-O-O-O from you? This is the message that you want me to carry to Mister Wulfric Pierce? Because I'm gonna be honest, it won't go over well. Killing of messengers and all."

"Why can't they make a recording and we take notes from that? And we could even slow the speed."

"There's a massive secrecy issue with new data models, like paper notes only. No electronics. But if you feel like this should be recorded, you're free to take it up with Wulfric. I'm sure he'd love to hear your point of view on that."

"Very funny." I grab a legal pad.

"On the upside, there'll be rosemary currant scones."

I follow her into the hall. "I'm not that fast of a writer."

"I'm fast. You'll pinch hit." She looks over at me. "I'm sorry you guys are having issues. I loved you together."

"I did, too."

"Are the issues...terminal?" she asks.

Charlie's words have been banging around in my head ever since our talk. I want Hugo to overlook my flaws, but I can't return the favor? And Hugo has my back—he really, really does. He was right there.

"I don't know," I say. "So what happens at a data model presentation?"

"Analysis. Kicking of tires. It'll be the two other quants and a few analysts. Plus Wulfric and Brenda. It's an internal review."

We head up the elevator and into the tenth-floor conference room with its sweeping views. A long, impossibly polished wooden table stretches down the middle of it with Brenda and a few people already there, and Hugo's standing at the front of the room next to the blank whiteboard where he'll reveal his magic.

Our eyes lock. Hugo smiles, and something pleasant zings through me.

He's excited, and I know sure as anything that he's cracked whatever problem he was having. He's not bringing his B-game data model; he's bringing his A-game.

I feel happy all over. He did it.

All the hate he was having for his pathetic iteration or whatever.

I follow Lola to a far corner. We grab scones and work out a strategy to get everything in. It'll be some tag-team note-taking where I jot down audience questions and comments and she'll write Hugo's parts, and I'm supposed to poke her if I fall behind, and vice versa.

Wulfric walks in and takes an open seat next to Brenda.

Hugo begins to speak. He's saying things about the previous data model—something about the goals of that model and the way it changed things over the quarters and years.

A door opens at the side of the room and three large men come in. They look more like weightlifters than finance bros. One carries a table, one carries a chair, and the third has a large box, which he sets on the table.

"What's going on?" Wulfric barks.

"They're assisting me," Hugo says.

The men take up position in the corners.

"I don't think so." Wulfric stands. "This is a closed meeting!"

"They're mine," Hugo growls. "And they're essential."

Murmurs go up from the group.

Wulfric shotguns a bunch of words that sound like the words *what*, *how*, and *fuck* all jammed together.

Lola goes over and whispers something to Wulfric. He blusters some more and finally sits down.

Everybody's looking at the box as Hugo rambles on. It's obviously strange to have brought a large box and three assistants.

Hugo goes on to talk about the previous data model's limitations and the need for a next-gen version. Wulfric follows along with intense interest as Hugo discusses the goals of his new model, throwing out phrases like "stochastic volatility framework" and "elastic net regression."

I'm glad Lola hasn't needed me yet. I don't know how she's getting it down, but she's a strangely capable human being.

Hugo's going on about extreme market scenarios and disruptive potential now. He seems to be laying the groundwork, building up to whatever next-gen thing he's about to reveal.

Wulfric's so excited, he looks like he's going to float to the ceiling. "Everybody! Hugo needs absolute silence!"

Hugo strolls to the table. He looks over at me. Our eyes meet.

My pulse begins to pound as I recall our jokey conversation. The garbage zero sculpture. The pineapple-eating.

No, I think. *No way.*

He smiles, as if reading my thoughts, and lifts the box off the table to reveal a cutting board with a knife and a partly cut-up pineapple on it.

Gasps go up around the room.

My jaw drops to the floor.

Wulfric stands. "Hugo! What are you doing?"

"Demonstrating the new data model." Hugo sits down in the chair and, cool as a cucumber, he tucks a napkin into his collar.

"What the hell?" Wulfric charges the front, but one of the burly guys blocks him.

People stand, whispering furiously.

"Hugo—no! It's not worth it!" Wulfric's trying to get around the guy, who seems to be using every wrestling move known to humankind to stop him. Another of the guys joins in, and the two of them manage to hold a furious Wulfric back.

"Somebody get that fucking pineapple away from him!" Wulfric shouts. "If it's an extension on the deadline you need, you can have it!"

Lola turns to me. "Why aren't you stopping him?"

"He's not allergic," I whisper. "He can eat pineapple."

Her eyes go wide as saucers. "Excuse me? He was faking his allergy?"

I shrug. "Yes?"

People are trying to get up there, but Hugo's guys are very effective.

He picks up a slice of pineapple and takes a bite. Utter mayhem breaks out.

"The pineapple might not kill him, but Wulfric will," Lola says.

"Hugo, stop!" Wulfric struggles to get free of the two men. "For fuck's sake, somebody stop him!"

People are shouting and trying to get to him. Somebody yells to call 911.

One of the analysts manages to get behind the guards and up to Hugo's table. He rips the fruit from Hugo's hand, but Hugo's already eaten a great deal of pineapple.

"My god, what have you done?" Wulfric bellows, still struggling to get free.

Hugo wipes his mouth and sets the napkin down on the table. "Questions?"

Wulfric looks on, aghast. "What the hell have you done?"

"I ate pineapple," Hugo says. "Next question."

"What the fuck?" Wulfric bellows.

"This was the data model," Hugo says, gesturing at the pineapple remnants. "Me eating the pineapple and not being allergic was the data model. Any other questions?"

"You're not allergic?" Wulfric asks.

"I never was. Next."

Stunned silence descends onto the room like a thick blanket. All eyes turn to Wulfric, who seems to thrum with pure molten fury.

Except for Hugo—Hugo's gazing at me, looking so wild and free. And I know that we joked about the data model, suggesting it be a garbage sculpture zero or him eating pineapple, but this is more than a joke.

Hugo cares about things too much for this to be a joke.

A deluge of questions has erupted.

Hugo, was this a critique of in-house bias?

Is this an emperor's-new-clothes thing?

Are you suggesting our basic assumptions need to be questioned?

"Hugo," I call out. "Why?"

He looks right at me. "I've been embracing the wrong goals. The wrong method."

I feel light as air. The wrong goals. I don't know what it means, but it feels big and important and hopeful.

Suddenly he's coming to me.

"I love you," he says when he reaches me. "And you need to know that I'll never stop loving you. And I'll never stop fighting for us."

"Hugo," I say. "I love you too, but..." I look over at his stunned colleagues. I look at Wulfric with his murder face.

I didn't understand the presentation, but I know it was Hugo fighting for us...in some elaborate and total Hugo way, and for that, I love him.

CHAPTER 58

HUGO

I pull Stella from the room. I want us away from here, away from all of these people who don't understand, or just aren't ready to understand. Away from Wulfric's roar.

I don't care if people don't understand.

I only care about Stella.

She's laughing as we rush into the elevator.

"Hugo, what have you done?" She stabs the door-closed button about ten times, and then the down button.

The thing starts moving.

She turns to me, face bright with wonder.

I kiss her. "God, you feel good," I say.

"Hugo!" She pulls away. "What was that?"

"I'm embracing imperfection."

"By blowing an important presentation in the most outrageous way possible? I don't think that's what people mean when they say to embrace imperfection."

I slide my thumb over the cool silk of her cheek. "I'm new at it. I might not have it right yet."

"Be serious, Hugo! This is your job! Should you maybe—I don't know, go back there and fix things or something?"

"No—this is what's important," I say. "Us."

She takes my hand. The look in her eyes is everything.

We get off on the first floor, blow past security, and race outside, breathlessly making our way down the crowded sidewalk toward the East River. Seagulls screech overhead as we near the seaport; the whipping wind smells like saltwater.

I give her my jacket to wear.

"I need you to know that you were right in everything you've been saying to me," I tell her as we get clear of the crowds. "I was enforcing impossible standards of perfection for everybody and everything."

"Hugo—" There's amazement in her voice. She links her arm in mine. "Just...wow."

"It's true. I was creating these ridiculous standards in every area of my life. So...I got this book on perfectionism."

"You went out and bought self-help books? You?"

"Yeah. And I started reading it, and it's given me a torrent of new insights."

"I never expected you would just...take what I said to heart."

"How could I not take it to heart? I was hurting myself. I was hurting us. This thing is important to me."

We stop by a railing in front of one of the historic ships. "So it was good? This book?"

"I've read multiple books on the subject at this point. All the classics, all the cutting-edge ones."

She grins. "Of course."

"Not that I'm planning on being perfectionistic about it. Or at least I'll try not to. I need you to know, I'd never look at you like I looked at that orb—never. I know you, and I love you and every one of your lost shoes."

"You love my lost shoes? Are you the one who takes them?"

I smile at that. "Those lost shoes are all you, Sparky."

She does an indignant frown.

I adjust the jacket lapels to better shield her from the wind. "You were right in that I was enforcing ridiculous standards on this relationship we've built. I was limiting the amazing-ness of us, trying to fit our experiences into an ideal. Our first kiss in the music room? It was wrong and unexpected, but it was ours. Fucking in the elevator? Ours. We're a team, forging this new path all our own."

"A team," she whispers.

"I need to be done with shaving the edges off of squares so that they fit into circles and vice versa. Maybe not in math, but everywhere else? I'm done. And no more things like flow charts that describe kids flopping on couches. It's reductionist. It's small."

She looks amazed.

"I can't say I'm cured," I confess. "Will it distract me to see you walking around with one shoe untied? Maybe."

She makes a fake surprised face.

I lower my voice. "But am I gonna get down on my knees and tie that shoe? And then sink my fingers into your sexy hips and eat your unbelievably delicious pussy on the way back up? Maybe."

She grins and lowers her voice. "Am I gonna walk around with my shoes untied more often now? Maybe."

"Well, Stella, am I gonna haul you up over my shoulder when you lose your keys or your shoes?"

"Hugo!" She grabs my lapels. "Are we gonna talk about the fact that you ate pineapple in front of Wulfric? Because I really need to talk about that."

"He wasn't happy."

"Umm...did you see his face? Mur-der."

"I know."

"Not a fan of your presentation," she points out. "The eating of the deadly pineapple."

"It had to be done."

"It looked like an elaborate way of quitting to me."

I tell her about my experience at the card game, how busting free from my usual play led to unexpected gifts. "My friend Leon said that you need to break things in order to level up. To disrupt things. He was right."

"I don't understand. Eating pineapple in front of Wulfric...it felt more like career detonation than disruption."

"It was a little of both. The data model was wrong. The data model approach needs to be disrupted—I know that's true, and I feel like the presentation suggested that. But Wulfric—I don't know if he and I can come back around."

She takes my hand. "You love working with Wulfric."

"I do. But things needed to change," I say.

"So...like, are you going to be a baker or something now?"

"Hell no. I still love the work, but I need a radical new framework. Our progress was being limited by that framework—I can't say exactly how, but it's something that I know. I'm going in a new direction, and it'll happen with or without Wulfric. Probably without, but that's definitely not my preference."

"And...will your new direction still have math?"

"So much math," I say.

"And what if I untie my shoe? What then?"

"We would go somewhere, and I would tie it for you."

"In the most tawdry way?"

I lower my voice to a rumble. "You have no idea."

Wulfric texts me an hour later requesting a meeting first thing the next morning.

"What do you think he's going to do?" Stella asks.

"No way of knowing," I say.

"You want me to text Lola and ask about his state of mind?"

"His state of mind now might not be his state of mind tomorrow," I say.

"Maybe he'll have calmed down," she tries.

I kiss her on the head. "Maybe."

"Or not," she whispers.

"Or not," I agree.

We play hooky the rest of the day, which consists of hunting down our favorite falafel truck and retiring back to my place to eat and binge on historical sleuths.

Stella tells me about Charlie's visit, and what Charlie observed about my having her back. I'm surprised at the one-eighty after the way he acted when he was here.

"He deserves another chance," she says. "He's trying. He's looking at things. I'm not going to relate everything he said, but I feel like these years in Japan have given him perspective. He really owned what he did."

Emotions crowd my chest. "Really."

"He's sorry."

I grab my phone. I need to see him. "Is he in town? Maybe we should meet him out."

"He's in Illinois by now."

I nod. That makes sense. He comes to the States so infrequently, of course he tries to get home. "He's probably helping your dad clean the gutters right about now." I set down my phone.

"What is it?" she asks.

"I miss him. I didn't realize how much I miss him. He's my oldest and best friend, and I want to make things right."

Stella announces that I absolutely *have* to come home with her. "I know you like to avoid your parents on holidays, but just stay with us the whole time. Don't even tell them."

"I'll stay with you, but I'll check in on my folks."

"If you check on your folks, could I come? If it wouldn't be too weird? Would that even help?"

"You'd go with me?" I tuck some hair behind her ear. "You don't have to."

"I want to. I love having your back and being in things with you."

I slide my fingers over hers, with this strange and good feeling in my heart. Everything feels new. "I'd like that," I say. "It would help a lot."

She grins. "Are we all in on a growth spurt? Instead of eating turkey, are we gonna have to put on lava lamps and hug?"

"Please, no."

She climbs into my lap. "We'll celebrate with commemorative Chia Pets."

"Better not," I grumble into a kiss.

"I'll tell Mom to start them growing so that they can be fully chia-sprouted by the time you arrive."

CHAPTER 59

HUGO

I head to Wulfric's office first thing, braced for the worst.

The madness with this pineapple demonstration and the flamboyant public nature of it was everything right for Stella and me, but I cringe to think of the Wulfric fallout.

Lola gives me an inscrutable look as I pass. "He's waiting."

I walk in. His office is bright and spare. My belly twists as he stands up behind his massive desk. This man who's always been able to see what I see when other people haven't.

"Jones," he growls.

"Wulfric," I say.

"You're a real motherfucker," he says.

"I'm sorry. I know you're angry. I understand why you would be. You're questioning our relationship—"

"Questioning it? That fucking demonstration was nothing short of brilliant!" he bellows. "Jesus, Jones. Yes, I was angry. I wanted to kill you. This outrageous, monumentally fucked-up stunt with the pineapple? All those years? Not even allergic. Unbelievable."

"Uh…"

"I buttonholed that protégé of yours and forced her to explain it all." He comes around and slaps me on the back. "The whole of Wall Street is buzzing. Somebody leaked what happened—with my blessing, of course. People are turning themselves inside out to guess at what you're onto. You want to take a guess at how many billions in pension funds slid our way in the last twenty-four hours?"

"A lot?"

He barks out a laugh. "A lot."

"So…Brenda explained it?" I blink. "What did she say?"

"The line of inquiry you're on; all this business about how the solution to accounting for irrationality cannot be arrived at through rationality."

I stifle a smile, thinking about my conversation with Brenda. *You can't pick up a rug you're standing on.* She put it into terms Wulfric would appreciate. He made her tell, and that's what she came up with. Genius.

"So you're not mad about the pineapple?" I ask.

"Everybody out there thinks you've been playing this outrageous long game. I know you—I don't think you've been playing a long game with the pineapple. I think you got flustered and lied when you met me. But everybody else thinks you've been plotting all this time to blow up the paradigms with it, and it's fucking hilarious. Perception is reality."

"Right," I say.

"But I prefer reality to be reality, so I'll count on you to develop something off this. I want you to attack this thing. Get me a timetable, though."

"Got it," I say.

"Whatever resources you need."

I promise to work up a list. I know one of the items already: a promotion for Brenda. Somebody else can staff the desk outside my office.

We shake hands. "A true motherfucker," he says.

"I know, Wulfric." I turn and leave the office.

CHAPTER 60

STELLA

On Thanksgiving morning, Hugo and I drive the thirty miles through snowy cornfields to visit his parents at their senior condo. They're already hitting the sauce when we get there, but they're sober enough. We've brought bagels with different toppings, and we dig in at their small table and eat while they tell us about the squirrel activity out the window, which they seem to extensively monitor.

"We have an early Christmas gift," his mother, Mara, announces, adjusting her bright red glasses.

"You could save it for Christmas," Hugo says.

"We want to give it now," she says, bringing out a gift-wrapped box.

His dad rubs his meaty hands excitedly. "We can't wait!"

Hugo carefully peels the tape off the wrapping paper and removes it in one perfect piece. Inside is a white box; inside that white box is none other than a torus paperweight—the exact kind he collects.

He stares at it, baffled. "Where could you have gotten this?"

"We watch the auction sites," his father says proudly.

"This is a rare one. Exceedingly rare." Hugo holds it up to the light. "A limited edition azure. In perfect condition."

His mother claps her hands. "We know our boy!"

Hugo seems deeply moved. He thanks them profusely.

I'm well aware of what this means. It's not the paperweight, but the fact that they had the wherewithal to find it for him. The perfect gift. Like olden times. Like better times.

His mother embraces me before we leave. "We hope to see more of you," she confides. "We think you're perfect together."

At dinner that night, I pass the candied yams over to Hugo. His handsome face glows in the light of the candles set across our Thanksgiving table.

He passes me back the mashed potatoes. He's looking worn out and happy. He and Charlie spent the afternoon outside fixing the shed door—and repairing their relationship, judging from the way they came in, warm and happy and laughing like old times.

I spent the afternoon helping Mom cook, and while the turkey roasted, we sat down and created a promotional reel for her math club. She's amazed at how quickly I edit her boring footage into a fun promo. She's never asked me to do anything like it. I loved helping her.

I pour gravy over my turkey and describe my creative-on-the-fly business.

Hugo is disgusted. "You're not describing it right at all. Your daughter has created a concept in response to the market, identified talent, learned spreadsheets…" He lists a lot of things I didn't realize I was doing.

They're all staring at me, looking as stunned as if our cat, Skittles, had begun performing brain surgery between rounds of chair clawing.

So very stunned.

Okay, so it'll take them a while to change their view of me, but the difference is that I don't care. Their ideas about me don't define me. They'll come around or they won't, but I think they will.

Charlie pours us sake after dinner, a special bottle he brought from Japan. I tell them about Greta from the Gourmet Goose, entertaining them with the story of how she wouldn't sell me a cheeseball, but now she's my favorite client. I went in and sold her on some ideas I had to promote her store, showcasing her weird passion for food.

Later on, Dad tells a math joke and I do my Muppet flail and then I look over at Hugo and smile. We're this family. It's kind of amazing.

Football comes on later. I pull Hugo into my bedroom and stretch out on my bed.

He gets on top of me and kisses me.

"This is a fantasy come true, I hope you know," I say, clamping my legs around him.

"Oh, you're not the only one," he says. "I spent a lot of time trying very hard not to imagine you in here; trying very hard not to imagine us in here. A lot of time."

We have sweet, quiet sex. The sex of knowing each other's bodies. Of being at peace with things. We snuggle happily.

The game is still on, judging by the cheers and coaches' whistles.

The next time I glance at Hugo, he looks really troubled. Like something's upset him.

My belly flops upside down. "What's wrong?"

He points up at the Hanson brother's poster on the wall. "What did you do to that poor guy's mouth?"

"I loved him too much," I whisper.

He slides a chunk of my hair through his fingers. "You can love me too much any day of the week."

340

I snuggle back against him. "I plan to."

~ The End ~

Thank you so much for reading Stella and Hugo! I love them so much; I hope you did, too.

〜

Q: Want more Hugo?

There's a special Hugo bonus epilogue out there that you can get!

Hugo is being a full-on sexy grump about going to the fab New Year's Eve ball. He doesn't understand why it's so important to Stella (Psst: she has a surprise for him!)

Will Stella go up against scary Wulfric to get Hugo there? You know she will. And will all the 45th St. women be there? Along with some of our fave growly guys? And will there be gossip? Yessssssss, friends!

Find it here:

https://geni.us/TGBbonusEpilogue

〜

This book is part of the Billionaires of Manhattan series, a group of standalone romantic comedies set in New York City. Turn to page to see the rest.

ALSO BY ANNIKA MARTIN

Find a complete list of books and audiobooks at www.annikamartinbooks.com

ABOUT THE AUTHOR

Annika Martin is a New York Times bestselling author who sometimes writes as RITA®-award-winning Carolyn Crane. She lives in Minneapolis with her husband; in her spare time she enjoys taking pictures of her cats, consuming boatloads of chocolate suckers, and tending her wild, bee-friendly garden.

newsletter:
annikamartinbooks.com/newletter

Facebook:
www.facebook.com/AnnikaMartinBooks

Instagram:
instagram.com/annikamartinauthor

website:
www.annikamartinbooks.com

email:
annika@annikamartinbooks.com

Made in the USA
Columbia, SC
28 November 2023

26811388R00212